ALSO BY RIN CHUPECO

The Girl from the Well

The Suffering

A HUNDRED NAMES FOR MAGIC SERIES

Wicked As You Wish

An Unreliable Magic

THE BONE WITCH TRILOGY

The Bone Witch

The Heart Forger

The Shadowglass

THE NEVER TILTING WORLD SERIES

The Never Tilting World

The Ever Cruel Kingdom

THE SACRIFICE

THE SACRIFICE

RIN CHUPECO

sourcebooks
fire

Copyright © 2022 by Rin Chupeco
Cover and internal design © 2022 by Sourcebooks
Cover design by Liz Dresner
Cover illustrations © Leonardo Santamaria
Internal design by Danielle McNaughton

Published by Sourcebooks Fire, an imprint of Sourcebooks
P.O. Box 4410, Naperville, Illinois 60567–4410
(630) 961-3900
sourcebooks.com

Cataloging-in-Publication Data is on file with the Library of Congress.

Printed and bound in Canada.
MBP 10 9 8 7 6 5 4 3 2 1

For the Scooby Doo Manila squad—until our next hunt

He who offers the sacrifice controls the Godseye.
The first to feed,
the second to seed,
the third to wear,
the fourth to birth,
the fifth to serve,
the sixth to lure,
the seventh to consume,
the last to wake.

ONE

THE CAVE

Nobody tells Hollywood about the screaming.

Nobody tells Hollywood about the curse. Or the way things walk across the sands here like they are alive enough to breathe. Nobody tells them of the odd ways the night moves around these parts when it thinks no one sees.

Nobody gives them permission to visit, and it's all the incentive Hollywood needs to permit themselves.

The people who live in the provinces nearest the island don't talk. Not at first. But money is the universal language, and the years have been lean enough, desperate enough. Tongues loosen. The words come reluctantly.

Yes, they say. *There is a curse. Yes; at least five people dead.*

No, they say. *We will not step foot on that island with you, not even if you gave us a million dollars.*

Hollywood crashes into the island, anyway; it's a new breed

of conquistadors trading technology for cannons. First their scouts: marking territory, measuring miles of ground, surveying land. Next their specialists: setting camp, clearing brush, arguing over schematics. Then their builders arrive with containment units, solar panels, and hardwood. In the space of a few days, they construct four small bungalows with an efficiency I'm not accustomed to seeing.

The noise is loud enough that they don't hear the silence how I've always heard it.

They scare the fishes away most days, and so I've gotten accustomed to idling, to watching them from my boat instead of hunting for my next meal. Hollywood does terrible things with machinery. They whirl and slam and punch the ground, and the earth shakes in retaliation. They dig perfect circles, add pipelines to connect to local supplies, and install water tanks. They set up large generators and test the lighting. They cut down more trees to widen the clearing to place more cabins.

None of them step inside the cave. The one at the center of the island, where the roots begin.

They don't talk about the roots that ring the island, half-hidden among white sand so fine it's like powder to the touch, so that they trip when they least expect it. But they talk about the balete. "I came here expecting palm trees," one of the crew says with a shudder. He stares up fearfully at one of the larger balete trees, with their numerous snake-like gnarls that twist together to pass as trunks, and at the spindly, outstretched branches above. "If trees could *look* haunted, then it would be these."

Soon they notice me standing by the shore, only several meters away.

"Hey, you there!" one calls out. He wears a Hawaiian shirt and dark shorts. A pair of sunglasses are slicked up his head. "You live nearby?"

I nod.

"Oh, thank God, you can understand us. We'd been having a hell of a time trying to translate."

"Most of the people here understand English," I say. "They probably don't want to talk to you."

"Ouch. Big ouch. Well, you're still the only local I've seen this close to the island. Even the fishermen stay clear. You're not afraid of the curse?"

I shake my head. Askal peers cautiously from around my legs, watching the foreigners curiously. "You?" I ask.

He guffaws. "I'm more afraid of my bosses docking my pay if we don't get this right." He peers back at Askal. "Cute dog. I've never seen the locals bring pets on their boats."

"He's used to the water."

Askal wags his tail, sensing he is being praised.

"Want to make some money, kid? We need someone who knows their way around the place. Everyone we've asked on the mainland has turned us down."

I row closer to where they stand, hopping out and dragging the boat through the last few feet of water. Askal scampers out after me.

"Not scared like everyone else, eh?" Hawaiian Shirt's companion asks, a guy with a goatee and bad haircut. Clouds of smoke rise from the little device he's puffing away at, and it smells of both cigarettes and overly sweet fruit. A half-empty beer bottle is tucked under his arm. His eyes are bloodshot, and I've seen enough drunks on the mainland to know what that means. "You hang around this place a lot?"

"You shouldn't be here."

Hawaiian Shirt scowls. "That's what the officials here have been telling us the past few months while we've been negotiating, but it's not gonna stop us. We have all the necessary permits. It's hypocritical, don't you think, telling us to leave when you've obviously been poking around here as much as we have?"

"I didn't ask you to leave. I said you shouldn't be here."

"Semantics. Look—we need someone to point out the mystery spots, maybe tell us about cursed areas on this damn island. Besides the Godseye. We've heard about that. We're on a deadline, and we need to get things moving before the rest of the crew arrive."

"The Godseye?"

"The cave on this island. The one where all those deaths happened. The locals didn't have a name for it, but we needed one for the show and that's what Cortes called it. You know why we're here, right? You must have heard the news by now."

Goatee blows rings in the air. "How are we gonna build three seasons around one fricking cave?"

"We'll figure it out, Karl. They say there's gold hidden in the cave that Cortes stole. Viewers love hearing about buried treasure. I'm sure Ethan's storyboarded more ideas." Hawaiian Shirt scratches his head. "You ever been inside the Godseye?"

"Yes."

Both stare at me. "All this time," Goatee mutters, "and he's been here all along. Kid, if you're who we think you are, then you're famous among the locals. You're like a ghost whisperer, they said. You're the only one brave enough to come here. We're hoping you could help us."

I look about pointedly and gesture at their building. "Do you even need permission anymore?"

"We signed off with the authorities. Well, we offered them a ton of money and they took it, so I guess that's permission. But we need more information, and that's the one thing they ain't selling."

"I'll give you five thousand dollars to come on board with us," Hawaiian Shirt says eagerly. "And another five if you stay the whole season, but that means you'll have to go on camera to talk about any creepy stories you have about the island. All the highlights of this place." He eyes my empty net. "That's gotta be more than you make fishing in at least a decade, right? I'll have a contract drawn up for you in an hour. You can look it over and tell me what you—" He stops. "You can read, right?"

I frown. "Yes."

"No offense, just checking. Get a lawyer to look it over for you if you want. It's got some terms and clauses you might not be familiar with—saves a lot of headaches later. So you'll help?"

I take my time, coiling my nets, making sure the boat's beached properly. Askal lingers near me, keeping a careful eye on the two men. "Have *you* been inside?"

"Well, no. Not till our legal department clears us to proceed. Or the exploration team gets a crack at it. Standard precautions."

Without another word, I head up the path, Askal keeping easy pace beside me. I can hear them scrambling to follow me.

No one can miss the cave entrance at the center of the island. It's two hundred feet high, built for giants to walk through. Limestone stains mar the walls. Something glitters in their cavities.

It doesn't take long for Hawaiian Shirt and Goatee to catch up, both looking annoyed.

"Ask it permission," I tell them, and they guffaw.

"The hell I'm asking some ghost," Goatee says with a snort.

"We can't go in until we get the all clear," Hawaiian Shirt repeats.

"A few steps in won't make a difference." I place my hand on the stone, which is cool to the touch. "Tabi po," I murmur, and enter.

The ground is softer here, and my sandals sink down slightly wherever I trod, leaving prints in my wake. Though reluctant at first, I hear them following, Hawaiian Shirt grumbling about all the trouble they could get into should R&D find out. Askal pads along, ears pricked as if he already senses something we cannot.

It's not a long walk. A stone altar lies a hundred feet in. Part of the ceiling above it caved in at some point, revealing a view of the sky. It's late afternoon, and the moon is already visible and silhouetted against a sea of blue.

The altar is more yellowing limestone bedrock, chiseled from ancient tools and carved with purpose. I look down at the ground and see, running along the sides, withered tree roots so old they've grown into the cave wall, stamped so deeply into the stones as to be a part of its foundation.

The passageway branches out, circles around to another tunnel that lies just behind the altar, leading deeper into rock.

"You said something before we came in," Goatee says. "'Tabi po'? That's how we're supposed to ask permission to enter?"

"It's a sign of respect," I say.

But the two men are no longer listening. They're too busy staring at the stonework, and then at the sky where the moon stands at the center of the hole above—a giant eye gazing down at them.

Askal whimpers softly. I lean down and stroke his fur.

"They weren't kidding about the Godseye," Goatee says, impressed. "How'd you have the balls to come here all by yourself, kid? Seen any of the so-called ghosts? See Cortes himself?"

I pause, debating what to tell them. "I've heard the screaming."

"No one's told us about any screaming."

I approach the altar but do not touch it. I hear a soft, rasping sound, and look down to see small makahiya leaves writhing quietly on the ground. From the corner of my eye, I catch the tree roots on the walls curling, stilling only when Goatee, sensing their movements, steps nearer.

I have spent enough time on this island to recognize when it's distressed.

"You all shouldn't be here," I say again.

Goatee snorts. "Let's wait until the cameras start rolling before you get all creepy, kid."

"The Diwata knows me. But outsiders are another matter. You can't stay here."

The smile Goatee shoots my way is patronizing. "Kid," he says, as the sounds of digging outside resume, "we're just filming a TV show. We have *permission*."

"Better drag Melissa here to do some initial shots," Hawaiian Shirt says happily. "This is gonna look beautiful in our promos."

"We'll still need to hook viewers for a second season," Goatee says. "Maybe something's haunting the mangroves on the eastern side of the island—a spirit that pulls people underwater. Or maybe a dead woman. Dead women are always hits."

He laughs. Hawaiian Shirt laughs along with him.

From somewhere within the cave, something mimics their laughter.

They stop, tearing their gazes from the eye above them to into the cavern's depths. But all I hear now are the faint reverberations of their voices.

"Easy to see why people think this place is haunted," Goatee says, with a nervous, quieter chuckle. "Makes you start imagining things." He raises his hand, which trembles slightly, and downs the rest of his beer in one noisy gulp.

They do not linger long. Askal nuzzles at my hand, lets out a soft whimper. "We're leaving, too," I assure him. Before I follow the men out, I look back at the tunnel stretching farther into the cave, waiting for a shift in the darkness beyond—but find nothing.

There's only the altar, which has borne witness to old horrors, blessed with the moon's quiet, unrelenting light.

TWO
VISIONS

THE ISLAND HAS KNOWN ME MY WHOLE LIFE. AS A CHILD
I raced along its shores and scavenged oysters hiding underneath its
rocks, caught the small fish trapped in its shallow pools at low tide.
I would lie down near the shore and while away lazy hours, diving
into the waters when the sun grew too hot for my liking.

My father taught me everything. How to catch fish with my bare
hands. How to scale trees for coconuts. How to quiet the voices on
the island. How to show them you mean no harm.

Except 'Tay hasn't been strong for a while now.

Occasionally I would see things. Things pretending to be one of
the trees by the coast, dangling from branches. Or crouched against
the stones by the cave, waiting for nightfall.

The creatures here leave me alone, and I've become accustomed
to their presence.

But I am no longer the only person on Kisapmata, and I can see signs of the island's discomfort. Now as I walk along the shore, small makahiya plants litter the soil, opening their leaves as I pass. They snap shut when Goatee or Hawaiian Shirt or the Hollywooders step through.

The island has not had this many trespassers before, and for so little reason.

I say nothing. I only stay close and keep watch. Askal refuses to leave my side. He's always been protective of me.

Goatee and Hawaiian Shirt give me little to do in the days after our meeting. "We tried looking for you, but nobody knew where you live," the latter tells me. "People said you were likely on one of the smaller islands, the ones that aren't even big enough for a village. Wasted ten months searching. Every lead we had of you was a dead end. 'Why not head to the Godseye,' Hemslock finally said. 'Sooner or later we'll find the kid.' And he was right, goddamn it. You don't live in Leyte?"

"I live nearby, with my father."

"He ever been to this island?"

I nod. "Taught me everything I know about it."

"You or he give anyone guided tours before us?"

"No."

"Because of the murders, right? I know they'd locked up access to this place afterward. Lucky for us the mayor decided our intentions were noble. The plan is to put you on camera without any prep, so you can tell us what you know of this place. Steve thinks it's gonna be more authentic that way, provoke better reactions from the cast if they're hearing the story for the first time. So he wants us to wait for him to get here for that. Just a heads up—sometimes we're gonna have to move your words around, to make a bigger impact for the show, right? That's specified in your contract, but since you've already signed it, I'm assuming you know."

Hawaiian Shirt sighs. "I'm gonna try and look out for you, all right, kid? I've worked enough shows to see how easy it is for producers to take advantage of someone for fifteen minutes of fame. We're gonna be the first people to stay on this island since, what? That plane crash? Whatever happened to that, anyway?"

Goatee shrugs. "Investigators tried to dig up the island till the locals put their foot down and said no. They couldn't find any bodies, other than that one passenger they found buried here. No evidence of plane debris, either. That's not stopping Gries, though."

"Who's Gries?" I ask.

"You're gonna meet him soon enough. Used to be a hotshot back in the day. Got some blockbusters under his belt, and I don't always mean in theaters. Broke up a few unions in his time. Ruthless. Then his wife died, and he lost his edge. This show's supposed to be his comeback as much as it is Hemslock's. Who knows? Maybe you'll get some fame from this too, kid. Get you on the circuit. Anything can happen in Hollywood."

I look at the cabins they're building. Pre-fab houses, he called them; they are a riddle of metal containment units joined together to create the trappings of luxury. "I don't want fame," I say.

Hawaiian Shirt grins, like he finds the idea hilarious. "That's what they all say at first. Look, I *want* the island to throw something at us. That's what we're here for. It'll be much easier to film hauntings than have to create them."

Slowly, and then very quickly, I watch them gentrify the island. Several generators are on standby to funnel electricity for a secure internet connection. There are water tanks and medical tents. A refrigeration system for food storage. There is even talk of paving part of the island to make walking easier, but the idea was thankfully discarded.

Hawaiian Shirt gives me a quick tour of the pre-fab houses. One for the showrunner/actor, two more for some executive producers who wanted to come with the production. Everyone else has to be satisfied with tents, which are nonetheless far more impressive in size and interior than what the name suggests.

There are more people than I expected. Aside from production there is the safety crew responsible for checking the equipment, a medical team, and a group of scientists keen to explore the Godseye.

A larger bungalow is the mess hall. It is where the crew gather to eat their meals and to plan the rest of the series. There is a large freezer inside the mess hall stocked with food flown from overseas, and the crew has employed several chefs.

But the island is surrounded by fresh seafood, and so I oblige when they ask me for a sampling of the local delicacies. On the days when Askal and I can catch enough fish, their chefs cook them over a makeshift grill. They're good fish—tilapia, galunggong, bisugo— and it helps endear me to the crew.

I negotiate with other fishermen, and they frequently supply us with other varieties of seafood—curacha, alimasag, and other kinds of crabs on luckier days, but more often squid, green mussels, and mackerel.

The crew offer me an extra tent. I accept but rarely spend nights there. *Sick father*, I say. *Need to look in on him. I live only several minutes away.* They are sympathetic.

Askal and I go home and spend time with 'Tay. He sleeps more frequently nowadays, though I know that is normal for his age. I'm not worried about the time I'll have to spend away from him. My father raised me and Askal after my mother's death. He's stubborn enough not to want help from anyone. Runs in the family.

'Tay was delighted when I told him about my new job. The money will be good. The Americans know the risks. It's not my fault they won't listen, and it's not on me to protect them.

While he dozes, and while Askal lies down beside him and does the same, I look at the contract I signed, the one promising me ten thousand dollars if I stay through their filming. It's more money than I've ever expected to have in my hands all at once.

And for a moment, I feel selfish, tempted. There are so many things I could do with this money. Leave the island. Make my own way in the world.

'Tay stirs beside me, and the thought dissipates. Ten thousand dollars can only get you so far. And I'm not going to abandon 'Tay.

But there are far too many people on the island. This will not end well.

"*Paano na?*" I ask myself quietly, knowing I don't know the answer to that.

⚜

"This island is almost perfect," one of the crew members gushes the next day, when I return. "Add a Panera and I'd be all set. Do you go to school on the mainland, Alon? You speak English so well, and I know there are excellent schools in Leyte for—"

"Harriet," another woman rebukes sternly, and Panera Lady gasps.

"I didn't mean that people here *can't* speak English *well*," she says hastily, unhelpfully. "I know most people here do because of, uhhh, colonialism, right? I wasn't expecting—I mean—"

"You need to stop constantly sticking your foot in your mouth, you know that?" the woman says, not caring for tact. She takes Panera Lady's arm and steers her away. She returns later to apologize, though I am mostly amused. Panera Lady isn't the first to assume that Filipinos don't understand English, and she's unlikely to be the last.

The nicer lady's name is Melissa, and she wears her hair in a style she calls an undercut, bleached pink at the roots but gradually blending to purple at the tips. She's got a tattoo of something called a roomba on her bicep—a private inside joke, she says, between her and her girlfriend. She's also a PA—a production assistant—a fancier name, she admits, for a glorified unpaid intern. She's only older than me by two years, and I like her best out of everyone so far. "But they *pay* me for being here," I point out. "And I do a lot less than you."

She chuckles. "That's not how it works in Hollywood—or a lot of other places in America. There're a lot of us desperate for a chance to break into the industry, and they know we won't complain. They pay us in connections, in introductions to bigger names who can poach us for positions with actual salaries. I live with my folks, so I don't need to pay rent. I'm lucky. I know people who'd be better at the work than me but can't afford the job."

14

It is a strange thing to say, to *afford* a job.

Melissa bends down and pets Askal, who likes the attention, his tongue lolling out as she scratches behind his ears. "What's your deal? The scuttlebutt is that you're the island whisperer. That you're one person the island won't curse."

"The island won't harm the people living around the area."

"But the others don't come here even so. Why do you?"

I stare in the direction of the cave. "I was five the first time I came here," I say. "'Tay brought me."

"'Tay?"

"Tatay."

"That means *dad*, right? So this was back when he wasn't ill?"

I nod. "You don't think about whether or not you should be afraid of this place when you've lived around here your whole life. Respect is key. But most foreigners don't have that for us."

Melissa winces. "Well, that's true enough. Is he doing all right, your dad? Is someone looking after him while you're here?"

I think again about my contract, the quiet way 'Tay breathes in and out. I want to stay on Kisapmata, but money and 'Tay are not the reasons I do. "He'll be okay."

Later, Goatee tells me more about showrunners. They pitch ideas to network executives in America. If the latter likes it, they receive hefty budgets for pre-fab houses and generators among other expenses.

"They're calling this show *The Curse of the Godseye*," he shares, offering me a cup of coffee. Melissa said the food's free, and the caffeine boosts are unlimited. "Or maybe just *Godseye*; we're still

15

deciding. Either should be catchy. Ever watched any ghost hunting shows before? You know—intrepid spirit investigators staying in haunted places and screaming at whatever's there to scream back?" Goatee doesn't take coffee. He's got another bottle of beer on hand, though I've already seen him drink four today.

"There have always been ghosts," I say. "Even when there's no one around to see."

"Yeah, but now there're cameras and CGI to monetize the shit out of them. You're in luck, kid. Hemslock's the best screamer in the business. Made ghost reality shows cool again. He had a couple of setbacks the last few years, but they're throwing big money behind him this time."

I know little of Hollywood, but I know directors are usually involved and hear no mention of one for this production.

"That's not uncommon with these types of shows. Hemslock made his name with the solo survivalist format—you know, the ones where you do all your own filming on a handheld camera, pretending you're the only one there? That's his brand—him versus the world—so it's par for the course. Twenty years ago, he would go this solo. But he's a big name nowadays, so we're here taking the risks for him first."

"You're friends with him?"

"Dunno if *friend* is the right word. Colleague, drinking partner. Know some of his family. Southern boy. His ma's big on church. Dad served in 'Nam. Joe—that's his younger brother—died in a car accident. Some uncles and aunts he likes to talk about—an Aunt Elle who was arrested for fraud and an Uncle Mal who was in the Irish mob or something. He always said he got his bravado from his uncle."

Goatee looks around at the crew working. "That group's gonna check the caves, figure out which caverns we can film. Then there are the cameramen for interviews, for following Hemslock, and for whatever B-roll footage we haven't gotten already. Light and sound guys to make everything watchable. Editors to make sure shit makes sense, figure out if we need more footage. Most are gonna head back to the mainland before filming begins. Hemslock wants as few people around for that as possible."

Some of the crew members are watching videos of Hemslock on his previous shows in the mess hall when I enter. Hemslock is a large man with a head of yellow hair and pale skin tanned from the sun. In one video, his hair is long and disheveled, and his beard is full, as he screams inside a temple in Cambodia for Khmer Rouge spirits to come and assault him. In another he is clean shaven with a crew cut, sitting in darkness inside a castle while making demands for unseen things to curse him. In one more he is being forced out of a shrine by several irate priests. Hemslock is shouting, accusing the priests of harassment.

"Kinda ironic," says one of the show's editors, a dark-skinned man who wears a wide-brimmed straw hat. "Considering all that shit that went down with him after this aired."

"He doesn't respect sacred places," I say from behind them.

The two crew members jump, their fear melting into relief when they see me.

"Don't sneak up on us like that!" a redheaded woman gasps.

"Causing outrage in sacred places is what made him popular," Straw Hat explains. "People eat this up."

Reuben Hemslock, as it turned out, is not his real name. They tell me that it is Paul Grossman, and that two years ago, eighteen women, including a few ex-girlfriends, stepped forward to accuse him of longstanding abuse. He has since taken a two years' sabbatical to distance himself from the scandal; this show will mark his return.

"Of course it turns my stomach," the redhead says. "But this is my paycheck. I've got three kids. I'm not going to risk my job for anything. Besides, I'm heading home when they arrive. Hemslock wants a skeleton crew, which is real bullshit because they're keeping the chefs."

Goatee takes a much more relaxed stance regarding Hemslock. He's drinking again, this time from a bottle of Red Horse, a local beer he must have brought from the city. "You get a lot of enemies when you're famous," he explains, after a long pull. His eyes are slightly unfocused. His fingers shake with the natural tremors of an unrepentant alcoholic. "That's what happened to Hemslock. These women want to make money off knowing him. Their tell-all books, talk show slots. But people have shit memories; dangle some new celebrity bait, and they'll forget the scandals soon enough. They'll forget this one, too."

"What are their names?" I ask.

"Beats me. I think one's an Audrey and maybe there's a Jill? Main girlfriend is Gail Merkan. D-list actor."

"Hey, wait," Straw Hat says. "Weren't there rumors that Gail

Merkan was visiting Cebu or something? Isn't that the next island—"

"That's all rumors. Tabloids getting a slow news day, trying to bait us into making a statement."

"If these women are making accusations for the fame," I ask, "then why doesn't anyone remember their names?"

Goatee scowls at me. "Yeah well, he makes money, and that's what we're here for. I've worked with him on other projects. He's fine. No idea what those bitches are going on about."

"You'll probably like Chase better," Melissa says cheerfully. "He's a celebrity, too. Sort of."

"Chase?"

"Leo Gries's son. Content creator or social media influencer or whatever. He's pretty popular." Melissa types on her phone then, grinning, shows me a video of a good-looking, shirtless boy wearing skimpy shorts and a plastic horse's head, tap dancing to music. "He got almost twenty million views from this alone and literally put *"I Need a Hero"* back on the billboard charts. He got some publicity for the horse head, but he's such a big goofball that it's hard not to like him."

I don't claim to understand the logic behind the video's popularity, but Askal seems to enjoy it, letting out staccato yips in time to the beat.

I hope Goatee is right, and that many of the crew will leave once shooting starts. There are far too many strangers on this island.

Two weeks before filming officially begins, a team of scientists explores the cave. I sit on a nearby rock and watch as they disappear inside. Askal seats all fifteen pounds of himself on my lap and barks. "They'll be all right," I tell him.

The sands feel soft underneath me. The nearby balete sway against some unseen wind. I watch their branches ripen; tiny makahiya leaves unfurl along their length. They are tiny and segmented like small feathers, and while they have no flower heads, the plants on this island can grow several feet long, resembling creeping ivy. I heard some of the scientists ponder taking samples; makahiya don't normally thrive on balete. Most things don't.

Makahiya close on its own from external stimuli, like when it's been touched. There is no one else nearby, but I watch the slender leaves fold in on themselves anyway, one after the other, as if caressed by something unseen.

One of the larger buds opens; something oddly familiar winks at me from within before the bud seals itself up again.

Soon, the scientists return. "It's breathtaking," one says excitedly, as they brief the rest of the team on their findings. "We've found writing to corroborate both Cortes's and Key's journals. We marked off areas inside. Make sure Mr. Hemslock and his team don't go farther than that. But he'll love what we've found. There may be a few more closed-off caverns in there, but we couldn't find a way to get in. Incidentally—Gerry, the maps those plane crash investigators provided were completely inaccurate. It's almost like they explored a different cave system."

"They seemed reliable," Hawaiian Shirt says. "Let me double check. They didn't find anything out of the ordinary when they were inside, either."

"None of you tell Hemslock," Goatee says dryly. "He wants to pretend like he's the first to discover everything." He takes another gulp of his beer—and then starts in surprise.

The bottle in his hand shatters.

"Jesus Christ, Karl!" The scientist moves away from the broken glass.

Goatee stares at something within the dense patch of trees just several meters from camp, and I see a glimpse of something moving within the copse.

A woman. Long brown hair, pale skin. She stares unblinkingly at him. The rest of her is hidden behind the gnarled lower branches of a tree; only her face is visible.

There is something odd about the way she tilts her head.

"Get me another drink," Goatee says hoarsely.

"Karl? You, okay?" The scientist persists.

The figure is gone when I look back. Goatee rips his gaze away.

"No," he says, voice trembling, only slightly slurred from the alcohol. "Does it look like I've ever been okay?"

And then he grabs another bottle from his assistant and downs its contents, until every drop is gone.

THREE
TRESPASSERS

It isn't long before there's another sighting, and the rumors begin. The witnesses, this time, are the redhead with the kids and the Panera Lady.

"We thought someone on the team was injured, so we called out," Panera Lady says, still shaking like a leaf. "Someone was staggering around like they were drunk. We thought it was Karl. We walked toward it—and then it turned and—and—"

"It had no face!" the assistant editor bursts out. "Like—you've seen *Texas Chainsaw Massacre*, right? Like Leatherface."

"Exactly! Its face was peeling off, and it was *naked*—"

Hawaiian Shirt raises his hands. "Well, what do you want me to do about that? Write it up for HR to sanction? Did it attack?"

"No," Panera Lady falters. "It disappeared. I can't stay here, Gerry. I want out, I want—"

"Look. Supernatural sightings are great for PR, but there aren't really any ghosts. People see all kinds of weird crap out in the boondocks. I know you're both scared, but my hands are tied till Hemslock gets here. Tasha, you'll be off the island soon, so hold on till then. Don't let Gries make it hard for you—he's fired people for less."

Theirs is not the only report made. The number of sightings grows as the days pass, giving Hawaiian Shirt more reason to worry. Something with tangled, dark hair skulking among the trees. Naked. And yet somehow *not* naked, either. No face that anyone could remember.

Until they could.

In the space of a day, the accounts shift again. There *is* a face, and it's the face of a cameraman's father, dead for years. It's the face of a staff writer's estranged brother, a production coordinator's best friend, a gaffer's school bully. The sightings last no longer than a few seconds. All happen within the vicinity of camp.

Frustrated, Hawaiian Shirt cancels filming for the day and sends everyone back to their tents. There are no new reports the next day, but one of the generators stops working, and it takes another half a day to fix. In the afternoon, one of the water tanks produces greenish, bracken-like fluid for an hour before reverting to normal. A check reveals nothing has been tampered with.

Next there's a scream in the middle of taping. It unnerves the crew, and this time Hawaiian Shirt hears it as well. The safety team does a check. Everyone is accounted for. No one claims responsibility.

"Are there animals on the island?" Hawaiian Shirt asks me, trying his best to act calm though it is clear he's unnerved.

"Only insects and fish. And Askal."

Askal barks importantly.

"It was a woman's scream, wasn't it? Wasn't that what you mentioned hearing before? When we first met?"

I nod.

"Equipment breaks down all the time, so that's to be expected. But some are claiming they've seen the ghosts of their grandpa or people who should be dead. What's that all about? How is that related to the screams?"

"Should I tell you now," I ask dryly, "or wait for the cameras?"

I am not expecting him to take me up on the offer.

Soon Hawaiian Shirt is hollering at the cameramen, for the light technicians to work their magic, for assistants to pin a mic on me and make sure they can hear every word. Askal dances in and around their legs, excited by the flurry of activity.

"All right," Hawaiian Shirt says, determined, once everything has been set up. "You can answer now. What's the deal with all these so-called sightings?"

I try to ignore the camera pointed at my face. "It's the Diwata's way of testing people, to see if they're worthy."

"Worthy of what?"

"Of being sacrificed. If you're one of the eight deaths that he's looking for. The ones who are kind—he won't harm them. The ones who are not—" I pause. "If you've done your research, you would have known this already."

"Have you ever had sightings like the ones my crew has been experiencing?"

24

I take a deep breath, not knowing why I am being so honest. "Not my own, no. But I see everyone else's. I know you're going to dismiss this as nothing more than superstition, but I'm telling you that the legend is just as real as you and me. And while I may not agree with your reasons for coming here, I don't want to see any of you harmed, either. Kisapmata is dangerous, and you should start treating it as such."

Hawaiian Shirt gazes steadily at me for a few more seconds. I can tell that he's more worried now, but he shakes it off.

"Nice work," he says. "We got all that, Rich? Do you mind saying everything again but in Tagalog, so we can decide the better version to air later?"

Hawaiian Shirt seems happy to pass off the visions as a form of mass hysteria. The psychologists on the team mandate that those who've had an encounter schedule an appointment with them.

Goatee, I notice, never reports his own experiences.

⁂

The VIPs reach the island two weeks later. The ship that brings them to shore is a bangka larger than mine, large enough for tours but small enough to get close to the shallower shoals. It anchors beside a small wooden pier built for the production. A dozen people climb out; they look around with curiosity, a few with distaste.

The first out is a man in his fifties wearing a suit despite the hot summer day. He glances about with misgivings, shaking off someone's attempt to guide him to the sand. "This is an *Armani*," he snaps. "Wash your damn hands first."

Reuben Hemslock arrives with eight men dressed in military fatigues and camouflage, all visibly armed. They hover around him like a moving barricade, stopping others from getting too close. Hawaiian Shirt quietly assures the surprised crew that this is normal, because Hemslock has specific stipulations for them in his contract. A flex in Hawaiian Shirt's jaw also tells me that some other clause has been broken, nonetheless.

"He's been in a few movies, you know," Goatee murmurs, words slightly slurred. "Ever seen them? *Infinite Space? The Fight at the End of the World?* That recent Star Trek movie? He's done a few popular roles in television, too. *Best Served Cold? The Con-In-Laws?*"

I shake my head.

"You're missing out. He's been nominated for several awards, for *Infinite Space* especially. He started out with reality documentaries, but it turns out he's a pretty great actor, too."

Reuben Hemslock is exactly what his shows depict him as—a six-foot-six-inch-tall behemoth of a man, with a handsome, smiling face. He wears no beard this time, and his sunglasses obscure his eyes. He strides down the wooden planks with an air of self-possession, surveying the shore like he owns the island and has come to collect taxes. The crew members applaud as he walks past—even Hawaiian Shirt and Goatee. Reuben Hemslock bows theatrically, his ponytail curling down one side of his neck.

"Appreciate the welcome. Who's ready to make an award-winning documentary with me?" he shouts, and more cheers greet his call.

"And who's this?" the actor soon asks, spotting me. Unlike the others, I do not clap.

"Name's, uh," Hawaiian Shirt taps rapidly on his phone to check. "I've got the signed contract here—yeah. Alon. Alon Budhi. Our official tour guide for the rest of the season. Dog here's named Askal—Az for short—but we haven't bothered asking him to sign."

"Here's a tip for you, kid," Reuben says. "Az is a crappy name for a dog. The other dogs are gonna kick his az if they haven't already." He chuckles at his joke. I don't. "Is this who we've been trying to find?"

"Yeah. Fishing nearby, if you can believe that. Knows more about the lore than anyone else and is willing to tell us on camera. We're waiting for Steve before we get the whole story, but kid's been inside the cave before. Eighteen years old, but dunno if we'd be all right filming a teen inside the Godseye. Legal tells us it's all good, but optics-wise it's dodgy, might get us some pushback."

"Nah," Reuben says. "Eighteen's an adult. If Alon here wants to come into the Godseye with us, then the kid's got every right to. And how many of these folks would kill for a chance to be on an American show? You agree, Alon?"

"If you say so, sir."

"See? I'm gonna crash for a bit at my cabin. Partied too much at Austen's last night. Why didn't anyone tell me it was gonna take fifteen hours to get to this goddamn island?"

"Reuben," Hawaiian Shirt says, smile fading from his face. "You promised you'd stop drinking. The press is already on your case for the rehabs, plus all that other news. I don't think you should be—"

Reuben yawns. "We'll talk about this later. After dinner. Where's my trailer?"

Hawaiian Shirt rubs the bridge of his nose after the actor

departs, his bodyguards trailing closely after. "You said he was going to clean himself up," he says to another man, the one wearing the Armani suit. "He's not taking off those shades because his eyes are bloodshot, right?"

"There's no paparazzi here to photograph his drinking bouts, Gerry. How bad could it be? Give him a day to wind down, and he'll be good to go. If you can handle Karl, surely you can handle Hemslock."

"We can't afford any more scandals."

"I've been his work partner for years. We fended off those hysterical women months ago. This is nothing."

"Bodyguards all look ex-mercenary to me. He said he was bringing in four people, not eight. Who does he think is gonna attack him here?"

"He paid them all on his own dime, so why not?" Armani looks back, as another man joins them. "Leo, the cabins for you and your son should be that way."

"Thank you," the newcomer says, stretching. Unlike the man in the suit, he wears a casual polo shirt and long khaki pants. His hair is graying, and his face naturally tanned but tired. "This is…a lot less gloomy than I expected."

At his side is a boy my age with yellow hair and bright green eyes, looking like he dressed for a beach party but caught the wrong boat. He's carrying a suitcase over his shoulder, oddly enough. He holds his phone in the air, grinning widely at it, and I realize he's taking a picture of himself.

"Dad, you didn't tell me this was *literally* in the middle of nowhere," he said, finally lowering it to blink at us.

"You said you wanted to take a break from home, Chase, so this is that. I told you this wasn't going to be a five-star resort."

The boy turns to look at me and nearly trips. His suitcase falls, and I reach out without thinking—and then grunt when the weight nearly sends me to the ground. The boy grabs it back with a sheepish grin, one hand holding the suitcase like it weighs nothing while the other helps me balance. He's stronger than he looks. "Sorry," he says. He takes another look at me, and his eyes widen. "I just, ah—hi! Who are you?"

"This is Alon," Hawaiian Shirt says. "Our tour guide."

"A tour guide?" The boy asks, sounding genuinely confused. He stares at me like I've grown another arm. "But I can walk around this island in like an hour."

"Chase, show some respect," his father says sternly. "It's very nice to meet you, Alon. This is my son, Chase. My name is Leo Gries. I'm the co-executive producer for this show. It's been a lovely visit so far. We stayed in Cebu for a couple of nights before coming here to Kisapmata, and I was so very charmed by the people there. I hope we're compensating you well for this?"

"Yes, sir."

"It's been difficult to find anyone local willing to tell us about this island."

"The island doesn't *look* cursed," Chase says, still in wonder. "Have you seen those waves? U-uh, Alon, right?"

Gries smiles at me, then shoots an exasperated look at his son. "Chase."

"Sorry, sorry. It's just—I know you told me about a curse, but I thought you guys were just gonna magic it all up in the studio. You mean, for *real* this is a cursed island?"

"Your son's right," says Armani. "We'll have to put some darker tones in, maybe a blue filter to set the mood. It doesn't look haunted if it's always this sunny." He shoves his suitcase into my hands. "Here. And get some coffee ready for me."

"Steve!" Leo Gries grabs the bag and shoves it back at the other man. "Alon isn't the hired help!"

Armani shrugs. "Well, my cabin's on the left. That's where I expect it to be by the time I get there."

"This is Steve Galant," Hawaiian Shirt says, with lesser enthusiasm. "Another of the show's executive producers."

Armani scrutinizes me. "So you're the kid Gerry's been going on about? Your English's impressive."

"Steve!" Gries exclaims once again.

Melissa takes the suitcase and shoots me an apologetic look as she lugs it away.

Armani laughs, pats me on the back. "I'm kidding. If Gerry's right, you're gonna be the hidden star of this show. Just don't tell Hemslock I said that. We're gonna talk shop at dinner. Stay and eat with us. I'd like to pick your brain about this place."

Leo Gries turns back to me when Armani leaves. "Can you give us an idea why so many of the people living nearby have refused to tell us anything about Kisapmata?"

"At least fifteen people have already died on this island, sir. The people here do not want to be blamed for any more deaths."

"Fifteen?" Chase breathes. "And it's not like, drownings or shark attacks? Like people were murdered? Even though no one actually lives here?"

His father sighs. "Yes, Chase. Actual murders took place here. If you'd read the articles I gave you, you would have known that. The murder of the poor woman by that cult is the one we want more information about. We've been asking for any related documents from the municipalities for months, but they only shrug and say they can't find any. Likely destroyed by now, they said."

"A woman's murder?" Chase echoes nervously. "Cult?"

"Apparently there was an active cult here a couple of decades ago. They were supposedly killed on the island before they could be arrested, but all we've found are rumors and secondhand accounts. No official case reports. I've been hoping that we could find someone here willing to talk. Do you know anything about this, Alon?"

I shake my head.

Askal ambles toward Chase, sensing his nervousness. The boy absently reaches down and scratches him behind the ears. "Nice dog," he says. "Is he yours?"

"Yeah."

"Some lab mix?"

"Maybe. We don't pay much attention to pedigrees here."

Chase smiles, and it transforms his face. The worry in his brow eases and he appears more relaxed. "Heya, Askal. You're a cute fella, just like—"

He stops and turns red. Askal yips happily and licks at his hands.

Hawaiian Shirt shoves his into his pants pockets and sighs.

"We've got more problems," he says. "Did Cameron tell you the local first responders won't be coming if we run into any emergencies? That we gotta fly in our own medics? They really hate this island."

"They don't hate it," I say.

"Could have fooled me."

"They aren't fearful of the curse. They're afraid of what all of you might do while you're here."

A soft indrawn breath from Leo Gries. "Then why are you helping us? Why aren't you warning us away like the others?"

"I've walked this island many times before. I've fished in its waters. I am familiar with the island's ghosts, and they are familiar with me. My countrymen will be blamed if anything happens to any of you. My presence might help."

"You are very kind. Thank you."

"We're not going to be intimidated by some old wives' tales," Hawaiian Shirt says. "We stand to make a lot of money from this show if we get the ratings we're after—or at least if we make it good enough for the network to give us a bigger push." He grins at me. "And when we do, we'll give you a bonus, Alon, and a nice treat for your dog, too. We'll finish out this season, whatever happens."

No sooner are the words out of his mouth than we hear a horrific crash.

The sound comes from the direction of the cabins.

I sprint toward the site before the rest of them can react. Crew members flee, screaming.

By the time I arrive, the damage has already been done.

One of the pre-fab cabins is gone, fallen into a sinkhole that has appeared, seemingly out of nowhere—a perfect circle on the ground, a mimicry of one of the many machines that the builders used for construction.

An ancient monstrosity stands at its center. A tree without a trunk. It is, instead, a fortress of webbed roots and slim ivy-like coils climbing up the pre-fab's foundation to spread its ossified tree branches. They reach up greedily, as if to claw at the sky above with their gnarled fingers.

Crew members gather at the edge of the sinkhole, unable to look away. Someone screams and points toward the thickness of the strange, twisted mass within the dead tree.

Within the cobweb of branches, a body lies huddled; its head is thrown back, and its mummified mouth is twisted open in an endless, soundless scream.

FOUR

THE CORPSE TREE

ARMANI IS BEYOND ELATED. "ARE YOU SEEING THIS?" HE
chortles, prancing around the sinkhole in unfettered glee. "What
are you all waiting for? Did we get footage of the sinkhole appearing? Were any cameras rolling when this was…? Why are you all
standing around? Go!"

The loss of the cabin has not put a damper on his enthusiasm.
The same is not true for Leo Gries, who is appalled to learn that the
destroyed bungalow was his. "Didn't you test the ground?" he yells
at the surveyors, visibly shaken. "If I'd been inside, I could have
been killed!"

One of the scientists speaks up, looking rattled himself. "The
chances of a sinkhole of this size…we ran every test we could, and
there was no way this was—"

"Well, run them again! Test the whole island!"

Goatee stares down at the hole, face pale. He mutters something about a drink and staggers away.

Askal hasn't stopped barking since the tree was unearthed, only calming down when I hug him. He's shaking.

Reuben Hemslock stands at the edge of the hole, fixated on the twisted tree and its grotesque fruit with the biggest grin on his face. He takes off his sunglasses. "I'm going down there," he says. "Hook me up."

Gries turns. "You're going to get yourself killed!"

"I've climbed down worse places, man. I'm not afraid of some dead dickhead on a tree. I want two cameras—head, face shot. Tape up the mic, don't clip it—strap everything tight so nothing gets dislodged while I'm down there."

"Reuben!"

"I know what I'm doing. I've been doing this for twenty years! You said you'd let me handle the show my way, so shut up and let me get you the ratings I promised!"

No one is listening to Leo Gries's protests. The crew is already outfitting Hemslock with cameras—one attached to a helmet on his head, another wired to face him—and hooks secured around his waist to help him rappel down. He tugs hard on the ropes tethering him to safety, nods. "Keep rolling, no matter what happens," he tells the cameramen, and then leaps backward, effortlessly, down into the sinkhole.

"At least take some of the security team with you," Leo Gries yells after him.

"Not waiting for them," Reuben shouts back. "And I'm not gonna film this twice."

Already there is a mad scramble among the safety crew to don similar protective gear, even as the actor lowers himself farther into the hole. Hemslock's bodyguards have gathered around the sinkhole. A few have their guns trained on the corpse.

"Do *not* shoot the damn tree!" Armani shouts, no longer pleased. "We'll need more footage of it before the day's out—I swear to God, Reuben—"

"Steve, they're doing what I'm paying them for." Hemslock angles himself toward the withered tree. "What a way to start the show!" I hear him exclaim as he begins recording. "This is how the Godseye welcomes me, literally on the first day I set foot on this island—with this beautiful corpse bouquet."

He keeps up the chatter, as Leo Gries and the others wait by a hastily set up workstation. Twin screens show the live recording— one focused on Hemslock's face and the other receiving feed from the camera on his head. The latter perfectly captures the gnarled tree as Hemslock gradually works his way toward it. The former shows the delighted expression on the man's face as he draws nearer.

I watch through the monitor as the camera swings downward, toward the hole below Reuben's feet. "That's a long way down," he notes. "I think I can see the ground from here, and something tells me I'm going to be exploring that before long, too—but that's a journey for another day." His viewpoint returns to the corpse tree before him. The other members of the safety crew are scaling down the sinkhole as well, their own cameras connected to more screens for us to observe with.

"Now, will you look at this beauty," we hear him whisper as he clings to the wall adjacent to the body, close enough for him to reach out and touch.

"Judging from the look of this, I'd say this is a balete—a parasitical tree that envelops and then kills their host's foliage, leaving a hollow center instead of a real trunk. It's a common enough species in the country, but the balete on this island looks to be a unique breed entirely. After all, how many trees can boast using the *dead* for its foundation?"

He's right. At first the body looked like it had been ensnared by the branches. A closer inspection afforded by Hemslock's camera shows that the corpse *is* the tree. It has no visible legs; its lower body appears to have fused with the roots surrounding it, so there is no clear distinction between where the corpse ends and the trunk begins. I can see strips of clothing still clinging to its person, tattered and nearly blackened with age.

"My God," one of the film crew says.

Hemslock is undaunted. "Almost looks like this thing was carved out of its trunk, doesn't it? The skin looks severely wizened, almost like bark. The corpse barely looks human at this point, if not for that face."

"But as odd as it sounds, this is exactly what I came here hoping to find. Many of the myths surrounding the Godseye delve into a strange, hauntingly symbiotic relationship between the trees and the supposed god who lives on this island. People used to worship balete trees here—they believed them to be the sacred groves of duwende, or the so-called fairy people. But here in the Godseye, the story gets even more fucked up…

"Hey, can I say 'fuck' or is Steve gonna bleep it out? Let me do it one more time, so he can choose.

"But here in the Godseye, things get even stranger."

The camera view swings closer to the corpse's face. Withered and desiccated, it looks halfway between a mummified skeleton and an embalmed body. Its eyes are long gone, leaving empty sockets and hollow shadows. The nose and mouth remain distinct, like a thin membrane has been stretched over its chin and cheeks to preserve its features.

Its lips are stretched and pulled wide, distorting the face's shape; its jaw is distended, like it died screaming. For the first time, we can see thin branches spiraling out from the corpse's mouth, like he's been impaled lengthwise through his body.

"According to the legends surrounding the Godseye and the island of Kisapmata," Hemslock continues, "balete trees are natural coffins. The locals would bring their loved ones to this island with balete saplings and bury them together. If the deceased is deemed worthy, or so the tale goes, the balete grows around them. The roots will pull them underground to some hidden cave beneath the island where the god, this supposed Dreamer, sleeps."

"And there the dead dream alongside the god, waiting for the day the god wakes—some say to heal the world; others, to destroy it and start anew."

"Do it, Hemslock," Armani whispers, as if the man can hear him. "Do it."

Hemslock edges closer and reaches out a gloved hand.

The tip of his finger sinks into the cheekbone. "Hey, you," Hemslock says. "Hey. How's it hanging up there?"

The corpse gapes back at the rest of us through the camera's viewfinder.

It moves.

The camera jerks away as Hemslock rears back in alarm. Gasps rise up from those gathered by the monitors. Through the other screens, I can see several safety crew members, hanging on their own lines, slowly inch toward the actor, intending to yank him out of harm's way.

The corpse's skull shakes. Insect legs stretch out of its left eye socket, and a large black spider slowly pulls itself out, climbing lazily up the decaying head.

Hemslock relaxes, chuckles. Nervous titters follow from the rest of the group.

"You got me there, old fella. You really got me." Hemslock pokes at the face a few more times.

I exhale slowly, sensing instinctively that whatever danger there would have been had passed.

"For the rest of you back home, that is most definitely not a tree carving. Despite all the stories claiming otherwise, no balete trees of this species have ever been recorded outside of Kisapamata Island. Some locals assert that balete trees grow *upside down* within the island. All you can see of them, they say, are the occasional roots sticking out from the sand."

He moves away, and the camera slowly pans to reveal the whole of the balete tree in its terrifying glory once more. "It isn't *technically* upside down," Hemslock says, "but it's not every day you find a whole tree growing underneath the ground either. Given the island's porous soil, I'd say there may be something to the legends after all. We shouldn't dismiss their stories. But here is the million-dollar question: Which of the so-called victims of the Godseye is *this* beauty? No one found Alex Key's body, did they? Or—and this is an even bigger speculation—is this the body of Oliviero Cortes, the famed Spaniard himself?"

Hemslock continues to film for another hour before climbing out of the sinkhole unscathed, grinning from ear to ear. He's brimming with energy, not lethargy. "I have a good feeling about this, Steve," he says. "This is a once-in-a-lifetime shot. And we're only on the first day."

"You got in some excellent closeups," Armani praises him. "That thing didn't even faze you."

Hemslock laughs. "This is the best in-your-face moment in all my years ghost hunting. We're gonna make a killing off this show, Steve." He strips off his gloves and tosses them to an assistant.

Hawaiian Shirt checks his pad. "We're going to ask Lachlan and the others to take a sample of the soil growing near the tree, plus whatever DNA they can scrape off the body itself to send for analysis. Maybe we can find a match during post prod, trace for any living family members."

"I'm betting money that it's the Spanish explorer," Hemslock says assertively. "Obviously not the local woman who was supposedly sacrificed. They only found Key's lower body, but they did find part of his hand. Unless he's got three limbs, this isn't him. You saw those pieces of rusted metal? That's gotta be *armor*, man. Cortes, or maybe another fellow conquistador. A few of them went missing during that expedition. Out of the five ships Magellan commanded, only eighteen men survived the voyage back."

"Impossible," Leo Gries says. "You're telling me that we may have found the body of someone that historians and governments have spent centuries looking for, just like that?"

"Why not? It's a known fact that Cortes went missing in the Godseye." Hemslock points a finger at the large cave in the distance. "Still don't believe the legends after everything, Leo? Didn't you come to this island hoping for the impossible? Don't you want to figure out what happened to your wife?"

Leo steps back, his face turning red. "Don't bring my wife into this."

Hemslock lifts his hands. "Hey, whoa. No offense meant. But you're lying to yourself if that isn't what you're here for. Like that isn't the reason you're producing this show with me. And what you're here for closely aligns with what *I'm* here for. I want to solve all the mysterious deaths on this island and throw it back at the naysayers who tried to sabotage my career. And you get your answer when I get mine."

Leo stares back at him, troubled.

"That sinkhole appeared for a reason. This island wants you here. It wants us to solve its mystery as much as we do, tell the world its story." Reuben Hemslock turns to me. "You're the Kisapmata expert. You agree, right?"

I stare back at him. "The Diwata doesn't like people on His island."

"Why not? Doesn't it need three more deaths to gain back its power, or so the curse goes?"

"He will take more than three lives the longer you all stay."

It feels like the crew is watching us, holding their breaths, waiting for the actor to respond to my lack of courtesy. A frown briefly mars Hemslock's face, but then it broadens into a wide smile.

"I like you," he says. "You've got guts. Hear that, Leo? We better not stay too long. Time to crack this case wide open."

"I want as many DNA samples from this thing as you can get," Armani calls out, his good humor restored. "Scrape all the flesh off the body you can, send it to Marvin's team ASAP. I want to know who this man is! If you're right about this, Rube, then we're one step closer to the treasure they say is buried here!"

"It would be easier if we could exhume the corpse," someone from the scientific team says. "If it's not too brittle. Would be fascinating to put it through an MRI scan, see if there're any more secrets we can find within it."

"Can we stick it back down there once you're done, though? I want more for our drone work."

"Not if the tree's fused to it, as Mr. Hemslock believes. But we can try."

That Hemslock escaped the sinkhole unscathed has boosted morale; soon other teams descend into the pit. Leo Gries remains by the workstation, staring in disbelief as Straw Hat, the friendly editor, begins reviewing the footage they've acquired so far. "I don't believe it," he mutters from time to time, though no one is paying him any attention.

Reuben has decided that the next place to film would be within the Godseye itself, by the stone altar within. The crew takes a shot of the exterior, and then more around the altar. Leo Gries stares at it and shudders. "What was this for?" he asks me.

"It was one of many places where sacrifices were offered."

"One of *many* places?"

"Seems like there are others within the cave," Hawaiian Shirt says. "The team hasn't found them yet, though. There are a couple of sketches from Key's journal that show how the ritual's done. No idea if it's accurate, but we'll run with it."

"Get on the altar, Steve," Reuben says.

"Me? Why the hell would I—"

"Just humor me."

Grumbling, Armani lies down.

"This is how they performed the sacrifice, according to what we've found so far," Hemslock says. He moves, placing Armani's hands and feet over the small holes on the sides of the stone. "They were bound like this, probably with rope." He points toward a larger hole at the center of the altar, between Armani's legs. "I've got a pretty good hypothesis about this one. I'm guessing that if the god accepts the sacrifice, it grabs the victim and drags it down through here."

"How?" Gries asks, appalled. "The hole isn't big enough for a human to get through…unless…"

"Unless the god doesn't care if they're in one piece when they do," Hemslock says, grinning.

With a grunt, Armani pushes himself off the altar, still scowling. "Get someone else to do the reenactment next time."

"It won't be as much fun."

Outside, I spot Chase taking photos of himself with his phone, flexing and grinning at the screen. Once done, he wanders back near the sinkhole, watching the crew circle their way around the tree, trying to figure out the best way to take out the corpse without destroying the roots that have grown around it.

"I promised Dad I wouldn't take any pictures that would reveal anything about the show," he whispers when I join him. Askal has calmed down but won't stop looking at the tree below us. "But I wasn't expecting this. Have you ever seen anything like it before?"

"It's not a good sign."

"It's not, like, some publicity stunt, right?"

"You're more familiar with that than I am."

"Yeah, it just feels freaking unbelievable that this happened, and I can't tell anyone. Did having so many people here cause the sinkhole?"

"I don't know. Kisapmata's never had this many trespassers before."

"Kisa-what? Oh, right. It's what y'all call this place."

His dismissive tone irks me. "It's what the island is called. At least care enough to learn how to say it."

He frowns at me. "What's your problem? Coming here to film ghosts wasn't my idea, you know. Take it up with the actual people in charge."

"Then why are you here?"

His phone buzzes again. "Well, my dad is one of the showrunners involved."

44

"Do showrunners always bring their kids?"

"I *want* to be here. So what?" He scowls at the still-vibrating phone in his hand, then ends the call without picking it up.

"Aren't you answering that?"

"It's my phone, and I'll answer it when I want." Chase turns to Melissa, who stands placidly nearby. "Who are you?"

"Your father asked me to stay with you," Melissa explains calmly. "In case you need anything."

"I don't need anything, and I definitely don't need a babysitter!"

"Gosh, that puts me in a real conundrum, because your dad's paying me to keep an eye on you. And his paychecks are the only ones I'm taking home for this gig, so…sorry. My girlfriend's birthday is next month, and I'd like to take her somewhere fancy when I get back."

"Check this out," Straw Hat says suddenly. "Leo, you seeing this?"

Chase lopes back toward the table, curious despite himself, and Melissa, Askal, and I follow. Straw Hat, it seems, has found a camera that was trained on the cabins when the sinkhole first appeared. Leo is already replaying the tape.

At first there is nothing out of the ordinary. The cabins stand as they were supposed to, with no inkling of what was to come. And then the camera flickers, darkness flitting through the screen for a few moments. When the veil lifts, the sinkhole is there.

"I've run it through ten times now," Straw Hat says. "The camera was most definitely not turned off. If you listen closely, you can hear sounds of the ground giving way at the 25:54 mark.

It almost looks like someone threw a blanket over the lens for a couple of minutes."

I stare at the screen as he replays it again. The darkness that fills the camera lens feels familiar. "Or someone moved in front of the camera deliberately," I say.

"Impossible. This camera's mounted to one of the trees overlooking the cabins. We were only supposed to use it for extra shots. Someone would have had to climb all the way up there, and even then, we would have seen who it was."

"We can't move it!" one of the scientists within the sinkhole yells. "Mr. Hemslock's right—we'll have to chop down the tree to get the corpse out of the hole."

"Under no circumstances are you to damage the tree!" I hear Armani yell back. "We'll find out who it is the old-fashioned way!"

Leo's face is inches from the monitor, as if a closer look would solve the mystery. "Faulty equipment?" he asks. "Or maybe sun glare that caused it to—"

Suddenly, from inside the darkness, the monitor before us breathes out a word, a whisper.

Leo, a woman's voice says.

Gries swears and jumps back, and Straw Hat upends his chair trying to get away from the monitor, pausing the video by accident in his haste. Chase leaps back with a yelp, sending some of the other crew running toward us, Reuben Hemslock included.

"Did you hear that?" Leo shouts, pointing accusingly at the camera. "*Did you hear that?*"

"Play it again," Hemslock says eagerly. "*Play it again.*"

But the whisper does not repeat in subsequent viewings, even when they use their expensive headphones and when they use equipment designed to draw out the most inaudible of sounds. Again and again, the darkness fills the screen; again and again, it says nothing.

FIVE

LORE

I SEE CHASE GRIES AGAIN BEFORE DINNER. HE'S FOUND an isolated spot on the beach some distance from the bustle of the crew, and he's dancing.

It's an odd dance. He's bare chested and in a tight pair of shorts, and he's letting his feet do most of the work—hard stomps on the sand with his heels and toes that somehow manage to look graceful. He'd set the camera against a large rock and it's clear he's filming himself.

In all the chaos of the sinkhole, I had little chance to assess the newcomer. He struck me as someone who was rather shallow, but now, watching him, his brows furrowed and his tongue sticking out of his mouth as he concentrates on the complicated routine, I recognize that it wasn't right of me to judge him so quickly.

Askal, as always, chooses trouble. He bounds gleefully toward Chase just as the dance ends. The boy sees him coming; with a laugh, he opens his arms and Askal jumps into them happily, sending both crashing into the sand. "Askal!" I call out, running toward them.

"It's all right! It's kinda sweet." Grinning, Chase gets back on his feet, then jogs toward his phone to end the recording. "That was a great way to end the post. Couldn't bring my horse head, but a pup's always a bonus."

"Is that all you think about?" I ask curiously. "About how you will look online?"

Chase cranes his neck to look back at me, but he doesn't seem at all offended. "I get to chat with my friends all the time," he says. "And all it takes is a scroll. And I can talk to people all over the world. Sure, there'll be some haters, but it's not like I don't get haters in real life anyway, you know? Aren't you interested? Aren't Filipinos like, some of the most active users online in the world? I have a lot of Filipino fans. People recognized me here."

"Being seen isn't my style."

"You're kinda weird," Chase says, smiling. "But in a good way. It's kinda cute." He checks his phone, gives a satisfied nod after he plays back the video. "Is that why you like staying here? Cause everything's quiet and stuff? How do you earn money if you're the tour guide of an island that no one's allowed to visit? Sell rocks to the tourists?"

"I... I fish?" I reassess my opinion of him again. He's nice and charming, but with two brain cells at most.

He grabs my hand unexpectedly. "Do you want to dance?" He asks earnestly, then realizes what he's doing and drops it. "I mean, do you want me to teach you how to tap dance? Or if that's not your thing, do you wanna hang out? Not like there's a lot to do—"

Up close, he looks almost like a puppy himself. The same earnest eyes, his obliviousness to his own appeal. "I can't," I say, not sure why I sound so regretful. "Need to check on my dad first. And I'm supposed to have dinner with the crew."

"Ah." He steps back. He's actually blushing. "Right. You're right. I'm gonna... go. I don't know why I keep putting my foot in my mouth, but—I'm sorry for bothering you."

"What? You're not both—"

But Chase's already sprinting back to the cabins, leaving me alone on the beach. Beside me, Askal sits and nudges at my hand, then lets out an exasperated bark.

⊰᯽⊱

"So nice of you to join us," Armani greets me with a smile, as I step into the mess hall. Most of the crew remain outside; lanterns hanging from nearby trees serve as their main source of light now that night has fallen. Filming is done for the day, and most of the crew linger at their tables with plates of food, chatting and swapping stories. A majority of the crew have left the island after the sinkhole incident, to my relief. Only a dozen and a half are left behind.

It's different when you're an executive. The others eat their meals outdoors with a hearty selection of sandwiches, fries, and cold drinks. But inside, the VIPs feast. Their menu has champagne and hors d'oeuvres—bite-sized sandwiches that are somehow more elaborate than the subs the crew receives, cold soup served from a turret, and fresh unagi and uni sashimi flown to the island from the seas of Japan.

I have to leave Askal outside with the rest of the crew, much to their delight. I can hear them cooing and fussing over him when I step inside. Askal has had a quiet life with me and 'Tay, and it feels good to see people give him the attention he deserves.

There is no one else here to impress, but Armani wears cufflinks and a new suit—a ridiculous contrast to Reuben Hemslock, dressed casually in a loose shirt with sleeves rolled up to his elbows and dark jeans. His bodyguards prowl the room, a few glancing offhandedly out the window, in case someone might think to ambush the group. They carry their guns like they're patrolling a military zone.

I would have preferred to remain outside, but Armani insists. "You'll learn how we do things around here soon enough," he tells me. "And as our local expert, it'll be good for you to be here, because we're planning the rest of the season tonight. We've got a pretty good idea of the lore, but we'll tap you for other details we need more of." He eyes my clothes. "You want me to lend you something nice to wear while you're here? That whole authentic look's great for when you're on camera, though."

His interpretation of *authentic* is not the same as mine, but I turn down his offer and keep my words polite.

"How've you been holding up so far, kid?" Hemslock asks from behind me. "Is all of this different from that island life?"

"It's more people than I'm used to."

"You'll ease into it soon enough. No one to keep you company?" His grin widens. "You look like the type to swing both ways."

"Reuben," Gries says, looking embarrassed.

Hemslock only chuckles. "Alon's old enough, Leo. And it's not like I'm flirting." For a moment his brows draw down, anger flashing across his face before he grins again. "Alon's hanging out with the heavy hitters now. Just pointing that out."

Leo offers the seat beside him. He introduces me to a few other people in the room, including the scientists who attempted to excavate the tree earlier, and a couple of the show's lead writers. Melissa is here as well, presumably to run errands for the producers. Chase sits beside his father and appears distracted, fiddling with his phone and scowling down at it, obviously in no mood to answer whoever's calling when it buzzes.

"The writing team will be presenting," Leo explains. "And we want you on hand to make sure we don't deviate from what the legends are really about."

He looks tired despite his friendliness. I wonder if he's still thinking about the strange video. Hemslock and the others decided it was a fluke since the voice couldn't be replicated, though it is clear that Gries does not feel the same way.

Several monitors have been set up on the walls, and a technical team is hard at work connecting them to numerous laptops. One by one, the screens light up, revealing three other important-looking men in business suits who sit behind large desks.

Melissa spots my confusion. "They're executive producers," she says, taking advantage of the opportunity to pile her plate high with the sushi. She lowers her voice. "It's kinda unusual. Most TV shows don't usually have more than two executive producers, but we've got five. Sounds like a lot of the studio higher-ups were insistent about buying in. Probably because of the stuff that happened with Mr. Hemslock—a show of support or something."

"Now that everyone's here," one of the head writers begins, after an approving nod from Armani, "we can start. As I mentioned before, we'll be improvising a lot for this show, mostly because we still can't completely separate the facts from fiction." He smiles in my direction. "I'd like to show you all the direction we're taking, and see if everyone is on board.

"All right, so we have this island, Kisapmata. Here's the mythology: something sleeps within it—a local psychopomp at the least, a venerated death god at most. There were definitely sacrifices made here—locals and historians have verified that. The ongoing lore is that eight deaths are needed to reawaken this god, and that his waking will usher in a" he raises his hands and wriggles two fingers on each, "*new beginning.*"

"What the hell is that supposed to mean?" Producer Number One asks from one of the monitors. "What new beginning? Some kind of rapture?"

"That is something we can't confirm. The locals believe the god will create a new world with no crime or poverty."

"But then how are we gonna do business?" another producer jokes.

One by one, heads turn my way. I blink.

"Well?" Armani asks. "Surely you know what this 'new beginning' is?"

"It's not the rapture," I say slowly. "We believe that the world is nothing but a dream of the Diwata. When He wakes, the dream will end."

"That's pretty vague," Producer One complains.

"If the belief is that the world is nothing but a dream," Leo says, "then what happens once the god wakes?"

I shrug. "We are born anew."

"So it *is* like the rapture," Producer Two says, chuckling.

"We don't need the prophecy to make sense," Hemslock says calmly. "People'll eat up those pseudo-religious theories and justify their own belief systems for it."

"What I don't get," Armani says, "is what the trees have to do with these sacrifices."

They all look at me again.

"Balete trees are sacred to the Diwata," I reply. "Burying family with their saplings is a sign of devotion. He gains nourishment from the dead as He sleeps, and they in turn are promised eternal bliss when He wakes."

"So He leeches off people in exchange for their peace of mind?" Producer Three sniggers. "Sounds like my ex-wife."

The remark is met with a smattering of laughter.

"Are there any known species of balete that grow underground?" Hemslock asks intently.

"No," a researcher answers. "But previous expeditions *have* found evidence of ancient burial sites here—nothing beyond traces of human remains, though."

"Any evidence of balete found with those bodies?"

"No—but the bones are old, several centuries in most cases, and none of them were intact when they were unearthed, so it's doubtful we'd find evidence of any balete trees buried with them as well. We can test the sinkhole for evidence."

"They found roots growing on Alex Key," Hemslock says, "They were balete. I checked."

"We're getting ahead of ourselves, Reuben," Producer Two reminds him. "Sam, continue."

The head writer clears his throat. "The plan is to give an overview of the curse and the legend surrounding it in the first episode, then focus on the known victims for the next three or four. See if we can get footage to tie fact and lore together more conclusively. We still don't have a lot of information about the first two deaths. The corpse tree was a godsend—we'll splash that for the first few episodes."

"How many victims have there been?" Producer One interrupts. "Didn't they record over fifteen deaths on this island already? So haven't they've surpassed the quota for the eight needed to awaken the god?"

"Most of those deaths won't count for the curse, sir. The deaths need to match very specific requirements. That we *were* able to confirm with the locals."

"A convenient explanation to keep the con going, don't you think?"

"Someone must be actively offered up as a sacrifice for it to count," Hemslock says. "I don't doubt though, that this god is not above killing anyone that it thinks is unworthy. If a serial killer sets out to kill eight women but kills men and children as well, then they're still his murders."

"The Diwata is not a serial killer," I say sharply.

"That his name?" Producer Three asks. "Diwata?"

"It means *god* in Tagalog," Leo says stiffly.

"Not that easy to remember. Let's call it the Dreamer. Better recall, fits in nicely with the rest of the narrative we're pitching."

"Getting back to the victims." The head writer taps on his keyboard and a projector flickers to life, displaying information on the wall behind him.

"Here we go. First two deaths, few details. Then the third victim, Oliviero Cortes. Those initial two deaths *were* recorded in his journal, and scholars have verified them. Cortes's life is a good chunk of known history, until his disappearance."

"I take it everyone here is aware of Oliviero Cortes?" Armani asks, looking meaningfully at me.

I set my jaw. "Oliviero Cortes was one of the many Spaniards who tried to colonize my country, sir. I am well aware of who he is."

"One of the crew members of Magellan's expedition, right?" Producer Two asks. "The one who tried to make off with the locals' gold. Allegedly hid it on the island. Now, treasure—that's what interests me most."

"We've printed out copies of Cortes's journal to pass around," the head writer says. "Other records mentioned that the chieftain Cilapulapu—better known as Lapulapu, a hero in this country— had this journal in his possession."

"The same chieftain who killed Magellan? How'd he get his hands on the journal?"

"Historians believe that Lapulapu killed Cortes for attempting to steal his people's gold. We think it's because Cortes had stumbled onto Lapulapu's supposed connection with this god. This Mactan chieftain was one of the most powerful rulers of the region surrounding Kisapmata, though very little has been recorded of him after Magellan's death. We'll spend a couple of episodes unpacking all of that before we move on to the cultists."

"What's this?" Producer One asks. "What cultists?"

An exasperated exhale from one of the other monitors. "Mark, weren't you paying attention during the last meeting?"

"Buried treasure was all I needed to sell me on this production."

"There was a cult," Leo Gries tells him. "They believed that by helping the god find the deaths he wanted, they would, in turn, gain powers beyond their imagination. So they sacrificed a woman inside the cave. A *pregnant* woman. We found her grave—not on the island, but she is buried in the town graveyard."

"Holy shit," Hawaiian Shirt mutters, shocked. "You mean the altar inside the Godseye was where they'd killed her? Damn."

The head writer clicks on his keyboard. The image behind him shifts to reveal a white woman, haggard-looking but defiant, staring back at us. She seems oddly familiar. *Watson, Lindsay*, is scribbled on the placard she holds before her.

"The cult leader," the writer says. "Lindsay Watson. Museum curator from Florida charged with embezzling funds. Turns out even *Lindsay Watson* was an alias as well. She didn't have any family we could find, nothing to suggest what her past life was. There are thousands of people with the same name across the US. She'd gotten her hands on someone else's social security and forged documents to make herself a new identity. By the time anyone realized that the real Lindsay Watson had been dead for twenty years, she'd already bailed herself out, fled the United States, and resurfaced at a museum in Cebu using forged references. It was the same museum with the Cortes journal. Colleagues said she was fascinated by Cortes's life. Seems like she was the one who found the journal in their archives and recognized its importance."

Another slide showcases a series of Watson's own notes.

"We checked out entries from the diary she kept. She talked about strange dreams and hearing voices in her head—we'll keep those details as filler. She referred to Cortes's journal as 'The Book' constantly, talking about it like it was the Bible. Said she'd been guided to this place from America. Like the god was going to give her powers if she carried out sacrifices for him. The irony was that when we first got her diary, no one had any idea what she was talking about. We hadn't found Cortes's journal yet—not until Mr. Hemslock suggested that we talk to the museum in Cebu where she'd worked, see if she'd been obsessing over any of their artifacts."

"And I was right," Hemslock says, with some satisfaction.

"What happened next plays out like some B-grade horror movie," the writer continues. "She gathered some like-minded expats she'd brainwashed into believing her claims, stole the Cortes journal, kidnapped a local woman, and then made for Kisapmata. Allegedly, none of the cultists survived. None of their bodies were found, either.

"I want to highlight something else we found in Cortes's journals, and then again with Alex Key's, the fifth victim. Some info on Key—he's an expat who'd been living in Cebu for ten years. Married a local, but disappeared when he came under suspicion after she was murdered. He was an avid scuba diver, so he was familiar with the islands and knew the lore, according to neighbors. Told them he wanted to explore Kisapmata one day, once the restrictions were lifted. Could explain why his body was found here. His death wasn't pretty, either—he'd been cut in half. Recovered his journal near his corpse but the entries were mostly the ravings of a madman. But here's what's unusual." Another click of the mouse, and new text pops up on the wall.

> He who offers the sacrifice controls the Godseye.
> The first to feed,
> the second to seed,
> the third to wear,
> the fourth to birth,
> the fifth to serve,
> the sixth to lure,
> the seventh to consume,
> the last to wake.

"We found this riddle in both his and Cortes's journals. Key's is mostly incomprehensible, but the similarity of his entry to the Spaniard's indicates he must have found something inside the cave."

"In the last meeting you said that you'd only found Cortes's journal a couple of months ago," Producer Three says. "Hemslock found it at that same museum in Cebu that Watson had worked at, right? But Key's been dead for four years. How'd he know what that Spaniard had written centuries before?"

"That's what we're trying to figure out. Since then, we've used Cortes's to formulate most of our theories regarding how these deaths are selected. The people here do believe that helping the god with these sacrifices endows his helpers with supernatural abilities. They think it's how Lapulapu was able to control these islands for so long. Cortes himself wrote about how Lapulapu killed some local criminal to appease the god—*the first to eat*. Another entry mentions a corrupt chieftain sacrificed during a time of drought, which he took to mean as the *second to seed*. And if that tree corpse is Cortes himself, then he'd be the *third to wear*."

"A tree, wearing what remains of him," Hemslock says. "Poetic justice. And it would explain why the cult would have chosen a pregnant woman to sacrifice. *Fourth to birth*."

"No local court records of the cultists, though," Leo Gries murmurs.

"We'll find more proof sooner or later," Hemslock insists. "Did you all know that the Godseye was the first documentary I ever wanted to produce? I couldn't get any of you asses interested in it then. Information has always been scarce. Rumors of the cult and Alex Key's journal were the only thing we had to go on at first, until the plane crash a few years back."

"The same plane crash where my wife died," Leo Gries says. "The plane went missing in the area. The island was searched, to no avail. And then—a body was found a year later. Giles Cochrane. He was on the passenger list. They found him *buried* here. No one knows who did it, or why. Authorities searched the island again but couldn't find anyone—or anything—else."

Silence descends on the table. I see Chase looking down with his jaw clenched, abject misery on his face.

"I'm sorry, man," Producer Two says sincerely. "I know coming back here must be hard on you."

"I want closure," Leo says. I glance at his hands, gripped in his lap, knuckles white with effort. "I want to know what happened."

"And we'll do our best to figure that out," Hemslock says reassuringly.

"So you're saying that the god caused the plane to crash?" Producer Three asks disbelievingly.

"That's one of the things we're here to find out." Hemslock looks at me. "Am I right so far? What do you know about the cult?"

"The cult were outsiders," I say. "That was long before my time."

"What about your father? He ever mention them?"

"Only with disgust, but he knows very little of them."

"The plane crash investigators found nothing inside the Godseye," Hawaiian Shirt says. "But that's part of what I want to talk to you about, Rube. Christie says the cave system is way different than what the crash investigators described. You're the cave expert, so thought you'd like to know."

"Thanks. Send word back to Jesse, see if he can grill the locals. It's only been less than a couple of decades since the cult died here, someone out there knows something." Hemslock points at the projection on the wall. "The fifth, and last known, death—Alex Key. He's the one we've got the most concrete proof about. We have

61

a body—half of a body, but it's a start. And as I said, he'd left behind a notebook full of ramblings that make the curse sound even more insidious. And again—Key died four years ago. How did *he* wind up writing the same riddle Cortes had hundreds of years before? *Fifth to serve* and damn if Key isn't living up to that."

"I'd like to get more stories about the island," Armani says. "Any more scary stories you can tell us about this place, Alon?"

"It would be easier to leave," I say frankly. "Conduct your research outside of Kisapmata. The corpse tree isn't an accident."

A long silence follows. Hemslock breaks it by laughing. Armani and the other producers join in. "I'm afraid we can't do that, kid," Hemslock says with a chuckle. "We've put in too much money to pull out now, and some withered old corpse in a pit isn't going to scare us off. We'll take our chances. So spit it out. Regale us with your scary stories. You do want money for your father's treatment, right? Is fishing going to be enough to support you both if we fire you?"

I look around, at the smiling faces, the amusement in their eyes. *This is how Americans make threats*, I think. "Fishermen have reported seeing a woman near shore. They also hear screaming from within the island."

"And have you seen and heard both?" Hemslock asks intently.

I meet his gaze. "Yes. Cortes, Key, the cultists—they still suffer here."

Leo Gries looks nervous, the others uneasy. I can see some hesitation on the three producers' faces. Only Hemslock and Armani receive this with delight. "Then it's our duty to know why they are being punished," Hemslock says. "Free their souls if we gotta."

"You're going to point us to where this so-called lady has been sighted," Armani adds. "We'll have you on tape to explain as well. We don't want to coach you on your responses, by the way—gives the anecdote a more authentic feel. Do you know what the riddles surrounding the last three deaths mean? *Sixth to consume, seventh to lure, eight to wake?*"

I shake my head.

"At this rate," Armani says, chortling. "I may as well ask for volunteers to be the last three victims so we can finally find the treasure and get the curse lifted. All the life insurance they can get. Heck, I'd pay for their kids' college if it comes down to it. I believe that—"

I never find out what he claims to believe, because at that moment, the power goes out.

SIX

DON'T LOOK

SHOUTS ECHO AS PEOPLE STUMBLE INTO EACH OTHER IN the darkness. I can hear chairs overturning, plates and utensils clattering as they fall to the floor. I hear Leo stand up, his chair falling. I hear Chase's startled cry beside him. "Dad?"

"I saw her," Leo Gries whispers. "I saw her—at the window—"

Armani is once again irate. "Who's in charge of the set?" I can hear him hollering. "Someone get the lights back on!"

"The generator should be functioning," comes the stupefied reply. "We did multiple checks—we have backups—"

"Then bring in the replacements! I want everything up in the next hour, or someone's going home without pay!"

Flashlights flicker in and out of the gloom. Leo Gries has a pocket light, and his terrified face is illuminated in the glow. Hemslock carries a much more powerful version, splaying the room with its beam. The screens before us are now blank gray slates, the producers wiped clean off their surfaces.

"What's the status of the generators?" Hemslock asks, a calmer contrast.

"We can't find anything wrong with them," one of the crew admits. "It's the ones for the mess hall and the other two cabins. But a team's swapping it out. It shouldn't take long."

"*My* cabin's one of those affected," Armani says hotly. "You better get your asses on it immediately. I'm going out for a smoke, and I want this resolved by the time I get back."

"Stay calm, Steve," Hemslock says. "This happens all the time when we're out in the middle of nowhere. The team knows what they're doing."

"It's only the *first day*, Reuben."

"Shit happens. If you wanted the Ritz, you could have stayed in California instead of bitching here. Roll with it."

Grumbling, Armani shuffles toward the door, the slam letting us know he's left.

"Alon," Leo says to me. "Melissa's going to be busy, so can you stay with Chase at our cabin while we figure out what's going on? They say the electricity there's still working. Chase, wait for me there until I return."

"I don't need anyone to escort me back," Chase grumbles.

"Unlike you, he knows his way around the island. Don't make this difficult."

"Fine."

I stand when he does and walk with him to the door. There

65

aren't many stars, though it's not as dark outside as it was inside the pre-fab duplex.

The crew has already scattered and is hard at work with the generator. The lanterns are still glowing. Askal waits patiently for us at the door. His tail is wagging—unlike the others, the darkness doesn't affect him.

The corpse tree is where we had left it. Armani insisted that cameras be trained on the balete, just in case. Some lanterns have been placed around the sinkhole, warning lights to ensure that no one accidentally falls in. They cast an eerie glow over the hole's inhabitant, illuminating the dark hollows of its face, highlighting the ruins of what it had once been.

Chase takes a glance at the pit and shudders. "That is so seriously fucked up," he mutters, though he can't seem to look away, either. "It's like a Halloween prank gone wild. Are you—have you ever seen anything like—?"

I keep my eyes concentrated on the sinkhole, half-expecting something to happen but not quite sure what. The body doesn't move. Its limbs hang loosely from the cobweb of branches it's impaled against, and the face continues to stare into the nothingness. "No," I finally say. "This is a first for me."

"I thought you were the island expert?"

"I'm not. This is the first time that I'm not the only one in Kisapmata, save for when I was with 'Tay." Movement. Makahiya are blooming along the edges of the hole, opening and closing as if buffeted by a sudden breeze. I am certain that they were not there earlier.

The rest of the regular balete around us look forbidding, spindly

66

shadows against a moonless sky. One of the branches slowly lowers, and I know it is from no wind.

I hear a faint creaking.

Something white and bulbous-looking emerges from behind one of the trees. My eyes have adjusted well enough to the night that I can make it out despite the dim lighting.

It's built the way humans are. Arms and legs. A dark head resembling a rat's nest, frozen against the air. But there is no face, just a stark whiteness that gleams, and with a strange depression at its center, a slight concaved twist to its lack of features. There are no hands, just a mimicry of the branches it hides against, long and gnarled and curled. I do not think that it has feet. It looks like a bleached white tree, but with long, moving, human hair.

I remember Goatee's fear, the way his eyes started when he saw the figure among the trees. The solemn girl who had stared back at him had looked like a different creature entirely, but she had tilted her head in the same way this being does, shuffles like it did.

It stops moving, content to stand and watch us.

Askal doesn't bark. He simply plants himself a few feet in front of us like he could shield Chase and me from this thing.

"Let's get out of here," I say. Chase's too busy looking down at the corpse tree to realize there is something else nearby. I reach out and give his sleeve a light tug. He starts at that, reddens, and then steps away in silent agreement.

When we are far enough away from the circle of lanterns, I risk a look back. This time there is nothing among the trees. Askal lets out a low, satisfied bark.

Chase doesn't say much as he follows me back to the cabin he now shares with his father, and neither do I. The place is ablaze with light from within, the complete opposite of the cabins beside it. I pause by the door, waiting as he fumbles with the key, accidentally dropping his phone in his haste. Askal reacts to the phone worse than he responded to the tree-like creature, growling and barking as if warning it away before he hunts it down. His shaggy body blocks Chase's path and his attempts to reach for it.

I bend down to pick it up for him. The screen is aglow. He's posted a picture of himself online—bare-chested and grinning, looking smug. The waves behind him and the setting sun tell me he took this sometime after the sinkhole but before dinner.

At one of the most secluded and most exclusive beaches in the world with a new love and new opportunities, his caption reads. Don't know what the future will bring. In the meantime—take a look at that view.

He must be popular, because the number of likes and replies are still rising as I look on. One of the latter caught my eye—answer my call!!! by someone named RileySmiley—and the growing comments gathered underneath it, some supportive and others mocking, indicate a debate has been going on for some time now.

> Maybe if you hadn't slept with Tad while Chase was at
>   football practice—
> You tell him, girl!!
> POV: watching someone throw a tantrum in the comments

while her ex takes a pic with someone new in a swanky
celebrity resort—
—I'd dumped my girlfriend too if it could give me that glow
up—

Chase snatches his phone back, red-faced. "Didn't give you permission to look," he snaps angrily.

"I didn't mean to—"

His phone lights up again, brighter this time. Someone named *Cheating Bitch* is calling.

Chase hits the Reject button hurriedly, his face turning even more scarlet. "It's my ex," he mutters. "She's been doing this almost nonstop since I got here."

"You haven't blocked her number?"

"I don't want to. I don't want her thinking she's won."

I'm not sure what he thinks his ex would win from doing that, but I stay quiet. After a moment, he groans aloud, running a hand through his hair.

"Blocking her wouldn't have done much unless I blocked her *and* half the school on all my socials, too. That's what she is—a cheating bitch. Turns out she slept with someone on the football team—one of my friends—for almost two months, and I found out only a week ago—on the last day of class."

"Why is she calling?"

"Probably to apologize and swear she didn't mean to do it. Like our relationship still means something to her. But I bet she's only calling because I posted that picture. I implied that I met someone else, but it wasn't because I wanted her back or anything. I just—I don't know. I wanted to make her mad."

"Why did you say you were at a glamorous beach resort?"

He looked embarrassed. "It sounded better than some boring film set with no one else but suits for company, you know? And I can't back down now. They won't let me live it down." He cleared his throat. "Look. I know you have no reason to help me. I'll understand if you say no. But could you get her off my case, at least for tonight? Just, you know—there's not many people my age on set, only Melissa and you. You don't mind if I post a photo of us hanging out or something?"

"Why?"

"Why?" he echoed. "Because it's what everyone else is doing. And pretending for a little while lets everything die down until they move on to some other gossip."

"Is this really what you want?"

He pauses. Hangs his head. "No. I don't."

As if on cue, the phone vibrates again. *Cheating Bitch.*

Chase shoots me a pleading look. "Just for a couple of days?"

I sigh. It's not like his friends would ever meet me. "Okay."

"Yes! Thank you. I owe you a billion." Chase pushes a button, his voice now stern. "For the last time, Riley, go away. I don't want to talk to you."

"Chase," the girl on the video responds, pleading. She's an attractive blonde with clear blue eyes and a dimple on one cheek. "Let me explain. I'm sorry; I know I fucked up. I swear Tad didn't mean anything. *You* mean everything to me. I—"

She breaks off when Askal inserts himself into the drama. He leaps up so that his front paw is practically on Chase's shoulders.

"Askal!" I yell. "Baba!"

Askal ignores me. He pushes his nose right at the camera and growls.

"Oh my God! What is that—"

"It's a *dog*, Riley. And it doesn't like you, either." Chase lifts the phone over his head, out of reach. Cheated of his prey, Askal barks importantly, and then licks Chase's face, who laughs.

"Like I said," he says, "I'm *busy*, Riley. Stop calling me."

From the phone's angle, Riley spots me behind Chase as Askal returns to me, nuzzling at my neck and yipping smugly as if to say, *See how I chased her out?* "Is that who you're with?" she shrills. "*That's* who you dumped me for? I *can't* believe that you would—"

"What I do here has nothing to do with you!" Chase fires back. "We're over. It's done. Go back to Tad or whoever else you want to be with. I don't care anymore."

"You love me," Riley insists. "I know you do. And I know that this isn't like you. If pretending to be with someone else is your way of getting back at me, then fine; I deserve that. But don't lie and tell me that you're hooking up with someone else. I love you, and I know we can work things out—"

"Who says I'm not with him?" I interrupt calmly.

Three faces look back at me—Riley's pinched face on the phone screen, looking shocked; Askal's cheerful expression, tail curled behind him the way it does whenever he's impressed by something I've done; and Chase's, looking stunned but rallying quickly.

71

"This is Alon," he says. "Alon, this is Riley, my ex."

Now I see real anger, the jealous possessiveness. "I'm going to get him back, you hear me," Riley shouts furiously. "You're just a rebound he's going to dump soon! It's me that he really—"

Still smiling placidly back at her, Chase ends the call. "Sorry about that," he apologizes.

"Like I said, it's okay."

"I can explain more inside. Guess I owe you that." He looks around nervously. "And I really don't want to be alone right now—"

One of the small electric lanterns that lines the paths between the cabins starts to flicker. I look down. More makahiya that had not been there before curl around our shoes.

There is something that stands shrouded just beyond the light, a figure too well formed by the night to be visible beyond a faint human shape and too swallowed by the darkness for distinguishable features.

It's followed us.

"Sure." I grip the door tightly, push it open. "I don't mind staying."

SEVEN

MOVEMENT

THE CABIN IS FAR MORE LUXURIOUS ON THE INSIDE THAN it looks outside. There are widescreen TVs and leather couches, dark mahogany tables, and a working kitchen that gleams from lack of use. I can hear the thrum of the air conditioner, unaffected by the power outage. There is a large living room that leads into two smaller bedrooms at the back; both had originally been for Chase's use, but after the destruction of his father's cabin, new arrangements were made.

There's a stuffed bear propped up against one of the couches. Chris reddens, snatching it away. "Gift from my mom," he says defensively.

"It's cute," I say. Askal sniffs tentatively at it, barks his approval.

We sit on one of the velvet couches. I angle myself to make sure that I am facing the window. Whatever has followed us is now gone. Askal makes himself at home on the small rug before us.

"Hope you don't mind me asking," Chase says. "He's trained not to uh, poop indoors, right?"

Askal makes an offended sound.

"He won't," I say.

"Okay. Just wanted to be sure." And then Chase groans, dropping his head to his chest. "Riley's dad is a Hollywood bigshot. A VP for one of the biggest studios in the US. Riley's always been spoiled. We started dating freshman year, over three years ago now. I don't know why I stayed with her that long. This isn't the first time I've suspected her going out with other guys behind my back. I ignored the rumors and trusted her." He laughs sarcastically. "Hits different when you're the one to catch them in the act, you know? I'm not the smartest, but..." He raises his arm, lets it drop. "I'll let my dad know, make sure she won't cause trouble for you."

I try not to let my amusement show. "What can she do to me?"

"I don't know. Try to get you fired? Your father's sick. You're getting paid a lot of money for this. Dad won't leave you hanging."

I shrug.

"That doesn't worry you?"

"We have a saying here. Bahala na. It means that you shouldn't worry about circumstances you can't control. I'll care for my father like I always have, regardless of what your ex chooses to do."

"I won't let that happen. Besides, it sounds like Dad and the others need you." He pauses. "Do you really believe what they've been saying? About that puzzle, riddle, whatever—and those eight deaths? About—about the plane crash not being a coincidence?"

"I don't think the Diwata is responsible for your mother's death," I say cautiously, and then add, "I am sorry for your loss."

"It's been four years. I'm doing a lot better than Dad. He's been— odd since. He thinks I wanted to come here to get away from Riley. I mean, I *do*, but—Mom died here. Or died near here. I want to know what happened as much as he does. Did you take part in the search?"

"No."

"But your father did? Was he the island's caretaker before you? Were you paid for it?"

"The local government gives us a stipend."

"So your dad's not a local politician or owns the island or something?"

"No one owns it. The local government pays us to make sure no one gets too close. At least, until you all arrived. My father's a teacher. I learned everything from him."

"But you're not in school?"

"No. The opportunities you have in America are not always available everywhere."

"Ah, right. Sorry. If you don't mind me asking—cancer?"

I shake my head. "Old age."

"Is that why you agreed to help? Because you need money to care for him?"

"No." I look around the cabin, at the luxuries I've never had. "I agreed because I don't have a choice. The show paid off the govern- ment, and now you're all here. The island doesn't want you here. I have—a very bad feeling."

Chase's phone buzzes again. He glances down at it with irritation, but that soon turns into relief. "Oh—it's Rory. You don't mind if I take this?"

I don't, and soon there are two faces beaming at us on video when he answers.

"Hey, how's Mauritius?" a curly-haired, pale boy with brown eyes asks cheerfully. "Or was it the Bahamas? You didn't say where you were exactly."

"This who you've been hanging out with?" asks the second boy, dark-skinned with close-cropped hair. He hones in on me before I can move out of view. "How're y'all doing?"

"Alon's our tour guide," Chase tells them. "Alon, this is Rory and Jordan. I'm at this island called Kisapmata. My dad's in charge of a show they're filming here, and I wanted to tag along."

"Never heard of Kisapmata. What are they known for? White sands? Gorgeous girls?"

Chase hesitates. "No. They've got white sands here, but it's an uninhabited island with a ton of ghost stories. Sorry for lying, I just really wanted to avoid any questions."

The boys don't seem angry by the admission. "I'd fly to Antarctica if that's the only option I had to get away from Riley Sedgwick," Rory says promptly. "I've been telling you from the very first date that she was going to cheat on you, man."

"I know," Chase says unhappily. "I should have listened."

"From where I'm sitting, it looks like you've got things figured out," the other boy says, still eyeing me. "Was that post all a lie, man, or did you really hook up with someone while you're there?"

Askal, always keen on inserting himself at the crucial moment, worms his way between us and the phone, rumbling contentedly at the two instead of barking like he had at Riley.

"And you got a pooch!" Jordan says delightedly. "Awww, look at you. This your friend's?"

"Yeah. This is Askal."

"Awesome name," Rory says.

"It means *stray dog*," I say.

"Dope. Look, Jordan and I called 'cause we're worried about you, dude. At least you've got yourself a vacation on some nice beach—"

"Even if it's a haunted beach," Jordan chimes in.

"—where she won't be able to fly to ruin your vibe. Dunno what the singles population is out there, but you better get a couple of rebounds in before you come back. Do something fun for a change."

"Seconding getting laid," Jordan adds mischievously.

"Do you want me to leave?" I ask Chase quietly.

He shakes his head and gestures for me to stay. I oblige, drifting to the kitchen. "Friend of yours looks way too young to be part of any TV crew," I hear Jordan say. "And way too cute."

I redden a little. Chase glares at his phone. "Alon's the only local who's willing to talk to them about this place; everyone else won't. You guys wanna come and hang out? I don't think Dad would mind much, but you gotta sign the usual clauses."

"Oh, hell, no!" That from Jordan. "Not on your life are you gonna find my Black ass on some ghost beach with a body count. That's a white people vacation spot right there."

"Well, you're not going to believe this, but literally minutes after

77

we arrived here, a sinkhole took out Dad's cabin, and there was an actual *corpse* at the bottom of it. Suspended on a tree."

Both boys stare at him. "And you're *staying*?" This from Jordan again.

"Yeah, no. I'm gonna need some pics," Rory insists.

"I can't—NDA—but you'll see it when the show premieres. It's just—it's unbelievable."

"No, it's not," Jordan says emphatically. He quiets down. "Hey. This is—I'm looking it up, and—this isn't where your mom died, is it?"

Chase takes a deep breath. "The plane crashed near here. Why do you think I came?"

"Yeah, yeah. Sorry, man. Didn't mean to joke earlier."

"No prob. Appreciate you, dude."

"I've found a short article about the island," Rory says. "There's some strange curse? A sleeping god? Sacrifices?"

"Five sacrifices. But at least fifteen recorded deaths. The others don't count toward the curse because they don't fit the god's requirements or something."

"Oh, no," Jordan says. "Hell, no. Chase, your dumb ass better be careful. And they got *tourist guides* in this hellhole?"

"Just Alon."

"I'm here to warn people away," I say dryly. "So far no one's acting on my advice."

"Reuben Hemslock's on this show, and he lives for this stuff. You can pry the cameras out of his cold dead fingers before he'll wrap."

"They only found *half* of one victim's body?" Rory bursts out, still reading the article. "The *lower* half?"

"Alex Key? Yeah, I don't know much about that, though."

"Chase," Rory says, "there is a hottie in your room right now and you're talking to us? I'd be hitting on that, man. Oh wait, shit, are you still on speaker??"

"Yes, you fucking pigeon brain," Chase retorts, and then lowers his voice. Rory's reply, on the other hand, is loud and deliberately so. "You know what they say. What happens in Kisapmata, stays in Kisapmata."

"Rory!"

"Has Riley been trying to call you, by the way? She's been blowing up Josh's phone."

"Yeah, and I'd appreciate it if Josh tells her to go to hell for me again."

"You know that the best way to piss her off is to get with someone else, right? You've never tried to be with anyone when y'all were on and off, so she assumes you're waiting around to forgive her. Show her she's wrong this time. Anyway, I gotta go. Josh's waiting outside for me, but I'm gonna call you once I'm back. And by the way—even Josh thinks this is for the best."

"We'll leave y'all alone," Jordan says mischievously. "Call you tomorrow. Tell us when you're gonna disappear next time. I know you're going through some things, but don't get us worried either. Know what I'm saying?"

The call ends. Chase grimaces. "Sorry you had to hear all that."

"I'm not offended."

"You sure? Those two are the worst flirts, and they like to meddle. I'm not—you don't have a girlfriend or a boyfriend, right?

Or any, uh, significant other? Rory always tells me to ask before I assume—you know, for gender—but I always mess up."

I smile slightly. "I don't really look at myself as either male or female."

Chase nods sagely. "Nonbinary. I've got a bunch of friends who are nonbinary. That's cool. No significant other?"

"No. Never had time."

"Because your dad's sick?"

"It's one of the reasons."

Chase looks down at his phone again and groans. "Ah, shit. Now she's back on social media yelling about how I'm lying. I mean, I did, but…"

"That bad?"

"I just want her to shut up. But her friends are amplifying her, making it worse. You don't have social media?"

"It's not really for me." I pause. "Will it help if we take another pic?"

He frowns. "You don't know what you're getting into."

"Why not?"

"Do you know how many followers I have?"

I do not. He clicks on his profile to show me, and my mouth drops. "Five million? You have five million people following you?" For tap dancing while wearing a horse's head?

"I'm like, an influencer? Sometimes companies will send me awesome stuff like clothes and sunglasses, and I talk about it. Like an advertisement. But mostly I post pictures of myself in fun places. The videos made me famous. My mom tap danced, and she got me into it when I was a kid. It's not common for people to do nowadays, I guess. So people follow me for that, and then for other stuff."

I think about my father, a teacher who had much to impart to the world yet fell into obscurity. "But why?"

He shrugs. "I really don't know. Maybe because I make people laugh? Maybe because of my dad, too. He's a Hollywood big shot, so I've got an advantage. But that's why you shouldn't get involved. People may not know who you are, but they'll find out if they want to."

He's very serious. Very earnest. I try not to laugh.

"I'm hoping you don't mind if I borrow Askal, though," he goes on. "Everyone likes pictures of dogs, and he's extra cute."

The flattery works on Askal. He wags his tail and poses for the picture he takes of them. I watch as Chase uploads it onto his social media, this time with a longer caption. On an undisclosed location in the Philippines with my dad today, watching them film a new show. You're gonna have to wait to find out what that is. In the meantime, I'm already in love. Look at this perfect mug. Sometimes we travel to far-off places so we can remember to find pleasure in the familiar things.

It's not exactly deep philosophy. But when you make a career out of aesthetics, I suppose it makes people feel better to think they can impart some deeper meaning.

It doesn't take long for Chase to get what he'd been hoping for, either. The comments come quickly, and most ooh and aah over Askal. A few make mention of how they never believed Riley, anyway. It seems that Chase's ex is an influencer like him, which explains his worry about the situation blowing out of proportion.

"Who's that behind you?" One eagle-eyed commenter asks. Chase's picture hadn't left me completely out of the picture. There's a shot of my legs in the background, barely out of focus.

"That was deliberate," Chase says sheepishly. "I don't have to comment about who I'm with on this island, but I can imply that Riley's making things up about me. They'll hash it out among themselves, and I won't ever have to respond. That's the beauty about having a truckload of followers." He looks back at the picture and frowns. "Well, that's odd. What's that?"

I look again.

My legs are evident in the picture.

But there is another set of legs farther behind me.

They're distorted enough that they could be dismissed as an odd wooden sculpture or some kind of abstract statue. But there is nothing resembling that decorating the room. It looks like gnarled roots shaped to mimic calves and feet...

I spin.

There is no one else there.

Chase doesn't realize the enormity of what we're looking at. He's glancing around too, puzzled but relaxed. "I didn't put on any filters; I don't know where that could have come from—"

A sudden cry from outside catches our attention. Chase rises to his feet, alarmed, and my instincts kick in.

"Stay here," I bark at him, opening the door and racing out before he can respond, Askal tearing at my heels.

The cry sounds again, but this time it's coming from the direction of the sinkhole.

There is no one else around when I arrive at the glowing lanterns and ropes set up around the hole.

But I see Armani. The man must've slid down into the sinkhole and found nothing but the corpse tree to cling to. The balete tree stopped what could have been a fatal plunge.

The man is all but gibbering in terror, though relief flashes across his face when he spots me.

"Kid," he shouts. "Thank god you're here. Get help, tell them to bring some ropes and get me the hell out of here!"

"Don't move!" I shout back, but he ignores me, struggling to free some of the smaller branches that are stuck to the sleeves of his shirt.

"Hey!" I shout again, this time in the direction of the other cabins. "Someone's fallen into the pit!"

There's a long piece of rope still strapped to a nearby tree, securely tied from the crew's previous excursions into the sinkhole. I grab it and throw the line down for him to catch. Askal is going nuts, running back and forth along the rim of the pit and barking like mad at the tree.

Armani wrestles to gain a better foothold against the sides of the hole, his hand reaching out to grasp the lifeline I threw his way. "I am going to fire *and* destroy whoever pushed—"

The corpse tilts toward him. Soundlessly the tree shudders; its thin branches rise, becoming wizened bone-thin fingers on either side of the dead body. It grasps at Armani's face and forcibly turns his head so that he is gaping, terror stricken, into the yawning mass of its mouth, the hollow void of its eyes.

Screaming, the man lets go of the rope. More tree branches wrap around his face, and Armani disappears under the tangle of brambles as the corpse presses its face against his, and both are lost from view.

I take the rope myself, and grimly lower myself into the sinkhole. The branches are still winding their way around the man like a grotesque cocoon, swiftly wrapping his waist, his legs still kicking uselessly in the air from adrenaline. One hand is still outstretched, grasping wildly for something to hold onto, and I grab at it, my hand latching onto his wrist.

I pull, prepared for a fight.

The branches give way almost instantly, the roots snaking away from Armani as it loosens its hold. I grunt as the sudden dead weight strains my shoulders, and the only reason we both don't fall into the sinkhole is because new hands grab at me from above, yelling at me not to let go even as they haul me, and then Armani, up over onto safer ground.

It's Chase. His muscles ripple as he hoists the both of us out. "What the hell?" He rambles, horrified, looking down at the pit. "It *moved*. I saw it grab him. What the—what the hell—holy—"

"The balete." I lay on the ground a little longer, trying to catch my breath, waiting for the burning in my upper arms to go away. "The curse."

"Get a hold of yourself, Steve!" Hemslock is now beside Armani, slapping at his face, getting him to focus on him. The other man responds by rolling his eyes up until only the whites show. He falls unconscious. Someone from the medical team is already with Hemslock, checking Armani's vitals.

"No injuries that I can find," she says tersely. "Bring him in and get him warm, he's as cold as ice."

A stretcher is brought out, and Armani is laid atop it. While the others carry him away, Hemslock remains, staring at the sinkhole below, at the balete tree that has fallen unnervingly, unfalteringly still.

The corpse does not move. Its eye sockets stare serenely back at us, at nothing and at everything all at once.

EIGHT

SCREAMS

ARMANI DOESN'T AWAKEN THE NEXT DAY. HE SUFFERED A severe shock to his system, the doctor tells us. But his heart is steady, and he has no difficulty breathing. He'll be up when he's ready, they tell Hemslock, and not a moment before.

The generators are working again, and the crew's managed to reestablish communication with the nearest city on the mainland, where other crew members are awaiting word. The executive producers have returned to their respective screens and urge Hemslock and Gries to bring the unconscious man to the nearest hospital.

"We've already sent for a helicopter," Leo tells them. He has yet to change out of his clothes from the night before. There are dark circles under his eyes. He doesn't look my way. "The locals are still adamant about not coming here to help us, but they've at least agreed to that."

"Did you see what spooked him?" Hemslock asks me.

I am quick with my answer. "The corpse."

"This isn't a joke, kid," Producer Two says angrily. "You could get hit with a lawsuit if you don't tell us exactly what happened."

"You know what?" Hemslock says unexpectedly. "I believe Alon."

"If you think that bullshit is going to fly with us, Hemslock—"

"There were cameras rolling on site. I got the tapes. None of them caught what happened, but they did record what came before. Steve was stumbling around, drunk. He fell in. Then Alon ran out and climbed down to save his ass. Steve might not be alive if not for this *kid*, and you're threatening to *sue*?"

The producers glower at Hemslock from three different monitors. "We can't have word getting out that he's been injured," Producer Three finally says. "The studio's going to pull back funding if they think we're being reckless. The unions are going to have a field day with this."

"Then it's going to be up to you three to stem any gossip. There aren't any injuries on set. Steve'll wake up, and he'll be fine. I'll send a few of the crew back with him when the helicopter arrives." He points at me. "Has anything similar happened on the island before?"

"There were visitors who used to ignore warnings not to stay on the island. After the first two or three deaths, local authorities stepped up, banned tourist boats from landing here. But this was before my time. Their bodies were found along the beach, but without any wounds to show what killed them."

"What about the fishermen?"

"The curse leaves them alone."

"Ah yes, your god hates outsiders."

"He hates trespassers. There's a difference."

"We didn't need a tour guide to get our crew onto the island," Producer One says to me. "Only ten thousand dollars in bribes. So why are we spending money to keep you on?"

"Because, like I've said before, the island knows Alon," Hemslock says. "I know that's hard to wrap your brain around, Conroy, but some things can't be bought with money."

Producer One sighs loudly. "We'll humor you, Reuben. But you better have something to show beyond a dead tree and an injured producer."

"Good job," Hemslock tells me, as we all log off. "Ignore those old fools. They haven't held anything sacred for a long while now. I know we've kept you away from your family. If you want to take this opportunity to go and visit your father, since you weren't able to last night—"

"Thank you. I will."

"Do you have anyone who can look after him the rest of the time we're here?"

"I'm making arrangements."

"You're bringing him to Leyte? We'll pay for the transportation if you like."

I shake my head. "I have family in Leyte. I've reached out to them."

"Good. We'd like you back after lunch. We're going to figure out what's wrong with Steve, and then we're going to start exploring both the sinkhole and the cave, which we'll need you for."

I wait until he's out of view before I move.

First, the distraction. Askal wanders toward the production crew, flops on his back to expose his tummy, and barks loftily. *Pet me*, is what he means. *Love me.* And while they're distracted, I sneak away.

Hemslock's cabin is easy to break into. The bungalow is locked, but I keep a few tools in my boat. The lock is a standard one with no special reinforcements. I carefully press at the small indentation underneath the doorknob and twist the plate behind it so that it loosens in my hand. Jiggling the mechanism within opens the door in seconds. It was a trick I had learned from a reformed burglar-now-fisherman.

The man keeps things neat; it's easy to find what I'm looking for. His notes and documents are spread out on a table. One catches my eye—the handwriting is different from the others on the desk, a translation scribbled underneath what appears to be a Spanish manuscript—the Cortes journal.

Still I persisted, and finally he relented. Eight sacrifices, Humabon had told him. To receive the god's blessing, sacrifice to the god. Take their hearts and sacrifice them to the Tree, and you will find eternity within the dream. Humabon swears that the god will have no choice but to be beholden to you, grant you control of the islands.

However, Magellan cautions me against such attempts, believing it to be the devil's work, another pagan custom to be eradicated. He intends to wage

89

war on Humabon's behalf against the chieftain of Matan, as they believe the latter knows the secret to such power. It is the only reason they can think of, why the accursed native and his lands could not yet be conquered.

But I am determined to unlock this secret for, myself. Not for the first time I curse Magellan. The mutinies against him have done us no favors, nor his arrogance. We could have overwhelmed these people quickly, if not for our own losses.

It is not so large a cave. I will warn the Matan chieftain, Cilapulapu, of Magellan's impending invasion. I will gain his trust, and that of his god's. And then I will kill him, sacrifice him myself.

More annotations across the page. A note that states Matan = old name for the Mactan island that Cilapulapu ruled. The number thirty-seven, carefully circled on the right corner. More scribbled writings in the margins, the handwriting different from Cortes's, with lines crossed through every word on the list save the one at the very end.

~~local woman~~
~~criminal~~
~~cheater~~
~~prostitute~~
pregnant

90

I turn the page to the next entry. The handwriting is more agitated, all but stabbing the page in places, causing tears from their force.

Sometimes I dream. Of trees and their eyes watching, their flowers opening and closing. They speak in the quiet. I do not need eyes to see. I do not need ears to hear. Sometimes I obey, set the knife against my eyes. I wake up screaming.

This cave. I cannot leave.

I am sorry for the woman I killed. I am so sorry, I am so sorry, forgive me, I am sorry, please

They scream for me. They are

The words end there.

I hear noises from outside. I don't stay. I arrange the pages back to how they were before and steal away before anyone notices.

✻✽✾✿❀

'Tay's still asleep when I return, which I suppose is for the better. Our home isn't much compared to the fineries of the Hollywood bungalows, but it's good enough for us.

I've already visited my family in Leyte, and they promised to help while I'm away. For now I make sure 'Tay's comfy, combing the wisps of hair from his face. 'Tay didn't have me until he was much older, and it shows. His skin feels leathery, but he's cool to the touch and not feverish.

I settle myself in a nearby seat and keep vigil, Askal curled against my legs. I absently trace at the wall, my fingers lingering on the old, familiar grooves.

I watch him sleep and think about the money Hemslock is paying me. How worthless it would be in the long run.

'Tay stirs, as if sensing my unease.

"Tulog lang, 'Tay," I whisper to him, and hold my breath until his evens out.

⁂

The first thing Leo Gries asks of me when I return is to check on Chase, who has yet to leave his cabin that day. The man somehow looks worse than before. "Do you want to talk about it?" I ask.

He starts. "I—how did you know?"

"Everyone who's seen the ghosts has that same look on their faces."

He hesitates. "My wife, Elena," he finally says, in a whisper. "I—I think I saw her last night. It was before Steve fell into the sinkhole. She was—staring at me from outside the window. Her face was—" He lifts his hands to his eyes. "Her eyes were—"

His breath stutters, and he inhales loudly. "I don't want to talk about it," he says roughly. "Can you tell Chase lunch is ready?"

Something moves amid the balete trees outside as I walk the path leading to the Grieses' cabin. I see something solidifying in the air by the window, and my heart rate increases.

There are tiny roots growing along the pane. As I watch, it moves steadily on, wrapping its ends around the steel bars.

A few of the vines lengthen; one trails against my hand and another touches me, friendly, on the cheek. I shake my head. "'Wag mo silang takutin," I warn it.

They don't listen. The vines grow, wrap around my wrist.

I always keep my hunting knife close, and it's as good to gut fish as it is to cut down strangler figs. I attack without hesitation, cutting through the buds before they can find permanent traction. The plants slide free, dropping back to the ground, and rapidly retreat until they are gone from view.

Breathing hard, I stare at the nearby balete. "'Wag," I say softly, though I'm not sure they'll listen.

I enter the cabin to find Chase awake in the living room. His back is turned to me, and he's hopping about, trying to put on his shoes. His phone is on the counter, the screen lit up with Rory's face.

"I'm feeling secondhand embarrassment for you, man," he says. "You got Riley to agree to date you after twenty minutes of knowing you. And that's all you could manage? An offer for a tapdancing lesson?"

"It's not like I've had much dating practice in the last three years," Chase grumbles as I freeze by the door, trying to inch out of the room without him knowing. "And it's different now. It's not some cheerleader looking to snag a football jock."

"So you're trying the sensitive approach? Now I gotta see that. How sure are you about starting a relationship, though? And with someone across the world, to boot? You've never been one for the short term. And what if the guide's a plant? Like I know your dad's done some illegal stuff for other shows, but do you really think they're gonna manufacture a haunting of this scale like—"

"Well, of course, they're not going to get one of the old rich guys into an accident to boost ratings for the show. They'd hire a stunt double for that. It really *was* Steve Galant we pulled out of that pit. The tree went *wild* on him, and I know it can't be real! Someone must have tried to prank someone else, and it backfired when Galant fell in. Dad's gonna kill me if I post pictures, so I can't show you anything yet. Look, the guide's hot, but it almost feels like it's some tourist scam arranged by the locals. Like they're working with the crew so they can rake in money for—"

He turns and breaks off, spotting me. "I have to go," he says hurriedly, and ends the call. "Hey, Alon—I wasn't expecting you here this early—"

"I'm sure you didn't," I say—coolly. "Your father wants you to know that lunch is ready."

"H-hey! Wait!"

I ignore him and return to the sinkhole.

Chase catches up a few minutes later. "I'm sorry. I didn't mean it. The guys have been coming up with the weirdest shit, trying to explain what happened last night. They wondered if it was some kind of scam to get Hemslock and those studio execs to cough up more money, but I didn't mean that you had anything to do with—"

"You don't have anything to apologize for," I say calmly—I suppose *too* calmly, because Chase looks even more horrified.

"What's this?" Leo asks curiously.

"Nothing," Chase says hurriedly, wisely clamping his mouth shut.

The daylight does nothing to detract from the corpse tree's sinister appearance. I scan the twisted trunk, trying to remember if its position has shifted, if it has moved from what I remembered of the night before. Another team of experts has ventured into the sinkhole to resume their investigation of the balete.

Chase looks down at it with a shudder. "It moved," he asserts. "I *know* that I saw it move. You saw it grab him. I take it back. It can't be a scam. How the hell would you scam your way into creating a tree inside some frigging sinkhole?"

"You should leave when the helicopter arrives," I say. "With your father. I doubt Hemslock can be convinced to go too, but at least the two of you will be safe."

"Wait, you're staying?"

"I have to."

"What if something happens to you?"

"Nothing's going to happen to me."

"*Nothing's going to happen to me* are popular last words. I'm not going to leave Dad here by himself. He won't leave until he learns what really happened to Mom."

"There's nothing you can do for him by staying here."

He scowls. "If there are real ghosts like you say, then there's nothing *you* can do, either."

"They won't harm me."

"Really? Have you talked to them? Had them sign a contract, too? Look—I'll go if you'll go with me."

"Why are you so concerned about me?"

He glares some more. "Because I am, all right? The call you

95

overheard—I didn't mean to—ah shit, just forget it." He marches off like *I* am the one at fault.

The accident has not delayed the production schedule, and plans to explore the cave are set to continue that day. Hemslock has thrown himself back into his work with relish.

"You're serious, aren't you?" he asks me. "You *did* see the tree move and attack Steve. This isn't something Leo's son cooked up on the spot and got you in on."

"He's not a liar."

"Hey, don't be touchy. I'm not accusing anyone of anything." He smiles. "I'd like you to join the expedition later. The experts we've hired have already marked off the places they've deemed safe. I don't know how far into the cave you've been, but I think it'll be good to have you around, confirm some of the things we might see."

I nod again.

"Your old man won't be worried? Got someone to watch him?"

"I can stay for as long as you need me. He gives his blessings."

Hemslock snorts. "Of course, he does. We're paying you a lifetime's salary for this. No aversion to being on camera?"

"No sir."

"Good. I think you're going to be the glue that ties this mystery together. Who knows? We might even work on something new with you if this takes off."

Leo Gries is not as confident as the star of his show. "I don't think it's appropriate to bring in an 18-year-old where accidents have already happened," he tells Hemslock angrily.

"Seems to me that Alon can decide that."

Leo Gries looks at me. "Are you sure about this?"

"I am, sir."

"See?" Hemslock says. "We're getting along great."

Melissa offers me a meal and I politely accept. The crew treats me like a hero and I, embarrassed, try to brush it off. Nobody likes Armani, I soon learn, but they appreciate my efforts, regardless.

We eat on one of the tables, and I absorb the conversations happening around me. Askal lays down and chomps happily on a large bowl of boiled chicken that the chef made for him.

It sounds like half of the crew are ready to leave the island, while the other half are optimistic enough to finish the season so they can get paid in full. Melissa finds that hilarious. "At least they're getting paid," she notes ironically. "But with my luck, I'm gonna get punted into some Real Housewives spinoff when we get back and *still* not get a paycheck."

Hawaiian Shirt is buzzing with excitement, the sandwich on his plate untouched. "It's too soon to tell, but we might have something," he says. "Remember when I said that Christie had mapped out a huge chunk of the Godseye's cave system? And that it's way different than the map that the plane crash investigators gave us? Christie's adamant that her work's accurate, but I've reached out again to the supervisor in charge of that crash investigation, and *he's* adamant that he hadn't made any mistakes. Hemslock's on a roll. His theory is that they're *both* right, and that there's something underneath the soil creating new tunnels and collapsing others, which would explain the differences between the reports. Wild as shit, but it'll make for compelling TV."

"You can't tell me this place *isn't* haunted," Straw Hat says mournfully, poking at his salad.

Goatee, who is sitting nearby and high on his fifth shot of whiskey, snorts. "We came to this island *knowing* it's haunted."

"We came here to make it *look* haunted for a show."

"At this point, I don't care if this whole island is standing on a bedrock of bones. I'm gonna have to remind you fellas that choosing to leave at this point means you're fired. Show gets pulled, nobody gets money."

"Mr. Galant's in a coma," one of the crew members says nervously. "What if that happens to us, too?"

"Steve isn't in a coma; he's just too soft for fieldwork. Hemslock never should've talked him into coming along. Anyway, they'll fly him to the nearest hospital soon." A staff member places another shot of whiskey by his elbow; Hawaiian Shirt downs it in a gulp. "You know what, Andy, leave the bottle. Don't you understand? We're getting all the footage we could hope for. I don't care about the curse. I care that we're getting enough shit to make the curse *believable*. And when we blow up on social media, on streaming sites—you're going to have the résumés you all need to work on whatever other shows you'd like."

He freezes, his eyes staring at something beyond Melissa's shoulder. Puzzled, the girl turns and sees nothing. But by that time Goatee has already left, taking the bottle with him.

I spot a familiar face marching up to me—Chase. He dumps his plate on the table across from me, slides into the seat without asking. "I'm staying," he says.

"It would be safer for you to—"

"Dad's not leaving. He wants me to. I won't. It's not about Riley anymore." He looks down at her food. "It's about Mom," he says defiantly. "We were really close. Dad thinks there's something here that can explain the plane accident. They fought before she left on her trip, and I—I don't want to leave him alone when he's in this frame of mind, you know? He's never gotten over her death. Frankly I'm not sure I have, either. And if you can't tell us anything about the crash, then at least give us time to figure it out ourselves."

"Hold up," Melissa interrupts, no longer pretending not to eavesdrop. "Can the Dreamer of this island cause plane crashes?"

I pick at my food. "The Diwata would never harm innocents."

"But if they can magically recreate a new world when they awaken, then they would be able to affect airplanes, right? Plus, one dude who'd been on the plane was found *buried* here."

"I'm sorry. I don't know."

Chase's shoulders slump. "You're really planning on going into the cave with them?"

"Yes."

"Have you been inside before?"

"A few times."

"*Willingly?*" This from Melissa.

"It's not so bad."

"You're weird, you know that? But in a good way."

That makes me smile. "I know."

Someone shouts Melissa's name. She groans and pushes her chair back. "Work beckons. Be back later."

"I wanna apologize for this morning," Chase says quietly. He pauses, then says all in one breath: "You probably think I'm some weirdo, but the truth is I've always felt a bit—pessimistic, you know? Hollywood tends to do that to you. I'm used to people with ulterior motives, and I was wrong to think you'd be the same."

He hangs his head. "And I'm scared, you know? Being here is starting to feel personal. I looked at that picture I took last night again. That wasn't some trick of the light. There was some weird—thing—in the room with us. I'm sorry I said it might be a scam. I'm not the smartest. That's why I like being an influencer. I try my best to have fun and vibe. But I put my foot in my mouth a lot, and people get hurt. Probably did that a lot to Riley—not like that gives her a pass for cheating. But I won't do that again. I like you, Alon, and I know you've got a right to be mad at me, but I was hoping... are we cool?"

Chase's phone rings again. He shoots an irritated glance at it but relaxes. "Jordan and Rory again."

"Feeling better today?" came the familiar cheerful voices over the receiver. "Find any more killer trees?"

"I'm serious, dude. Alon saw it, too."

"Did it seriously attack one of the producers?" Rory asks. "Cool."

"Hey dude, this is serious. People could have died."

"Didn't I *tell* y'all to get off that haunted beach," Jordan grumbles.

"Has Alon seen these corpse trees before?" Rory asks.

"There's never been a sinkhole on this island," I say.

"But this tree attacked the old man?" Rory persists.

"Yes."

"You must be one of those sensitive people who can see and feel things," Rory says wisely. "Those new age hippies with third eyes and lactose intolerance."

"Did you know that there's pirate treasure buried on the island?" Jordan asks. "Is that why they're making a show about it?"

"It's not pirate treasure. Some Spanish explorer with Magellan's crew stole gold from the locals and allegedly it's still inside the cave where he hid it."

"And he was also allegedly killed by the ghost, right?" Rory says eagerly. "Have you seen him?"

"I'd rather not, thanks. Some of the scientists here think the corpse tree might actually be his body."

"Alon!" Hawaiian Shirt shouts. "We need you!"

I push back my chair. "If you'll excuse me," I say politely. I nudge Askal with my toe, but he's finished his food and is intent on eating the scraps people are still handing him under the table.

"So what's the deal with you two?" I hear Rory ask impishly as I leave, "If I didn't already have Josh, like damn it's great to be bi!"

Chase's embarrassed. "Rory, shut up!"

I walk faster, so that Chase doesn't see me turn red.

What Hawaiian Shirt and Goatee want from me, as it turns out, is as many details as I can provide regarding the strange female ghost and the screams.

"We'll set up more cameras to catch any supernatural activity that we don't spot ourselves," Hawaiian Shirt explains. "Orbs of light, things moving on their own when they couldn't have, disembodied voices—all that stuff. We're hoping for actual apparitions, of course—most shows don't get much beyond shadows, but one time in Cambodia, Hemslock caught an actual humanoid figure running down a hallway. Any chance you saw that episode?"

I did not. Goatee frowns at me like that insults him somehow. "We want something a lot more concrete than that. We're starting off strong, what with the sinkhole and that godawful tree, so we'll need something to follow up with that same punch." He sets the now-empty bottle on the ground. "Where do people usually hear the screams?"

"Near shore," I say, painfully aware of the camera trained on me once more, recording everything I say.

"During the day, or mostly at night?"

"The day. Many don't travel here at night."

"But you have? Seen it at night, I mean?"

"I take care of my father most nights."

"All right, then. Can you, you know, repeat everything you've told me, but in Filipino?"

"Tagalog. We have many other dialects that fall under *Filipino*."

"Well, whatever you call it. Galant wanted you to lean hard on your accent, but this is better, no?"

I fume quietly but do as he asks.

Goatee gestures at the cameraman to move closer. "Show us which part of the beach they've heard the screaming, and maybe we can—"

The shriek that fills the air sounds like it's coming from the empty space between us. It arrives with the force of an explosion. I tense, and Goatee jumps back with a shriek of his own, as does Hawaiian Shirt, the cameramen, and the boom operator.

Just as quickly, the shrieking stops.

"Shit," Goatee says; he's breathing heavily, visibly shaking from more than the drinks he's consumed. "The fuck was that? Tell me you got it on tape, Harry."

"Yeah," the man responds, looking about ready to drop the camera and run. "Holy shit, did I get it."

I scan the area. From behind the ring of balete, I see a pale face looking back at us. Unlike the figure from last night, this one has a face.

It opens its mouth. Something blooms out of it, like makahiya. Then it retreats into the trees and disappears.

"It is believed that when people hear the screaming," I say, "someone is about to die."

Goatee looks down at his pants, where a dark stain is spreading. "Pissed," he says. "Fuck. I went and pissed my damn pants."

NINE

WRECKAGE

THE BOOM OPERATOR SWORE HE CAPTURED THE SCREAM, but a quick review of the footage yielded nothing. There was only me talking, Goatee jumping back, and then jittery motions from when the cameraman jerked away. But nothing had been captured in the recording, our reactions to it the only evidence.

Goatee is frustrated, but there's nothing to be done. Already the team is shifting their focus to the next phase of production.

"We've got two drones on standby," says the man in charge of the show's IT team. He pats one of the robots affectionately—a tiny helicopter with quad rotators and a list of specifications that makes no sense to me but does to everyone else. "This one will give us a bird's eye view of the island; it's good for any overhead shots for promo and will also keep a lookout in case anything strange is going on that we can't see. We've got a station devoted to its feed, so we'll see everything happen in real time."

"This one, though." He crouches down and shows us another kind of robot. This one looks like a small tank equipped with a large camera lens. "It's the SZ-132. It's built for rockier terrain. We're going to lower it down the sinkhole and see how far into the tunnel it can go. See these?"

Two small handles on each side of the robot lengthen and retract. On each end is a small knob with finger-like articulations that could apparently be used to grip objects. IT Guy demonstrates, using a complicated-looking remote control. It grabs at a tuft of grass on the ground, pulls it out. "Are we clear to explore the sinkhole?"

"We've gotten what we can from the corpse," one of the scientists says. "Like most strangler figs, balete grow from the top down on host trees that are already thriving. Eventually they consume the latter, and, in many cases, kill them. But this one—" He pauses dramatically.

"Well, what?" Leo asks irritably.

"There are no host tree remains. It's hollow. The balete tree grew around the corpse. The corpse *is* the host tree."

"It grew *on* the body? But—"

"From the upright way it has taken root and from the unnaturally slow way the corpse was decomposing—it's almost as if—"

"Almost as if the person was still alive when the balete consumed it," Hemslock finishes for him.

"You can probably suggest that for the show. Improbable, of course. That means the balete would have grown around it at supernatural speeds unknown in any other plant species—"

"And how far does this sinkhole go down?"

"We made some initial measurements. Surprisingly it's not that deep. Thirty or forty feet at most, and then solid ground. We're relying on SZ-132 here to be our eyes."

"Practically the most advanced in the market today," IT Guy says proudly. "If there's anything worth discovering here, it'll find it."

"You think you can get this ready to go?" Hemslock asks.

"We have everything in place, but we weren't sure if we were doing this today, after what happened to Mr. Galant—"

"Mr. Galant would have wanted the show to go on. He'll be happy to hear we're making money for him while he's asleep."

I hang back and watch as the robot is lowered into the pit. At the same time, I hear a faint whirring sound as the helicopter drone is sent up, its figure retreating into the distance and disappearing among the trees.

"If this wasn't such a cursed spot," says one of the crew piloting the drone, his eyes on the screen before him, "this would be a real gorgeous place."

He's right. The airborne drone gives us a beautiful angle of the island from overhead—a stunning view of the trees spread out before it, the white sandy beaches that circle the shorelines, the crystal blue of the sea.

But Hemslock's attention is focused solely on the robot tank. I move nearer so I can see the camera from its point of view as it descends, its night vision mode kicking into gear when it finally hits bottom.

"Excellent landing, Rick," Hemslock says. "Spin it around for a bit. Give us some bearings."

The drone's camera swivels. I expect to see nothing but the walls of the sinkhole and the base of the balete tree. Instead I see another small tunnel looming on its left, large enough for a person to pass through. The roots of the balete tree do not end on the rock floor, but instead twist themselves westward, straight into that new passageway.

"Christ," Leo Gries says.

"What are we missing here?" Hemslock asks.

"The tunnel isn't a result of the sinkhole," one of the scientists confirms. "It's the other way around—the sinkhole happened *because* of the tunnel. Judging by how long these roots are and how far they appear to go, it must have been growing upward like this for some time. Which is, again, puzzling. Balete latch onto a host tree and then grow *down* to the ground."

"Rick," Hemslock says. "Think you can drive that thing down the tunnel, see where it leads?"

The little tank wheels around in reply and whirs down the passageway. From within a hidden compartment, a flashlight flickers on, allowing us to see its surroundings more clearly.

"Does it look man-made to you?" IT asks doubtfully. "The tunnel, I mean. Maybe this was part of some mining pit that got filled years ago?"

"The ground was solid when they tested it. Logan was very sure about that."

"The sinkhole proves him wrong though, right?"

There is little conversation after that. By now, other crew members are watching, curious. I see Chase lingering awkwardly on the edge of the group; our eyes meet.

Wordlessly I incline my head toward the space beside me. A smile lights up his face as he makes his way toward me. "Does that mean we're cool?" he whispers.

"We're cool."

He looks relieved. "What are they doing?"

"Are those pieces of paper?" Hemslock asks. "Go nearer."

The tank scoots nearer, picks up one with its robotic arm. The handwriting looks familiar to me.

"I'm sorry, forgive us," Straw Hat reads. "I'm sorry, forgive us. It's all that, filling the rest of the page over, and over. Damn creepy, man."

"There's something else." Leo Gries points at the screen.

The tank edges closer. One of its small arms reaches out, digs into the soil, and comes away holding something white and metallic in its hand. The camera zooms in on it.

"Doesn't look like a rock to me," Hemslock says.

"It's too small to be—hang on." IT Guy guides the robot nearer. This time it finds a larger, heavier piece, and drags it out.

"It looks like it's made of steel," Leo muses. "Some kind of ancient machinery?"

"Machinery, yes," Hemslock says. "Ancient, not likely. Rick, go right."

IT Guy complies. This time, they find something that looks like paper, parts of it burned as if by some fire, but the remainder is otherwise intact.

"Inch it closer. I think I can make out writing."

The camera zooms in again and refocuses.

"All that's discernible are these numbers: 245. What does that mean?"

"245?" Leo leans forward, until he's almost plastered to the screen. "Rick. There's something beside that large rock over there, on the left."

The robot dutifully finds it, raises it up for a better view.

It's an earring. Though covered in grime, there is no mistaking the sparkle of cut diamonds glistening back at us despite the gloom.

"No!" Leo rears back, clutching at his head in disbelief, as if he can't believe what he's seeing. "No!"

"Calm down, man," Hemslock says sharply. "What's gotten into you?"

"245," Leo says, nearly hysterical. "That's the flight my wife was on. RWY245. And those earrings—my wife wore those earrings. I gave them to her as an anniversary gift. *What are my wife's earrings doing on this island?*"

"Those are Mom's?" Chase cries out, horror-stricken.

"A plane ticket," Hemslock says with sudden understanding. "I see now. And all these metallic bits strewn about—plane wreckage? How did none of the investigators find—why would the wreckage be so far underground? When someone buried Giles Cochrane here, did they also—?"

Leo grabs at Hemslock's collar without warning. "Why are my wife's things down there?" He shouts, "If this is some sick joke to get ratings, Reuben—"

Several inches shorter than the actor and with far less bulk, the producer is no threat. Hemslock lifts his hands in a gesture of peace.

"Leo," he says, in a calm, conciliatory tone. "I don't know why your wife's possessions are underneath the island. This isn't a prank. I want to know as much as you do, but that's not going to happen if you lose your temper. You hear me?"

Still trembling, Leo releases his grip on the man. "They searched here for weeks," he whispers. "They didn't find anything. There isn't a—why would—"

A sudden grating sound from the incoming video gains our attention. The robot tank isn't moving. Something else appears to be making the noise, but there is nothing else down there.

IT Guy manipulates the controls. The tank spins around, trying to find the source of the noise. "How should I go about this, sir?"

"Keep following the trail of roots as far as you can," Hemslock orders. "That's where we're going to find answers."

The robot sets off again. Chase is by my side, struggling not to cry. Awkwardly I let him lean against my shoulder for support, though my eyes never leave the monitor.

If there are other plane detritus inside the tunnel, we do not see it. Instead the roots splayed against one side of the wall grow thicker as the robot travels deeper.

"This is promising," the scientist says, eagerly. "Once we find out the base of this balete tree, we can get a better understanding of how it could thrive underground, far away from any—"

The robot's flashlight dies abruptly, leaving only its night vision mode. Hemslock curses. "Now what?"

"There shouldn't be anything wrong with it." IT Guy fiddles with a few buttons. The drone lurches forward in brief sputters. "I don't think it's stuck. Let me restart the system and see if we can—"

He cuts himself off this time when a shadow slips across the upper part of the robot's screen. The robot raises its camera toward the ceiling.

"There!" Hemslock shouts, pointing. The camera stabilizes, honing in on a dark figure that crawls through the balete's roots toward us, barely visible in the darkness despite the robot's night vision. "Get it out of there, Rick," he urges. "Come on, come on. Get out—"

The robot backpedals noisily, speeding away, but I already know it's hopeless. The figure's movements quicken, arms scrabbling, grasping at the roots as it makes for the drone at twice the speed.

The flashlight flickers on.

We catch a glimpse of the thing. Straggly, twig-like hair. A bare body made up of roots rather than skin and bone but still grotesquely human in shape. A face that curves inward—with an expanding mouth, rows of teeth lining its cavities, parts of it flapping up like flesh that has been flayed and distended beyond its jaw to be bigger than even its head should be.

Leo, the thing says.

It lunges at the camera—*screeching*. Something within its face extends—

The screen goes dark.

"W-we lost contact," IT Guy stammers after several seconds. "SZ-132 isn't responding."

<hr />

There is no film. There's no footage of Flight 245's remains, no shot of the dark figure that destroyed the robot. There's no record of the creature's face, none of its terrifying form that we all so clearly saw in the flashlight's glare.

"No," Hemslock says desperately. "We *saw* it. We all saw it. The camera should have captured it. Run it again."

Straw Hat tries, and then tries again, and then several more times.

The screen is black for all of the tank's run.

Hemslock does not take this failure well. He stalks off, pausing only to punch at the mess hall's outer wall. Gries sits on a chair, head in his hands, trembling.

"Did Mom survive the plane crash?" Chase asks his father quietly. "Did she wash up here? With no one to rescue her?"

"I don't know, Chase."

Chase gulps. "Dad. Do you think that…maybe that was Mom—"

"No!" Gries shouts. "She died when the plane crashed. No one could have survived a landing on…" Leo closes his mouth, realizing he's only making the situation worse. "Have you seen anything like that…*thing* on this island?" he asks me instead.

A shriek interrupts my reply. It's one of the crew. "That was the ghost that Lydia and Trish saw on the shore! It was her! Oh my God.…"

"We have to go inside," Leo Gries says, desperately. "I want to know why my wife's belongings are buried here."

"Are you kidding?" IT Guy sputters. "That thing's still down there! It could kill you!"

Hemslock returns, a determined look on his face. "We're going into the cave."

"What?" IT Guy is about to have a conniption. "Why?"

"We might have lost one robot, but we still need more footage." Hemslock strides to the other station, still monitoring the helicopter drone, and moves the monitor so we can see what it had recorded. Its flight over the island reveals a dark figure standing just inside the cave, disappearing from view when the drone's camera shifts down for a closer look. "I want some answers, and it looks like this is the best place to start."

TEN

ENTRIES

"HERE YOU GO," HAWAIIAN SHIRT SAYS, DUMPING A SMALL stack of papers before me. "Figured you might like copies. These are from Alex Key's complete journal. *These* are for the Cortes journal, pages numbered one through thirty-six. The museum wouldn't let us take the original. They're what Hemslock's using to base most of his theories, so you can expect us to ask questions about these on camera."

I scan through them quickly. The Cortes journal had been translated for the crew's benefit; the writing is faded but legible. Ironically Key's journal is harder to read. There is no organization to the wild thoughts the man had scribbled on paper, veering chaotically from one unrelated topic to the next, writing over his previous words in the same way his own thoughts seem to have lain on top of each other.

Hawaiian Shirt points to one of Key's entries:

MY EYES CANNOT SEE MY EARS CANNOT HEAR YET I SEE
AND I HEAR AND THE VOICES IN MY [INCONCLUSIVE] HELP
IS THE THREE OF THE EYE AND THE EYE OF THE THREE AND
THE HEART IS HERE THE HEART THEY TAKE THEY WILL COME
BECAUSE OF ME AND IT IS HERE IT IS A VOID THAT CONTAINS
BOTH NOTHING AND EVERYTHING AT ONCE I AM [INCONCLUSIVE]
NOTHING AND EVERYTHING THE EIGHT ARE READY THEY ARE
COMING FIRST TO FEED SECOND TO SEED THIRD TO WEAR
FOURTH TO BIRTH FIFTH TO SERVE SIXTH TO LURE SEVENTH TO
CONSUME EIGHT TO WAKE [INCONCLUSIVE] I AM FIFTH I SERVE
MY EARS I CANNOT SEE MY EYES I CANNOT HEAR

"Absolutely batty, right?" Hawaiian Shirt says. "Notice the similarities? Like the writers already told you, the journal pages reference the same riddle, despite the Key journal being written before we discovered Cortes's. Not even the museum curator thought it would be so significant—she only thought Lindsay Watson's obsession with the journal was odd. The locals knew about the eight deaths, but nothing more specific as Key wrote about it. The Cortes journal has some pages torn out, more's the pity. But look at this."

Hawaiian Shirt jabs at one passage. "See this entry by Cortes? Read it."

This is what the people here believe. Typically a priest or chieftain performs such rituals, but anyone with the strength can do so (for the god prizes strength rather than its own

115

people) to achieve power beyond their wildest imaginings. For every sacrifice, they gain abilities beyond imagining. Control of the demons in the woods. Invulnerability. But most importantly—rulership of all. The command of an eternity within a dream, as these people say.

Yet they describe little of this god they worship. An eye, they say. It sees you. Perhaps it is a demon that wears nothing but an eye, though that paints a disturbing image. A Godseye. It incites the imagination.

If there is a strange power here, then it is our duty to find out more lest it be used against us.

I sought out Magellan for what information he could provide, for it was Rajah Humabon himself who explained the phenomenon to him. That is why the chieftain wishes for us to wage war against Cilapulapu, for the latter knows its secrets and worships this strange god. It is believed that Cilapulapu has already done two of these rituals; Humabon believes that he wields the god's power and is impervious to their bolos, and it is why he remains invincible. His people claim they saw Cilapulapu control certain creatures within the forests soon after the criminal's sacrifice—strange monsters fashioned from the god's own sacred tree.

Our muskets shall soon put that boast to the test.

But Magellan had only shaken his head mournfully, told me that such power is not for humans to enjoy, only for God to administer—

His finger moves toward the ragged tears in the next section of the journal, the pages missing. Hawaiian Shirt grunts. "And just when we were getting to the good part, too. Like Cortes, Hemslock thinks this Lapulapu fella may have learned how to manipulate the Godseye, and that's why he was able to kill the Spanish conquerors. Jessie from the team in Leyte says they've got some promising news—they might've found people who'd talked to some of the Watson cult members. Hopefully we get answers out of them."

He turns to leave, pauses, then hands me something else. "It's a grisly picture, so give it back to me if you don't wanna look."

It's a black and white photo, but that doesn't hide the bloodbath. I can make out a pair of legs, a bloodstained wall behind a heap of flesh.

The corpse doesn't appear to have an upper body.

"Haven't seen this yet, huh? Alex Key had a Filipina wife. He killed her and fled to the island, and they found him outside the Godseye like this, days later. It's why the authorities didn't do much else after finding his body. *Part* of his body, anyway. Closed the case as quick as they could. Local government didn't want an investigation, either. Always thought that maybe he'd run afoul of some local mob boss or something, and they'd dumped him there. Seemed like he had a running debt.

"Gries wants to feel better about his wife and Hemslock wants to clear his name and I don't know why the hell so many of the higher-ups are interested in producing this show—but when I first heard what Key had done, I thought good riddance. I still don't believe in all this god and ghost stuff, but if something really is out there, then I want to tell its story. Good job, you know? Hell of a good job."

And then he wanders off, to discuss the upcoming episode they're planning to film with one of the crew.

I remain where I am. My eyes flick toward the trees out of reflex, though this time there is no one watching. Small makahiya leaves slowly fold themselves shut, bashful against the wind. "Parang awa mo na," I say quietly all the same, though I don't know if anything hears, either.

❀❀❀

A fight breaks out, strangely enough, between two of the bodyguards accompanying Hemslock. "I fucking saw it!" The soldier shouts angrily, pointing toward the shore. "He was there! Bastard followed me here! I'm gonna fucking kill him!"

"He was about to charge into the water when I stopped him," the other soldier reports uncertainly.

"What the hell are you on about, Kyle?" Hemslock demands.

"My fucking stepfather, that's who. He's right there."

"Your stepfather's not in a condition to be here, Kyle. You told me so yourself. In the time it would have taken to get here, the hospital would have reached out."

The soldier stares out at the sea. "But I could have sworn I saw him," he whispers.

They send him off to the doctor's tent.

Melissa sidles up next to me. "The studio did background checks on everyone coming to the island," she murmurs. "I read some of the paperwork. That dude's stepfather is in a coma at a hospital in Colorado. He'd fallen down the stairs in the dark or something. Wild. Wish they'd thought to do mental health checks on the mercs. Not really the people I want to have guns."

The second time, it's someone from the medical team who approaches Hawaiian Shirt, visibly shaking, to tell him that he's seen his mother. Hawaiian Shirt stares at him for a good three seconds before venturing, "Your mother?"

"She's been dead for six years." The poor man looks terrified. "It's not my imagination, Gerry. Sam claims he saw his father, and I overheard one of the bodyguards say he'd seen his brother who died last month. There's something on this island. Maybe there's a gas leak, but—"

"There is no gas leak," Hawaiian Shirt says firmly. "Don't let the ghost stories get to you. Take some Ambien or something."

"Guy was an army medic in Afghanistan," he grumbles to me when the man leaves. "Went through all that bad business there and came back with an impressive psych eval, but *here's* where he hallucinates? He wasn't on good terms with his mom when she died— toxic relationship, from what I've heard. Still, not like him to get this jittery."

He winces. "Heard screaming again last night. That alone would scare the crap out of someone, but I'm not the one who decides when we get to leave. I—"

And then he straightens, eyes going wide. "Hey. Is this Dreamer haunting only *bad* people?"

Excitedly he fishes out the photocopies of the journals from his satchel, thumbs through them rapidly. "Here's the early Key journal entries"—HE KNOWS YOUR DREAMS. HE KNOWS YOUR FEARS. HE HAS

SEEN MINE. HE HAS SEEN MY FATHER, AND NOW HE HAS SEEN MY WIFE. I HAVE HAUNTED HER THROUGH THE YEARS AND NOW SHE HAUNTS ME. HE SEES ME. I AM NOT WORTHY. I AM AFRAID. THE EYE IS UPON ME, AND I AM AFRAID.

"He went downhill from there. Your god knew that Alex had killed his wife. It deliberately targets people like him, doesn't it?"

I look him in the eye. "I said he would never harm innocents."

He pales a little, then laughs half-heartedly. "If he's gunning for villains, then the whole slot of producers on this show alone would—that's just too—maybe there's something on this island making people hallucinate things. Wouldn't hurt to talk to the science team to make sure before we consider anything else."

<hr>

I spot Goatee and the girl again. She is behind another series of trees near the water, her face the only visible part of her, and he is on the path leading to the small pier, staring at her. The can of beer slips from his fingers and stains the sand a dark brown.

As if on a whim, he rushes toward her, his fists bared. I race after him.

The girl waits, serene and sad as she has always appeared. But when Goatee reaches her, his fury has turned to despair. His hands unfurl, and he reaches out toward the girl. "Tabitha," he says brokenly. "I—"

The girl gazes at him silently. Her lips move, but I don't hear what she says.

She pitches forward.

Her head drops into his hands.

With a loud cry, Goatee lets go and leaps back. But nothing falls to the ground.

He spins around. There is nothing in the space around him.

"Did you see that?" he cries out at me desperately. "Did you see her?"

He stumbles back in the direction of the cabins; his hands shaking, his face red, snot running down his nose. He trips, falls to his knees, but Hemslock is suddenly there. The man hauls him up, none too pleased.

"How are you this drunk at one in the afternoon?" he shouts. "Where the hell were you? We've got call time in half an hour and you're not even fucking ready! I was willing to give you the benefit of the doubt, Karl, but if you're only going to get wasted—"

Goatee stares at him. He looks hopeless, like he's given up on everything. "I saw her again, Rube," he whispers. "Tabitha. She was waiting for me by the shore. Said she was going to see me soon."

Hemslock casts a quick glance around them. "You need help, Karl. It's been years. As soon as we get home, I'm marching you straight to rehab. Pollock's a discreet place; they'll treat you right."

Oddly enough, Goatee smiles. "I don't think anything can help me anymore, Rube. And you know that? That feels—it's a relief."

He straightens himself, brushes off the man's help, and lurches toward the cabins.

Hemslock gazes after him, frowning. "What did you see?" he asks me.

121

I look back at the trees. "Consequences," is all I say, knowing Goatee is lost.

❊❊❊❊❊

The call to gather in front of the cave occurs half an hour later, and it takes another hour to set up everyone with the necessary equipment. A crew member straps a mic on me, while the others are outfitted with small cameras on their helmets and body vests. There are ten of us: me, Hemslock, Goatee, Gries, a scientist, a researcher, and four of Hemslock's bodyguards. Chase is talking with his father, trying his best to dissuade him from joining. "Please, Dad," he protests, "I don't think this is a good idea."

"Nothing's going to happen," her father says reassuringly. He puts up a brave front, but I see the dark circles under his eyes, proof that he hasn't had much sleep. "A team went in yesterday, and they were fine. I've been spelunking for years, and the network of tunnels they've mapped out isn't extensive enough to worry. We'll be okay."

"If it's okay, then at least let me go inside with you."

"Absolutely not. You know nothing about caves. Why don't you go and take more pictures of the beach for your followers?"

Chase glares at him. "You think I'm shallow for doing what I do, but you think what you're doing isn't insane?" he snaps at him, then stomps off.

"He may be right, sir," I say softly.

"I'm just jet lagged. I'll be okay."

"Seeing your dead wife isn't jet lag."

Gries starts violently. Wipes his forehead with his sleeve.

122

"I need to know what happened to her," he says. "I'll do anything to know."

"We've marked off parts of the caverns that are safe to move through," the scientist tells us. "There'll be luminescent paint and some physical markers we've placed inside so you can see the boundaries. Everything beyond that is still unexplored territory, and I advise you not to wander. That said, I don't foresee any problems."

She smiles. "You're really going to like what we've found there, Mr. Hemslock. The cave system we've plotted is very, very different from the one the previous investigators provided us with. I can't explain it. Caves don't shift like this in a few years' time. It's almost as if we're exploring an entirely new system, and that's impossible. There's at least three more caverns inside that aren't on the plane crash reports, and we haven't even explored it all."

"That's music to my ghost-hunting ears, Christie," Hemslock says with a wink at her. "While I appreciate the effort, I wish we could have gone into the cave blind."

"We're expendable and you're not, sir," the woman says dryly. "Once Mr. Galant wakes, he would agree."

Goatee cleans himself up well and is back to his impatient, slightly sneering facade. He's smoking, likely an attempt to ease his nerves, but at least there's no bottle in sight.

Chase wanders to me, taking in my appearance. "You look like you could blend in with the rest of them," he says, an attempt at humor.

"I hope not." I don't know why I sound so defensive.

Chase raises his hands. "I'm not here to argue, okay? I just wanted to tell you to be safe." His gaze drops to my hands. He moves like he wants to take mine in his, and then stops himself. "Be careful in there," he says instead.

"I'm always careful."

"Would it kill you to say thanks, for a change?"

I grin at his obvious sulking. "Thank you." I start to turn, stop. He still looks far too tense, like he's using great effort to rein in his temper. This mood didn't start from his argument with his father. "What's wrong?"

"Nothing," he says, suddenly evasive.

"I don't think so. Tell me."

He gives in. "It's Riley again. She's spreading rumors that I was the one cheating on her first. With you. Before I even got here. Before *she* even cheated."

"I met you only a few days ago."

"Her new theory is that we met in California, then I flew you out here so we could have some privacy. And all because she saw a fucking pair of legs in my selfie."

"I'm sorry."

He sighs. "You have nothing to be sorry about. This is all on her. That's why Jordan and Rory have been calling me all morning—to let me know. People are going to believe her even though she's the one who cheated!" Chase whirls toward the cave entrance. "Fuck you, Riley!" He shouts, the echoes receding into the darkness. A few of the crew members look our way, startled, but Chase doesn't seem to care. "I hope you get an STD, you cheating ho!" He shouts, and then marches away, kicking angrily at a few rocks in his path.

Askal crouches beside me, whining questioningly. "Go with him," I say. "Make sure he's okay."

He understands and trots off after the boy.

Hemslock chuckles nearby. "Teenagers, right?" His gaze drifts toward the cave's entrance as well, and then starts, as if he's seen something there. I look, but only darkness beckons us.

Still staring hard, Hemslock takes a step into the caves, and then another. Gries reaches out a hand to stop him. "What are you doing? The team isn't ready yet."

"I could have sworn I saw..." Hemslock frowns, but never finishes the thought.

"We're ready," someone from the safety team says. "You're all wired up so anything you say we'll hear in real time, and you should hear us loud and clear through your earpieces, too. Everyone gets walkie-talkies in case of an emergency. If you run into any kind of trouble or if communication shorts out, use those to reach us. We're ready whenever you are."

"We're ready," Hemslock says. "Keep a lock on us at all times." He glances at the rest of us. Goatee nods, as do the scientists.

"You got weapons?" the actor asks me.

"I have a machete, for chopping wood. That's all I'll need."

To his credit, he doesn't mock me for it. He only inclines his head, looking oddly thoughtful. "I got a feeling we'll be needing all the protection we can get." He turns. "Let's roll."

ELEVEN

ELENA

THE ALTAR LOOKS EXACTLY HOW WE LEFT IT WHEN Goatee and Hawaiian Shirt stumbled into the cave with me that first time. I go through the motions, laying my hand on the cave wall close to the stonework, murmuring "Tabi po." To my surprise, Hemslock does the same. The short clips the crew showed me of him screaming at Taoist priests, being forcibly removed from sacred places, made me think he would be just as discourteous here.

He sees my face, grins. "That's show business for you. Getting riled up, causing controversy is what gets you the clicks. I can be respectful, if I must." He looks at the altar, and then up at the open sky above us. It is early enough that the moon is not yet visible; no eye stares down at us yet. "Let's see what the rest of the cave has to offer. How far in have you been, kid?"

"It's dangerous to go beyond this altar."

He only grins. "Talk to me about this place. How did anyone

even know about the curse to begin with? Did any of the locals know about Alex Key?"

"Not the details." We are moving along a smaller passageway, enough for two people to pass, shoulder to shoulder. I find myself beside Gries with Goatee behind us, while Hemslock walks in the lead, tossing questions over his shoulder at me. The bodyguards tail closely behind, the scientists bringing up the rear. "The Diwata's story has been passed down for generations, longer than even we know."

"What do they think about Cortes?"

"That he stole gold from the people is known. The Diwata punished him. Legend says that roots grew around Cortes and pulled him screaming into the ground."

"See, Karl? We didn't know this about Cortes. There'll be more stories that people haven't told us yet."

"It's not something you'd find in history books, obviously," Goatee says shortly. This close, his breath stinks of alcohol. "It's probably an old wives' tale that lingered with the locals but never got written down. Who knows, though? Maybe we'll be the one to find all that missing gold."

"Was that the case, Alon?"

"The Spaniards destroyed much of our precolonial history when they came here as conquerors. Your American armies arrived afterward and destroyed most of the rest."

"Don't blame us, kid," Goatee snorts. "I wasn't even alive back then."

"But we reaped the benefits of that past all the same," Gries replies. "It's likely that Lapulapu was as responsible for Cortes's death as Magellan's. It explains why he has the journal."

"I have another question for our tour guide," Hemslock says. "Those tourists who tried to explore the cave wound up dead or missing. That's why *fifteen dead* is an estimate. We haven't found all the bodies of those who'd disappeared yet. But the science team explored the cave without any mishap. Same with the aviation accident investigators. Now don't get me wrong—I'm glad. But what makes them different?"

I keep my eyes on the ground, careful not to stumble over the loose roots in the path. "The Diwata only punishes the cruel. They were curious, but respectful."

"And it doesn't consider *us* respectful?" This from Goatee. "I mean, it fucking screamed at me!"

I don't say anything, choosing diplomacy. Hemslock laughs. "Guess that answers your question, Karl. Hang on. This must be the area."

He whistles low as we step through the passageway into a wider cavern beyond. There are no altars here, but there is something else.

Staring back at us is a wide, glaring eye carved into the wall, easily twenty feet high. There are crude lines around it, as if to symbolize rays of light. Underneath the eye is a stick figure's body, simple, almost an afterthought in comparison. One hand is raised, as if to strike.

Jagged-looking drawings of trees surround the figure. "Balete," Hemslock notes quietly.

"Damn," Goatee says, staring. "How the hell did they draw them so high up?"

"The size of the cave entrance didn't clue you in?" the historian points out. "The Diwata was a supposed giant."

128

"Hey Denny," Hemslock says, speaking into his mic. "Are you getting all of this? Beautiful, isn't it? Portrait of an Artist as a Young God."

"We found some writings in the cave last time," the researcher says excitedly, gesturing at the others to draw nearer. She points at a series of inscriptions below the massive figure. "We sent photographs off to be translated—it's an ancient script, a syntax that I believe is based on Baybayin. This likely dates to what we know of precolonial society in this region."

"What does it say?" Hemslock asks, reaching out to touch one of the crudely carved letters.

"They're not sentences, so much as words. This one says 'Feed.' This one, 'Seed.' The third, 'Wear.'"

Hemslock grins. "*First to feed. Second to seed. Third to wear.* So you're telling me that these writings, likely to have been scrawled here centuries ago, maybe even thousands of years ago, exactly depict the eight deaths riddle."

"It's too much of a coincidence not to be. I don't know how the aviation accident investigators missed all this, but—"

The actor lets out a loud whoop. "Do you hear that?" He laughs into his mic, speaking to the people back at the command center, and addressing some unseen audience at the same time. "We're on the right path. We now have independent evidence of the eight deaths' curse beyond Key's and Cortes's journals. We're one step closer to unlocking the Godseye's mystery. Anything else can we expect to see here?"

"Nothing much, I'm afraid. We explored the next cavern, but we haven't found any more carvings or drawings. Ground penetrating radar tells us that there's a couple more tunnels farther out, but there doesn't seem to be a way for us to get to them from this end. Either those passageways have been blocked off since these caves were formed and there's no way to access them short of tunneling through the walls—or there's another entrance to the Godseye that we've missed."

"Did you hear that?" Gries asks suddenly. His face has gone pale in the semi-darkness.

"I don't hear anything," Hemslock says intently, watching the other man. "Describe it to me."

"I can hear someone calling my name." Sweat streaks down Leo's face, and it has nothing to do with the heat. "I—it sounds a lot like Elena's voice."

Hemslock gestures sharply at the rest of us to fall silent. We wait, tersely, straining to hear.

"There it is again." Gries is shaking, leaning against the wall like all his strength has been sapped by the sound. "I—I need to find her. I need see who's been making this—"

"That's the last thing we're going to do, Leo," Hemslock interrupts—firmly, confidently. "Take deep breaths. We didn't hear anything. Maybe your mind is playing tricks."

"Our scans are clear," Goatee says. "Leo, if you're not feeling well, I think one of us should escort you out, see if—"

"No," Gries says, shaking his head. "I'm fine. I can go on."

"No changes in oxygen levels," the researcher adds. "We haven't gone deep enough within the cave for any drastic changes. But it might be better to return to the surface, regardless, Mr. Gries. Mr. Hemslock, maybe you should get one of your bodyguards to accompany him to—Mr. Hemslock? Are you okay?"

Hemslock is not okay. He focused on something in the gloom, and there is a very peculiar expression on his face. "You bitch," he whispers.

"What are you doing?" Goatee yells, but Hemslock is already moving. The camera light on his head winks out without warning as he steps into the darkness and disappears.

Goatee swears and dashes in the actor's direction, then utters a startled cry. "He disappeared into the wall! No, wait—there's another passage here!"

He's right. It's a narrow squeeze, wide enough to allow only one person through at a time, and half-hidden by some bramble hanging down from the limestone.

"Wait," the scientist says, alarmed. "We haven't seen this cavern before. We need to make sure it's stable—"

No one's listening. Hemslock's bodyguards are already pushing through. Goatee swears noisily again and stumbles in after them, his gait uneven.

"Stay here and wait for us," Gries barks at the alarmed scientists, finally returning to his senses. "Darren? Lamarr? Damn it." He slaps at the walkie-talkie, but it responds only in bursts of static. "See if any of you can reach the others. Tell them we need backup." He looks at me. "You're free to stay here, if you like."

But I am already shaking my head. "I'm going after him."

We make into the new cavern by forcing ourselves through the opening in the rock sideways; the tightness feels oppressive, like the walls could crush us at a moment's notice, the ceiling flatten us. Somehow we make it through and find ourselves standing before another tunnel, larger than any we've gone through so far. There are several forks in the path leading to three different passageways, all similar in size. Hemslock stands at the crux where they all meet, unsure of which one to enter. His bodyguards crowd behind him, their hands on their guns.

"What the hell is wrong with you?" Goatee bursts out, finally catching up. "Reuben, you're the last person to lose your head like this, what do you think you're—"

Hemslock lifts a finger to his lips to silence him. We wait, but we hear no other sound.

"I know what I saw," Hemslock says, as if trying to convince himself. "No way she—"

He breaks off. When he speaks again, his voice is calm and controlled once more. "You're right, Karl. Bad of me to have come in without thinking. Denny, do you still copy?"

Apparently outside communication now works despite having traveled deeper into the cave, because he continues talking. "Yeah, thought I saw something and wanted to verify. No, not exactly a ghost—more like a bad memory. Look, that's not the point. We'll head back to the first cavern. I—wait. What's this?"

He crouches down over what looks to be a large briar patch of thorns, his mouth hanging open as he makes another find. "Goddamn. Look at this, Karl. These aren't rocks. There are *remains* here. Parts of them, at least. Can't see a skull, but these bones are human, all right."

Makahiya plants from within the patch are blooming over the bits of bone, opening and closing, contributing to the blanket of moss.

"No shit," Goatee says again. "Let me see."

He leans forward. One of the makahiya plants turns slowly toward him. Its leaves open.

Within, a wide eye stares back.

Goatee rears back with a shout.

Another cry bursts upon us without warning. "Leo!"

"Elena?" Gries spins in a circle, trying to discern where the sound is coming from.

A sob comes from somewhere to my left. "Leo, I'm so sorry."

I see blonde hair, a flash of a blue dress at the end of one of the tunnels; everything else is obscured by shadows. Without thinking, Leo sprints toward her.

I give chase and grab his arm before he makes it halfway through.

Gries fights me. "What are you doing? I need to get to her!"

"No, sir," I say, keeping my grip. "I don't think that's your wife."

He stares at me like I've spoken in another language, so I repeat myself, emphasizing every word. "Sir, I don't think that's your wife."

He shudders and then this time looks, *really* looks, at the figure waiting for us at the end of the tunnel.

It doesn't move. The screaming has stopped. It stands there watching us, waiting for our next move.

"It's not Elena," Leo whispers, finally understanding. "What—what—"

The dark figure screams again, and this time it sounds inhuman.

It is a horrendous, earsplitting shriek that shakes the cave, sending bits of stone scattering down upon us from the ceiling.

The shriek is followed by strange crackling sounds, like that of twigs and dead leaves being trodden underfoot.

Hemslock jerks his flashlight toward the noise, illuminating a face.

Or what should have been a face.

A large, cavernous mouth takes up the whole of what should have been eyes, nose, ears—it's a Venus flytrap of a mandible. Something like hair snakes around its head, but the similarities end there, because it moves like every lock is alive. The skin is a brownish gray stretched thickly over bone—if it is truly bone that keeps it upright.

It wears something that could pass for clothes, likely a memory of what Elena Gries used to wear, yet in the next instant shifts into a bareness that has nothing to do with nudity. More branches twist and braid together to create a human form. Makahiya leaves wrap around its shape; they open to reveal eyes within the center of its flowers, lidless and bulging, gazing back at us.

The light catches it again. Something slides out of its mouth, far too long to be a regular tongue.

The figure seems to stretch for one long second—its shape extending toward the ceiling, distorting and lengthening—before it drops to the ground on all fours, arches its back, and crawls toward us, shrieking. Its movements are jerky, crackling—but it's fast. Too fast.

I haul Gries with me as we flee down to the tunnel where the group is waiting. Hemslock's bodyguards have all drawn their weapons, and for a moment I think they might start shooting while we are still within their line of fire.

We hit the floor just as the thing dogging our steps jumps again, before Hemslock's bodyguards start firing.

Their bullets catch the creature squarely in the stomach. It flies backward, crumpling into a heap on the ground.

"Move!" I can hear Hemslock yelling. He grabs me by the arm and hauls me up, watching one of his guards do the same for Gries. Goatee is already through the tight passageway, squirming desperately to scrape himself through the narrow space. Hemslock shoulders his way through with lesser difficulty. Gries is next, and then me, the sounds of gunfire as the bodyguards continue to unload on the creature still ringing in my ears.

We are back in the first cavern, where the stick figure drawing of the Godseye gazes down upon us. Goatee isn't waiting—he's already racing for the exit, stumbling slightly, splaying his flashlight frantically around him without looking where he is going. The historian and the researcher are frozen, goggling at us.

"Get out!" Hemslock roars at them, and they scramble to obey.

Another shout, this time from Goatee. He's tripped over something and sprawls on the ground.

His fingers find roots. They wrap around Goatee's wrist, multiplying rapidly until they encircle his whole arm. The drunkard yells in horror.

"Karl!" Hemslock grabs at his friend. We all watch as something emerges from the ground before us, the swarming roots and tiny branches reforming into a shape that resembles the monster in the tunnels, but this time it no longer requires a human-like head to manifest a wide mouth.

For a moment it looks like Goatee can get away. Hemslock has whipped out his knife and is trying his best to cut the gnarls from Goatee. He says something to Goatee, but it's too low for me to hear. I only see Goatee's face, panicked and afraid, staring wildly back at his friend.

A shadow moves behind them both. Hemslock freezes and looks up—right into the faceless tree creature.

Goatee screams one last time. And then the sea of writhing tendrils fling Hemslock away and descend upon the other man, forming a massive ball of branches that hide him from view.

Hemslock drives the blade frantically into the grotesque, frothing tree-mouth—and it disperses almost immediately, the tangle of tree limbs unknotting, returning to individual roots and giving way, skittering back into the ground.

But as the vegetation recedes, there is empty space where Goatee had once lain—like he had never been there.

"What happened?" Chase gasps as we stumble back outside the cave. Gries is a mess. His shirt is stained with dirt, and there are scratches on his face. Hemslock is doubled over, panting, his hands on his knees. The historian and the researcher who had accompanied us collapse on the ground, their knees giving way as they stare listlessly toward the cave, no longer boasting of their discoveries.

"What happened?" Hawaiian Shirt runs up to us, taking in the scene before him. "Reuben, what's going on?"

"They're real," Hemslock says, raising his head. "They're real, Gerry. What Key claimed, what Cortes wrote—they're all fucking real."

TWELVE

PLAYTHROUGH

"**WHAT DO YOU MEAN WE CANCELED THE FLIGHT?**" LEO Gries yells into the phone. "We didn't cancel shit! You promised us that helicopter *two hours ago.*"

He pauses, fuming quietly, as the person on the other end of the line attempts to explain themselves. "I don't care who screwed up at this point," he shouts. "There is a person missing from my crew and another still unconscious. We need someone to fly us to the nearest—" He stops. "The line went dead. Dammit."

"I can't believe it," the historian stammers. Most of the crew has clustered themselves inside of the mess hall, unwilling to venture out unless in larger groups.

"This island is honest-to-god cursed," Melissa says nervously, and there are a few murmurs of agreement. "We can't work under these conditions, Mr. Gries. We need to get the law involved. Maybe the FBI or something."

"What we *need* is to get off this island," someone else wails. "I don't want whatever got Karl to get me!"

A babble of voices respond, the noise growing louder with every second. Hemslock raises two fingers to his mouth and whistles shrilly, breaking through the mayhem.

"Anyone who wants to leave the island is free to do so, as soon as the helicopter arrives," he says. "I won't stop any of you. I'd ask Alon here to ferry you all back to the mainland if you don't want to wait, but that boat isn't going to hold more than three, maybe four people at a time—"

"No," I say, interrupting him.

"What?"

I point wordlessly at the sky, where dark clouds have been looming on the horizon since our return. Askal whimpers quietly beside me, staring upward as well. "It's coming up fast. We'd be caught in the storm before we're more than halfway across."

Hemslock scowls. "Which means the helicopter isn't likely to make it here in time, either."

"We're delaying filming indefinitely until we find Karl," Gries decides.

"I'm not going back in there!" the researcher says violently. "I don't care if you don't pay me. I'm never going back in that cave after…after *that*!"

"I got it running," comes the breathless response from the workstation where Straw Hat is hunched over, running through the footage that the group had recorded inside the caves before everything turned to chaos. "Here we go, Mr. Gries, Mr. Hemslock."

Hemslock is by his side soon enough, with Gries close behind. At least half the group follows, gathering expectantly around the screen as Straw Hat plays the video.

The night vision built into the camera casts the cave in black shadows tinged with an alien green. Hemslock's voice echoes across the wide cavern, loud and clear and sounding pleased with himself. The lens is from his point of view; I see his hand press against the cave wall, right above where the ancient script had been carved into the surface. "We now have independent evidence of the eight deaths' curse beyond Key's and Cortes's journals. We're one step closer to unlocking the Godseye's mystery."

As he continues to talk, his flashlight plays against the strange letters, highlighting the word the historian had confirmed meant *feed*.

The scream Leo heard does not register on the playback. I catch sight of myself on the screen, my head jerking toward the producer over a sound that isn't picked up by the recording. The camera shifts wildly away from me, focusing on Gries's face, which is as pale as paper. "I can hear someone calling my name. I—it sounds a lot like Elena's voice," he says.

And then it is Hemslock's turn to behave erratically. Something on the rightmost corner of the camera catches my attention—a shadow where there shouldn't have been, idling by the smaller tunnel the historian said had not been there before. It flits out of view.

"I don't understand it," one of the scientists says shakily, staring at the screen before him. "We were thorough. There wasn't an entrance there. It couldn't have magically appeared—"

140

Leo's voice on the recording cuts through his words, crying out Elena's name, and I hear Chase start beside me. I lay a hand on his shoulder, and he leans toward me.

The strange dark figure that emerges is only a speck in the lens, not enough to make out what it truly was. We watch as I grab Gries, dragging us to safety as Hemslock's bodyguards open fire at something behind us. But there is nothing on screen to show beyond shadows, even as we all retreat.

And then, Goatee—again from Hemslock's perspective—runs up ahead, sliding and skidding, until that last fatal trip sends him sprawling to the ground. The screen goes blank as he begins to scream.

"What's wrong with the recording?" Hemslock demands, nearly beside himself and livid.

"I don't know, sir!" Straw Hat frantically types on his keyboard, trying to sort out the technical difficulties, to no effect. "It's not that there's anything wrong with our equipment, it's just that the camera didn't film shit!"

Images return abruptly, but by then it's far too late. We can see Hemslock's hands digging frantically into the ground, desperately searching for his friend. But Goatee is gone.

Hemslock yanks off his mic and throws it on the floor before stalking off, his bodyguards silently following.

Straw Hat leans back in his seat, looking like he ran a marathon. "I don't understand," he says. "There's nothing wrong with the—"

"Play it again," Gries orders.

"Sir—"

"Play it again."

Straw Hat flinches but obeys.

Nothing changes in this second playthrough—Leo and I escape with our lives and the soldiers fire at something that is never caught on video. Goatee runs, falls, and then—nothing but the sounds of his screams.

"It was a woman," Leo says, as if trying to convince himself of his own words. "No—a creature with a woman's shape. Only there was—it had no face. None at all. But it had a mouth. A wide, carnivorous—you saw that too, right? Tell me I wasn't hallucinating."

"I don't know what that was," the historian says, her hands trembling. "Nothing like that should exist—"

"I want to look through the rest of the footage," Gries says abruptly. "Surely one of the cameras we wore will show more."

Wordlessly and unwilling to prove him wrong, the crew looks through the rest of the recordings—all at different angles and multiple viewpoints, none showing us the creature that had chased us or what had taken Goatee.

"Impossible," is all Gries can say each time. "This is impossible."

"Did you see it, too?" Chase whispers to me. "Have you ever seen any creatures like that on the island before?"

"Yeah, kid," Hawaiian Shirt says, overhearing him. He looks exhausted. "You've been inside the cave. You told me you've seen figures moving around this place. Tell us why it isn't showing up on our cameras like some fucking vampire."

"I've never seen it up close," I say.

All eyes turn my way. "Explain," Gries says tersely.

142

"I've seen them, but they've never come near. They often stand among the trees and watch me until I leave, but they've never come this near before. Fishermen have sighted them in the past, but it's considered bad luck to talk about them."

"Guns seem to be effective at scaring them off," Hemslock says as he returns to the group, his temper under better control. He looks hard at me. "Bastards won't catch us off-guard a second time."

Gries turns to Melissa, still irritable. "Where the hell is the damn 'copter?"

"I've been trying to contact them," the girl says, nervously. "There's a storm on the mainland right now, which must be affecting our communications—we can't establish contact with the rest of the team there, either."

"Find a way!"

Melissa rushes off. Hemslock reaches into his jacket and pulls out a gun. "We're going to search the caves again for Karl," he says grimly. "Robert's already planning our approach. If any of you want to volunteer, you're going to have to go in packing heat."

Gries hesitates. Then, "I'll go."

"You have got to be shitting me, Dad!" Chase cries out.

"I'm sorry. But they need all the help they can get, and I'm experienced enough with caves to be of some use. I—" His jaw flexes. "I heard her, Chase. Your mom. She's somewhere inside. Alon—"

"Askal and I will stay with him, sir," I say, before he can finish the sentence.

"Brick, Leo's in," Hemslock says brusquely, nodding at one of his soldiers. "We'll keep up the search till nightfall."

"Mr. Hemslock, Mr. Gries." The medics approach them, troubled. "Mr. Galant is awake," one of them says.

"Finally some good news!" Hemslock exclaims, his face clearing. "How is he?"

The medics glance worriedly at each other. "Sir," one says carefully. "I think it would be best if you see for yourself."

A large tent had been set up near the shore to handle any medical emergencies during filming, and the medics have been treating Armani there since he'd fallen unconscious. I accompany Hemslock, Askal tagging a few feet behind us.

Armani lies on a large cot, staring up at the ceiling. He blinks, slowly. "Reuben?" he asks, as Hemslock sits on the chair beside him. "Is that you?"

"You gave us all a scare, Steve," Hemslock says reassuringly. He reaches down and grips the man's shoulder. "A lot has happened while you were unconscious. Karl's missing, and it's been a mess with the other—"

Armani grabs at Hemslock's arm without warning. His fingers score deeply into his skin, with a strength that makes Hemslock recoil.

"The fuck, Steve?" He struggles to throw him off, even as the man clings to him stubbornly.

Askal begins to growl and bark at Galant, leaping for him with teeth bared. I haul him back by the scruff of his neck just in time. "Baba!" I say sharply and he acquiesces, though he continues to snarl and snap in the man's direction.

The medics are quick to pull the injured man from Hemslock.

Armani fights them, but he then shudders, hands dropping without warning. He lets the medics settle him on the cot. His eyes continue to stare blindly ahead, never once looking at Hemslock, the doctors, or the rest of us in the room.

"I can't see, Reuben," he chokes. And then, he begins to scream. "I can't see! I can't see who it is, but I know it's here. It's telling me things I don't want to hear. God help me, *help me, stop telling me what I can't see, stop telling me what I can't—*"

THIRTEEN
BEHIND YOU

GRIES FINALLY PATCHES A CALL THROUGH TO THE helicopter rental again, only to be told that the flight had once more been canceled.

"Someone's sabotaging us," he says in disgust, as he ends the call. "Someone keeps calling and pretending to be me. It's useless at this point. There's a full-fledged storm in the area, and they can't send help until it passes."

Hawaiian Shirt looks at him, and then up at the cloudless blue sky, the sun shining down. "Doesn't look like bad weather to me," he says.

He says it again later that afternoon, staring out at the sea. The dark clouds that loomed over the horizon earlier are gone, and we have a clear sight from the island's shore of the mainland some miles away, without even fog to mar the view.

"Maybe it's just me," Hawaiian Shirt says, "but there ain't no fucking storm out there. It's not only the helicopter rental playing us. Leo's right. Someone is screwing around with us for fun."

"No," Straw Hat says quietly. "We're getting reports from our team back in Leyte. It's a full-on downpour there. They're waiting it out because the streets tend to flood. They're not lying to us."

"But we're not lying, either," Hawaiian Shirt says desperately, looking at the bright sky and warm sun. "They see rain, but we don't. What the hell is going on?"

Armani has been sedated; the medics found nothing wrong with his eyes—beyond the fact that he couldn't see through them—and suggested temporary hysteria, PTSD as a cause.

Hemslock does not sit well with this diagnosis. "Nobody gets PTSD from a damn tree," he spits out angrily, cleaning his guns again. Their search that day had turned up no signs of his friend, and the frustration is clear on the survivalist's face. He soon retreats to the mess hall, where he has set up multiple infographics detailing everything known about both the island and the curse. The riddle is scratched out in capital letters on a white board, scribbled notes linking five of the eight prophesied deaths on another.

"Tell me what you think," he says to me. "Tell me if there's anything here that I'm missing."

I scrutinize the boards. The corpse tree takes up much of his theories, along with his belief that the dead body is the ill-fated Cortes. Lindsay Watson's mugshot stares back at us.

"Third to wear," Hemslock says. "My gut tells me I'm right. I'm thinking your god's snagged Karl for the sixth sacrifice. Sixth to lure.

Because that's what he is, eh? He's bait for the rest of us to enter the Godseye again. But why him? What makes him so special?"

I look at the photos the crew has printed of the corpse tree, and then at a painter's illustration of Oliviero Cortes. He doesn't look as intimidating as one might think, whatever his exploits with Magellan. "Cortes wanted to steal the Diwata's power," I say, finally. "This is his punishment. The eight deaths aren't rewards."

"Karl didn't steal from your god."

"He drinks."

Hemslock chuckles despite himself. "Your god preaches sobriety? He's mad that Karl likes beer?"

"He drinks because he wants to forget. Because he committed a terrible thing."

Hemslock's face grows more serious. He sits on a chair across from me.

"How did you know?"

I gaze down at my hands. "I saw her, too."

A long silence stretches between us before he speaks again. "You're right. He did do something terrible. Hit and run. A teenage girl. Her family was poor, and he paid them off to settle out of court without press. He's been drinking ever since. He does his job well enough despite it, so we let him be. But it was an accident. He didn't even know her."

"No," I say. "He did."

Hemslock doesn't look surprised by that revelation. "And how did you find that out?"

"The living bring their own ghosts to shore, and only the latter are honest about why."

He nods. "Yeah, you're right. He knew the girl. Didn't want to make him look bad while he's still missing. I was told that they argued. He got into the car, and she tried to stop him from leaving. He didn't see her when he—it was still an accident." He sighs, spreads his hands. "He started drinking after that. Only so much we all could do to help. We're gonna find him. We have to. You think he's a candidate to be the fifth sacrifice, don't you?"

He takes my silence as confirmation and turns back to the board. "*Fourth to birth.* I thought at first that the pregnant woman was the sacrifice. I was wrong. I think she was collateral damage. It was her all along." He points at Watson's picture. "The god chose *her* for the fourth sacrifice. The riddle doesn't talk about the sacrifice's condition. It talks about what is the sacrifice's purpose. Ironically Watson killing that woman qualified her to be a sacrifice herself. And now she's birthed all these fucking tree monsters that keep coming after us."

I say nothing again, and he smiles, satisfied. "And you knew all this, didn't you? I can believe that you didn't know anything about the cultists since that was before you were even born, but you would have known the specifics of the ritual. We're paying you to tell us this shit. So why didn't you?"

I meet his gaze. "There have been far too many people trespassing here, hoping to recreate the ritual. The cultists came the closest, but they weren't the first."

He nods. "Cortes was one of the first recorded, I assume. But there would have been other Filipinos on the island who'd tried to wrest control from Lapulapu. Just like Watson. She learned what

Cortes had. She tore the pages of that journal because it showed her exactly how to perform the ritual. But it backfired."

He turns back to his board. "I keep coming back to your hero, Lapulapu. Took a deeper dive into the history. The records make him out to be some kind of superman. Powerful warrior who prevented the Spaniards from encroaching on his territory, protecting his subjects. But here's the problem."

He slams a fist against the table. The pencils jump and the cups rattle, but I don't move.

"There's scant history about him before his fight with Magellan, and even less afterward. But I'll bet all my money that Lapulapu *did* perform those first two sacrifices, and then sacrificed Cortes. And in exchange, the god rewarded him. The Spaniards couldn't defeat Lapulapu, despite their superior weapons. Watson had it right. Her only mistake was in choosing wrong—"

He shoots to his feet, startled, as if he's seen something by the window. I turn, catch a quick glimpse of a face, a flash of yellow hair. But all too quickly it's gone, leaving only more makahiya growing over the pane.

"What we need," Hemslock says, his voice strange, "are some more fucking guns, so we can descend into whatever level of hell this god is sleeping and put a bullet through his head."

⚜

Chase paces by the entrance of the cave, refusing to wait while his father and the others are searching inside the cave. Askal keeps close, copying his movements.

150

"Is Dad in danger? Is that why he can see Mom's ghost?"

"The others mentioned that your father was a ruthless business-man," I say, carefully.

"But—but he's not like that anymore! Yeah, I was royally pissed when I learned the shit he'd done before, and I know Mom was too, but he'd stopped..."

He trailed off. "It doesn't matter, right? A lot of people lost their jobs because of him. Even if he was sorry, it's not like that's enough." He froze. "Did you think that he was—violent—to Mom? He wouldn't—I would have *known*."

His phone buzzes.

We stare at it. Chase excitedly picks up.

"Look," Rory's voice comes over the receiver without waiting for an acknowledgment. "I have finished my investigation—"

"You haven't investigated shit," Jordan rebuts, laughing as his video feed pops up beside Rory's.

"I have finished my investigation, and I have determined that you need to tell your delicious tour guide that you're interested. Alon seems like the type to hate beating around the bush. I—oh, hello, Alon." The boy doesn't even look guilty, like he was planning for me to hear. "'Sup?"

Chase turns red. "Rory, thank God you're here, I—"

"Also," Rory rattles on, without waiting for Chase to finish, "I don't know how you put the fear of God in Riley, but I am *living* for it. Josh says she's been all over social media admitting she lied about you and your hottie, and that she is begging for your forgiveness. I don't know what you two told her, but she's getting wrecked for what she's done, and I am enjoying this far too much—"

"Rory!" Chase shouts. "Shut up for like a sec and listen! You need to get someone to send a helicopter to us as soon as you can! We've got injured people here!"

"Oh! Wait! Hold on!" Faint noises, then Rory yelling indistinctly.

"Yo, wait, wait, wait. Slow down," Jordan says. "Injured people? Are you serious? The hell's happening over there? Is it that damn curse again?"

"We think so! Our phones aren't working. I don't know how you got through, because my phone's had no reception since this morning. We don't have a way to contact the local authorities to tell them we're stuck on Kisapmata!"

Rory returns. "I told Dad. He's calling people right now. He plays golf with Paradigm's CEO. They should have people on it already."

"Tell him to call one of the producers. Stanley Brosnick, or Don Huessman or—"

"Wait, Don Huessman? Not gonna happen. Didn't you hear? Oh, wait—if you don't have working phones there then you wouldn't have. He's gone missing."

Askal whines quietly, looking at the nearby trees.

"What?"

Jordan clears his throat. "Yeah, no one knows where he is. Went into his home office and then never came out, his housekeeper said. It's all over the news. The police aren't sure if it's foul play yet. They think he fled the country or something. I could ask Dad to call Stanley Brosnick, but dude must be fielding a ton of calls. Everyone knows he and Heussman are best buds."

Don Heussman. Producer Two, who stared at us from the monitor, chuckling about how the Kisapmata curse sounded like the rapture.

"I don't think he's left the country," I say slowly.

"Well he was seen dining out in LA earlier today, so he should still be in California. The police checked the flight records. He hasn't flown out."

"No. I think you'll find his body soon."

Chase stares at me. "Your god can do that?" His voice shakes. "Can he reach all the way around the world and just—kill—someone?"

I take a deep breath. "He sees your thoughts. He can find you that way—even through a computer, I think, as long as a connection has been established from the island. If the Diwata did that, then it means that he's getting...stronger."

"Because Karl was sacrificed? Are you saying Karl's dead?"

"Who's dead?" Jordan gasps.

"Hold up, hold up," Rory shouts. "What is—"

The call cuts off abruptly. Chase taps at his phone but receives nothing but an automated voice telling him that Rory's number can no longer be reached.

"At least we're sure about the rescue this time," he grunts. "And I just realized—*you* could go home. You said you live nearby. Isn't your dad or the rest of your family worried that you've been gone for so long?"

"They know what this job requires."

"Your family never told you to stay away from this place?"

"Kisapmata isn't dangerous to us."

"The cultists disappeared the same way Heussman did. But why would the Diwata kill Karl?"

I remember Goatee and his e-cigarettes, the way he tried to drink himself into insensibility every chance he had. It was as if the miles of sea he tried to put between him and the past that haunted him were not enough. I remember the scream and the way he had jumped back in fright, the girl lurking among the balete. His slow but steady spiral into despair in the days that followed. "He's not innocent," I say slowly. "But..."

When I don't say anything else, Chase grunts. "All the big studio heads make these decisions, but they're getting off scot-free. You can't say that your Diwata is handing out justice when there're so many people who never get the punishment that they deserve. I—" Chase's voice dips low. "Mom didn't deserve to die. Nobody on that airplane did, least of all her. Why was that one passenger on their flight discovered here, on the island, but no one else? And why didn't anyone else find the plane wreckage underground before the crew did?"

"The Diwata didn't cause the crash. He honors innocents who die on Kisapmata."

Chase stares at me. "Are you saying that the Diwata buried the passengers as a sign of respect? Then what's the deal with Dad seeing Mom's ghost? Is she suffering here?"

"I...I don't think it's your mom that your dad sees."

He shudders. "Then where's Mom's grave?"

"I don't know. I'm sorry."

"If the Diwata favors you, can't you, like, entreat them to protect us or something? Protect the people who are here because they need a paycheck, like Melissa? Will it attack me?"

I remember the figure in the trees watching us, and the makahiya leaves on Chase's windowsill. "It won't. But I'll keep you safe."

Chase snorts. "Not like I don't appreciate it, but…I mean, I've seen all the movies. It's always the jock who gets stabbed, right? Plus, we're the ones making money off your legends. And you're still trying to protect us, even if we don't deserve it."

"You deserve it," I say seriously. I am astounded when his eyes fill with tears.

"You're a good person, Alon," Chase says earnestly. "You really are. We've only known each other a few days, but I feel like—like I—"

Askal barks, startling us. He's running in circles, pausing every now and then to backtrack a few feet and look at us, as if insisting we leave.

A chiming sound comes from Chase's phone. "We got reception back?" Chase eagerly swipes to see the message.

And then he yelps in fright, dropping the phone to the ground.

I reach down for his phone to see what scared him so badly.

It's a message from Rory. "THERE'S SOMETHING BEHIND YOU," he has typed, in all capital letters, followed by a screenshot he took of Chase and me during our video call with him.

Behind us something lurks in the trees—a dark figure with a twisted white face that looks like its skin is being wrung dry.

I help Chase sit on a nearby rock, and then move toward the copse of trees to search for the culprit. Askal follows me, still visibly agitated.

"It might get you!" Chase yells, but I ignore him.

I reach the spot where the apparition should have been but find nothing there. I turn to wave at Chase, who stares at me, worry straining his face—

—and see that same white face lurking just over his shoulder. Its shriveled flesh makes its eyes larger than they should be, and its steepled, twig-like fingers caress at Chase's hair, gliding down toward his neck—

I take off toward Chase, running as fast as I can, shouting "'Wag mo siyang hawakan!"

Chase doesn't understand, but I know the creatures does. Askal is faster than me. He closes the distance rapidly, leaping at the creature behind Chase with a bark. But suddenly the shapeless figure and its unblinking gaze is gone.

Nothing else moves around us. Askal calms, returning to my side with grim satisfaction.

Slowly, still oblivious, Chase reaches out for my arm and gulps. "I didn't understand what you were shouting."

With effort, I force my lips to move. "I said, *Don't touch him*," I say hoarsely. "I told it not to touch you."

FOURTEEN
INTERVIEWS

"THE BAD NEWS IS THAT THE STORM ISN'T GOING TO LET up anytime soon," Gries says in disgust, staring daggers at the bright sky outside the window. "As unbelievable as it sounds, there's a full-on tropical monsoon going on out there. We were able to establish communication with the crew in Leyte for a half hour before the connection went down again. They've confirmed the severity of the storm—the city's flooded, and many neighborhoods are without electricity. We won't be able to do much beyond waiting it out and hoping the power comes back quickly, so they can send a rescue team."

"Askal can't take his boat to get help?" Hawaiian Shirt asks.

"Let's not risk it. I don't want anyone getting caught out there, even if looks peaceful."

"We're not that far from the mainland," Hemslock says. "If there's a storm out there, then we should fucking well see it from here."

"This damn island's cursed," Straw Hat mutters again, an opinion the rest of the crew agree with, based on the growing murmurs. Askal whines quietly beside my chair, and I stroke his head to calm him down.

Gries raps loudly at the table for silence. "There's little we can do. We're in one of the few places in the country with good weather right now, so we may as well take advantage of it while we can. My son was able to get in contact with friends earlier, so there are people back home who are organizing to get us out of here. Have a little more patience. Once the storm's passed, we'll leave."

"I'm staying," Hemslock says abruptly.

"Reuben," Gries protests, "this isn't the time to—"

"On the contrary, Leo, I can't think of a better time to do this. We now have goddamn physical proof that these ghosts are real. We've all seen them. We could find power beyond our imagination here, the one that Lapulapu wielded and Cortes wanted. And you're choosing to *leave*?" He sounds almost disbelieving. "This is our chance to become household names, be set for life. And you're turning down the opportunity? For what?"

"The ghosts got Karl, Reuben," Hawaiian Shirt says nervously. "And from the looks of things, they're going to get Steve soon enough. We can't put our lives on the line for a show—"

"It isn't just a show!" Hemslock shouts. "It's *my* goddamn show! This is my chance to prove all those worthless Hollywood suck-ups wrong! All those glorified shitheads who laughed at me, told me I was playing Ghostbusters! If this show hits, we're all gonna be rich! More than that—if the so-called power that this deity can bestow is real, then we can be like gods ourselves! Or will you all be nothing more than cowards?"

The others look nervously at each other.

"Reuben," Gries says firmly. "They have every right to want to go home. We're all professionals here. The crew will do their jobs until help arrives. This is about more than you and your legacy. If you care about Steve or Karl, you know that everyone's safety should be the priority. No one signed up to be attacked by these tree creatures, whatever they are."

"No one?" Hemslock asks, with unconcealed venom. "You didn't give a fuck about this show, Gries. You still don't. All you cared about was solving the mystery of your wife's death. Are you ready to leave this island without knowing how that plane wreckage came to be underneath the Godseye? Or what is that *thing* hoarding keepsakes of your wife in the caverns?"

"I said to leave my wife out of this."

"But isn't that the problem? You can't leave her out of this, Leo. Not when she's tied to what's down here. You know they just found Dan Heussman's body? I got an email from one of the producers before we lost the connection. Guy was stripped naked, huddled underneath some banyan tree in his garden that his gardener swears wasn't there before. He never even set foot on the Godseye. What makes you think these spirits won't follow us back to LA? We've got to deal with this here."

Hemslock's words hit home. I see the fear on the crew's faces.

"Alon," Gries says. "What do you suggest we do?"

I wet my lips, knowing that my words will not be popular with them. "The time to act has passed. We need to stay put until help comes, then we all need to leave."

"That's not an option," Hemslock says. "The Diwata will pick us off, one by one, before the storm clears. You and I know that the secret to stopping our destruction is within the Godseye, kid. I suggest we all arm ourselves and stay in groups. I'll arrange another search for Karl."

He looks around at everyone. "You're gonna have to trust me on this," he says, in a gentler voice. "That's what I'm asking. For all of you to trust me. You know I'm right. You know I'm the only one with enough experience with these monsters to get us all out."

No one speaks for a few moments. "So what do we do now?" Hawaiian Shirt asks nervously.

"The Leyte team managed to send us a few files." Hemslock moves to his laptop and calls up a video. "Rupi and Maryjun spent the whole night translating and transcribing so they could send this to us. Let's see what they have. In the meantime, I suggest not going anywhere alone."

There are four videos.

The first is a short clip of a no-nonsense–looking woman who is introduced as the retired curator of the museum Lindsay Watson worked at in Leyte. "She came to us with excellent references," she says. "She was friends with several other American expats living here, but she was very quiet at work. Her specialty was our collection of Spanish-era documents, and she was very good at finding the links to other firsthand sources we have in the museum. I had no idea her qualifications were forged, and that she only wanted the Cortes journal, the poor woman. That poor family."

The second video is of a sad-looking man, the mayor of the city. "It was before my time," he acknowledges, his command of English crisp and fluent. "I don't know anything about a cover-up. Any official who destroyed documents concerning the cultists' case should be arrested. I only heard the story as a very young boy."

"You told us that you found something on the island after the aviation accident investigators left," someone off-screen says.

"Yes. I didn't know how important it was at that time." The mayor pushes a piece of laminated paper across the table toward the camera.

It's a one-page note. *I'm sorry forgive us I'm sorry forgive us I'm sorry forgive us* is scribbled all over the paper.

"Oh shit," someone on the crew mutters by me. "That was also in Key's journal. And in the sinkhole."

"Different handwriting, though," Gries murmurs.

"I wasn't sure if the paper was trash someone left behind," the mayor says, "but there have been no tourists at Kisapmata since."

"Until us."

"Until you," the mayor acknowledges, after a significant pause.

"It's been confirmed that the letter matches the handwriting of one of Watson's friends," Hemslock says. "One of the missing expats. We've been in touch with his family back in Arkansas. They've been hoping to find out what really happened to him, and they provided some specimens. Looks like the Godseye got them all."

The third is an interview of an old woman in her seventies or eighties. People behind her, likely part of the production team, fiddle with the lights and adjust the sound. "Mag-uumpisa na tayo, Lola," someone says, and small English subtitles pop up below the screen for the viewers' benefit: "We're going to start, grandma."

The old woman merely inclines her head and waits.

"All right," someone else says. "Rolling in three. Two. And."

"Grandma," the translator says formally, speaking in Tagalog. "Can you please state your name for our viewers?"

"My name is Katrina Teresa Bantay. I have lived in Barásoain for close to seventy-four years."

"You told us that your daughter was sacrificed by the cultists at Kisapmata many years ago."

A series of gasps erupt from the crew around me. Chase's mouth drops open. "They found her," he whispers, awed. Hemslock sits by, looking smug.

"Yes." The old woman doesn't look upset or anguished by the revelation. She talks as if she is reciting from memory, albeit an unpleasant one. "God has already punished those who were responsible."

"And by God, do you mean the one that supposedly sleeps within the Godseye?"

"Yes. I remember as a child, making offerings to the island. When our beloved pets die, we would bury them there, ask Him for His blessing. They used to bury people there too, until the local government sixty, sixty-five years ago decided it was bad for tourism. Times have changed. But time has no meaning with Him."

"Can you tell us what happened when you first realized your daughter was missing?"

"Oh. So, so terrible. We searched for hours. And then she—the American—arrived at our house. Our daughter's body was with her. 'I am sorry,' she said. 'Forgive me.' Over and over." Mournfully the old woman shakes her head. "As if that could bring my child back to me."

"Then the American died," she continues, with a quiet, bone-chilling finality. "We saw balete roots encircle her legs, wrap around her waist. It took her. The ground opened and the balete took her down, down, underneath the soil. They killed my daughter for nothing. Those people—your people—killed for nothing. All you do is take, take, take."

"Do you know what happened to the other cultists?"

"I heard rumors that some escaped Kisapmata. They had guns, the American told us. Guns were the reason the Diwata could not protect us from the Spaniards or the Americans or the Japanese, my great-grandmother said. She lived long enough to see them all."

"Hear that?" Hemslock says triumphantly, pausing the video. "Whatever supernatural shit is on this island, bullets *are* effective. And I have more than enough to spare. We're as prepared as we can be until we reestablish communication with the mainland."

This seems to satisfy the rest of the crew but not Gries. "But how did you know to bring all these guns in the first place?" he asks, suspicious, after the others had left the hall to await contact from Leyte. "And bringing this many bodyguards is no coincidence, either. There's something about the Godseye you haven't told us."

Hemslock smiles disarmingly. "You know me, Leo. I'm a regular Boy Scout. I like to come prepared. You should be grateful that I planned ahead."

"What do you know about this island, Reuben?"

"Enough for me to take the lead on this one. So sit your ass down and let me do what I gotta do."

Leo turns without another word and leaves the mess hall. Chase and I follow him. Askal trots beside me as Gries reaches the cabin he shares with Chase.

"He's hiding something," he says abruptly, striding toward his desk and opening his laptop. "I have the shared password to the files on our server. I want to take another look at the videos he showed us. There's a reason he didn't play them all the way through."

He finds the first recording and clicks on it. We stand behind him to watch. Askal claims the rug again.

"She sent someone care packages all the time," the museum curator says. "The police already questioned us about it—I believe it was to a PO Box, but it was all done under her name, and they couldn't trace who received them." She also talks at some length about the Cortes's journal but doesn't say anything that we didn't already know. Gries switches to another video.

"I don't think they found any bodies on the island," the mayor says, exasperated. "It isn't about covering up any evidence. Yes, the villagers here are protective of each other, especially of the family involved, but my predecessor couldn't have made any arrests if there wasn't anyone to—"

Another video.

"—She was the true death the Diwata wanted," the old grand-mother was saying. "As punishment for taking my daughter's life, it is she who suffers. The poor woman."

"How do you know this, grandmother?"

"How do I know?" For the first time since the interview started, the woman grows passionate, angry. "A mother knows. My family worships the Diwata. Most of us here still do. We know He is just, and that He punishes the guilty. When He took the American woman, we started hearing of strange things on the island—things that were always crying, always suffering. That is her punishment. She is not the only sufferer there. We can do nothing but pray."

She stares off into space for a few minutes. When she speaks again, her voice is wistful. "The Diwata knows. He knows all who come to his shores. He remembers us after we die."

"What do you mean that 'he remembers'?"

She laughs. "He sees into the heart of those who enter his domain. He can create dreams and nightmares to show you what lies there. My daughter is not the only one who has found bliss in His mercy. Over the years, He has given many sanctuary. Fishermen and travelers who did not survive our worst storms have found eternal sanctuary with Him. They are different from the sacrifices he demands. They are loved."

"The legends state that the god will create a new world when he awakens."

The old woman only smiles.

"Have you ever dreamt of him before?"

"I dreamt once of a plane that fell from the sky, how some of those poor souls found their way to His shores. And then I woke and saw what they say in the news."

Gries makes a strangled sound.

"Do you think He was responsible for the plane crashing?" the interviewer asks intently.

"No. He is not a vengeful God. The passengers were unfortunate. He gave them peace." She leans forward, her eyes on the camera. "You do not understand," she says, more urgently. "Because of that American woman, the Diwata knows there is still too much cruelty in the world. He sleeps, but He is no longer lenient. He is—angry. He wishes to awaken."

"I understand, grandmother," the translator says, undeterred by her warnings, "that this is the first time you've chosen to speak of this. Many have come asking questions over the years, but you refused to talk with them. Why speak to us now?"

The woman gazes steadily at the interviewer until the latter repeats the question. "I want to pray for you," she says gently. "You do not understand, hijo. We *want* him to wake. But he is hungry. He will need food. There is food on the island now."

The video ends and Gries sits back, dazed.

"If the Diwata didn't cause the plane to crash, then why all the wreckage on the island?" Chase asks his father, though his eyes are on me.

"Because he believes I'm a sinner," Gries says. "This—this is my punishment." He stands and pulls on a thicker jacket, picks up a safety helmet.

"Where are you going?" Chase asks, alarmed.

"Hemslock isn't telling us everything, but that doesn't matter. I'm going to help him look for Karl again."

"Dad, *no*. After everything, you're still going to—?"

"If there's anything to learn about your mother here on the Godseye, then I'm going to find it. And if this god feels like he has to punish me first to know the truth, then—" He looks back at her pleadingly. "Please understand, Chase. I have to."

Chase turns away angrily. "Yeah, sure. Do whatever the hell you want."

"Chase, I—"

But it's too late. The slam of the door tells us that he's gone into his room. Askal lifts an inquiring head up from the rug, then flops down with a small grunt, quickly losing interest.

Gries turns back to me. "Are you going to risk returning to your family?"

"No. My father is being cared for. This is more serious."

He clasps my shoulder. "I know I'm asking too much of you again, but I need you to promise that you'll stay with him while I'm gone. Keep a weapon near."

I know nothing I can say will change his mind. "I'd do that even without you asking me, sir," I say quietly. "Come back quickly, for his sake. He doesn't deserve this."

Gries laughs—a hurt, painful sound. "No," he agrees. "Chase doesn't, but I do. That's what you're not saying. And I agree."

FIFTEEN
THE CABIN

"HOW LONG ARE YOU GOING TO STAY IN THERE AND SULK?"
I ask.

No answer. I rap on the door. Still nothing.

I sit on the couch and survey the rest of the room, placing my small machete on the table by the door. The living room had been commandeered for Leo Gries's use; there is paperwork in small piles on the table and another area that has been allocated for his study, as neat as any clutter could manage. His laptop had been left open in his haste to leave.

I move toward it.

It's confusing. There are emails: conversations between Leo and other staff, other producers of the show. There are discussions regarding how long they expect to stay on the island before filming wraps, the associated costs and expenses, along with bullet point presentations of how they expect to plot the show. I search for the emails that specify the Kisapmata and the Godseye, and find a thread dated four months ago.

Hemslock's emails make up over half of the discourse; arguments over which parts of the island to focus on filming, the documentation and research they have for each episode, conjecture to make up for gaps in their knowledge.

"The Godseye is the real key," Hemslock wrote. "There's more than just treasure in that cave. If there's any truth to what these myths say, then maybe we can figure out what they mean. There's an eternity within a dream in there."

"Surely you can't believe these things?" one of the producers—Heussman, ironically—wrote back.

"We're not ever sure of much in this world," Hemslock responded. "And I've got bigger dreams beyond the treasure you're all interested in. More than the supposed gold and trinkets that Cortes stole from the natives."

"What are you doing?"

I turn. Chase stands in the doorway with his arms folded, frowning at me.

"Are you snooping through my dad's stuff?" He marches over and shuts the laptop. "You know you'll have to sign more than an NDA to read those, right?"

"I'm sorry. I was curious."

"I'm not angry," Chase says, sounding exactly that. "I just—I want to get off this freaking island, but everything's conspiring to keep us here. Including Dad. Are they back?"

I glance at the time. "There's another hour before sunset. I can get you an early dinner."

"I'm not hungry. You don't have to wait on me hand and foot."

"I told your father I'd stay with you."

"You didn't tell him you would look through his stuff, and you did. I won't tell if you won't."

"Are you trying to blackmail me?"

Chase turns back to me, fury on his face, and then the ire leaches out of him. "I'm not trying to do anything," he says wearily. "I just—I just want to go home. Home where I can post some clown shit on my socials and not care about anything else. I want all of us to go home."

He stares down at his phone and then thumbs through the gallery of photos he'd saved there. "You see this?" He waves it at me, and I see the image Rory sent him with that dark figure in the background watching us. Except now it's an abstract blotch in the scenery. The background is inconclusive now, though it had been so clear the first time we saw the photo.

"Why is it stalking me? I haven't had any visions like the others. Why is it toying with me? Didn't you say the Diwata won't harm the innocent? Am I guilty of something?"

"Absolutely not—"

"Hey!" He turns and shouts at nothing in the room. "Are you here? Do you want to kill me?" He pauses as if expecting an answer. "Then stop fucking around and say that to my face!"

"Chase!" I say sharply.

"I'm tired. I'm tired of Dad chasing after Mom's ghost, him never having time for me. And I'm scared. I'm beginning to think that maybe Dad has more to do with all this than I thought he did. Am I going to be punished for being his son?"

"No," I say, with a fierceness that surprises even me. "The balete creatures aren't haunting you because you're next. They're haunting you because of me."

He looks at me, puzzled. "What do you mean?"

After a pause, I make my decision and share. "They're curious about you."

"Curious?"

"I'm the only human this island has a longstanding connection with. When you arrived, it wanted to know more about you. Because of me."

"Are you saying that the island is *jealous* of me?"

I gape at him, then surprise myself by laughing. "No. Maybe. I don't think it's capable of those kinds of emotions, but it can mimic them. It doesn't understand personal boundaries the way you and I do."

"And how do you know that?"

"Have you seen hallucinations of your ex on the island?"

He shakes his head.

"If He thought you were guilty, He would have used your conscience against you. What we've been seeing—they are manifestations of the god. I see them all the time. They can feel invasive if you're not used to it." I set my jaw. "I won't let Him do that to you."

"You're a good person, ya know?" Chase says quietly.

I look away, not sure how to answer that. "I don't know if I can claim that."

"We're here trashing your island, and you still want to keep us safe. I'm not used to that, you know? In California everyone just gets…caught up. We don't think much beyond how we want people to see us, like us. I guess that's what got me into posting videos. I just wanna be validated, you know? But being on this island's got me thinking about a lot. My friends tell me Riley's always been shallow—but maybe we got together because I'm also shallow."

The boy's starting to get a little weepy. I'm not sure what to do.

"You're—you're gonna laugh at me. But after saying this? My immediate thought is *Hey, that would make an awesome caption for my next photo.* I'm living my life to make goddamn posts on social media so I can get engagements for advertisers to pay me more. If I die, is that all people will remember of me? Some dude who got 'hot boy summer' trending that one time? Is that my biggest achievement?"

Askal, far better at offering comfort, pushes his nose into Chase's arm. The boy lets out a choked, teary laugh, and then reaches down to pat him.

"It's all right. S'alright. Saying it out loud kinda helps me feel better, you know? You've been helping from the very first day. You could have gone back to your dad and left us all here to die." He hugs Askal with one arm. His other hand reaches out to pull me into a hug. "Thanks. I really, really appreciate it."

I pat him on the back. He chuckles. "You're not used to this, either, huh?"

"I don't have many friends."

"Can we be friends? Like, if everything here is done, I still wanna hang out with you. I can come here easier than you can fly to America, plus we've got the internet to connect. Do you have any social media yourself? I don't mind emails or telephone calls. You can charge them to me."

I don't know why that makes me laugh, but it does. "I can find a way to stay in touch with you. But I promised your dad that I was gonna get you dinner."

His arms tighten around me. "Rory was right. He said you sounded like the perfect package, and now that I think about it—"

His voice goes husky, deepens. "Now that I think about it—"

I don't know what happens next. Only that he feels warmer to the touch. His thumb moves across my shoulder, and something inside me sparks electric at the friction. His face is close. Then he shifts and draws nearer.

"Alon, I—"

I shove at him.

Stunned, he falls over backward, flat on his butt.

"I'm going to go get your dinner," I say brusquely, marching toward the door. Askal lies back on the rug and huffs.

"Alon wait, I—"

But I'm already outside and into the night, the door slamming behind me.

⚜

The dinner table is nearly deserted when I arrive. Most of the crew has chosen to retire early, and only a few linger in the mess hall, half-heartedly picking at their plates. Straw Hat is still at his workstation, going through the film footage and trying to make sense of the last few days. Melissa is behind him, studying the screen with a puzzled frown. Hawaiian Shirt is there too, and he gives me a miserable nod when I enter.

"I'm gonna go out on a limb here and say this show is as good as dead," he says. "I don't care what Hemslock thinks. It's been nothing but one disaster after another. Lamarr's looking through what we have—maybe we can scrape together enough for an hour, two-hour feature. Try to salvage something out of this."

"We still got cameras out there rolling," Straw Hat says despondently. "Gonna take them down when rescue comes. Still no contact with the Leyte team, but from the reports they sent before communication went down, the storm's due to clear tomorrow afternoon. A rescue team should be on its way as soon as it lets up. We gotta wing it till then."

"I'm not getting paid for any of this," Melissa says miserably. She's been carrying around a thick piece of driftwood for protection. The others have armed themselves with similar makeshift weapons. She had also taken to carrying her mace "because assholes always turn up at the most unexpected places," she says, and it sounds like she says this from experience.

Hawaiian Shirt glares at the camera feed trained on the corpse trees by the sinkhole. "I hate that thing," he says irritably. "That's the one image we were hoping would sell the rest of this. I *despise* it. Everything's been trouble since that sinkhole."

His voice drops. "I…I…"

I see what stuns him. On the screen, the corpse in the tree slowly moves and stares directly at us through the camera.

174

Hawaiian Shirt backs away. "Shit," he keeps saying. "Shit, oh, shit. Oh shit."

"What's gotten into you?" Straw Hat asks crabbily. Neither he nor Melissa have seen it.

Hawaiian Shirt points a finger at the monitor, his hand trembling. "You see that?" He cries. "It's looking at me. It's goddamn, fucking *looking* at me!"

But the corpse tree has already turned away, as if it has been that way this whole time.

⚔⚔⚔⚔⚔⚔

Something's wrong.

I exit the mess hall with two plates of food, and I can't shake the feeling that I'm being watched. I turn slowly, watching the trees, watching the shore, watching for anything that moves.

I see it soon enough. It stands just beyond the circle of comfort the electric lanterns provide, but there is no mistaking its bent form, the wet spindles of branches of its body, glossy against the brightness. It's half obscured by shadows, but I know that it's looking at me.

It's the same tangled hair and the same pale absence of face. It's the same jittered shape. It's slightly hunched, the way Lindsay Watson must have crouched, prostrated on the ground when the roots had first taken hold of her, dragged her into the soil while the old grandmother bore witness.

Something at the center of its face opens—a long tongue snakes out from a row of tiny, thorn-like teeth within its flytrap mouth.

Forgive me, the thing says, distinctly. *Forgive me*.

We stare at each other, neither of us moving. Then I see the balete shift and twist, until they become other faceless women borne of a similarly twisted seed, all with the same elongated, hollow maws. Crooked against the unyielding straightness of the trees, they lurk, gathering behind the pale, broken form.

Slowly, the first creature takes half a step toward Gries and Chase's cabin.

I'm surprised at my anger. "Huwag," I say, my voice loud in the dim. "Hayaan mo siya."

The spindles withdraw, but only briefly. The mouth opens and closes.

Gusto mo siya? it asks. Do you like him?

The Diwata is curious about Chase. Curious about what I think about him. Wary. Suspicious. Possessive.

"He's not like the others," I say.

It doesn't believe me. The pale thing takes another step toward the bungalows—still keeping out of the light, its movements deliberate. It tenses, as if about to run.

"'Wag!" I shout.

I throw our dinner at it. It disappears, and the plates crash to the ground, shattering upon impact.

Melissa and Hawaiian Shirt run out of the mess hall. A few other crew members poke their heads out of their tents.

But Lindsay Watson is already gone, and the withered forests with her.

"I saw," Melissa said, visibly shaking. "Those *things*. You told them to stay back, like in the footage—"

"You saw it, Melissa?" Hawaiian Shirt asks, placing his hand on my shoulder. I spin at the touch, ready to fight, and he jumps back. "Hey, whoa, whoa. It's me. We've got a few cameras trained on those woods. We can—" He breaks off, starts laughing, a little hysterically.

"We're sitting here, waiting to be picked off by spirits, and I'm still thinking about the show," he gasps. "Fuck this."

"Stay inside the mess hall," I instruct him. "Don't leave until I return, whatever you might hear. If you need to go to your tents, do it in groups."

"We will, but what about you? Hey, where are you—"

I ignore him and run back to the cabin.

⁂

I arrive just in time.

I can hear Askal's angry howls and Chase's terrified shouts before I turn the doorknob, and I burst into the room where both sit huddled at the end of the couch.

Tree roots grow everywhere.

They hang down from the ceiling, probing through the roof's material to infect every space and crevice they can reach. They grow over the walls, wrapping thick branches around the table and furniture. Gries's laptop is nearly hidden under brown, withered bark. They surround Chase and Askal, moving closer.

A creature hovers before them, dangling upside down before Chase's terrified face. Chase tries to shield Askal with his body, lashing out at the air before them with a clenched fist.

177

The tree makes an odd crooning noise. Its branch-fingers reach out to caress Chase's hair, moving down toward his shoulders and neck.

Huwag mo siyang saktan, it says.

Askal reacts. Snarling, his teeth find bark. The thing rears back, but Askal refuses to let go, bravely engaging it in a tug of war, distracting it from Chase. The rest of the balete circles nearer.

I grab my machete and swing.

I chop at the nearest root, and it breaks easily, the cut branch shriveling. I lift the axe again, and this time bring it down on the largest of the roots that I can see. A fountain of ugly, black, sap-like liquid spurts from the gaping wound, seeping onto the floor.

"'Wag!" I shout.

More roots spring out from below. Only this time, the larger, thicker vines block the thing's attempts to close in on Chase, who is frozen, gaping as the tree mutinies against itself.

I plant myself in front of it and swing my ax again.

The thing turns away from Chase and grabs at me, roots circling my wrist. Up close it shares similarities to a Venus flytrap; the sides of its head fold in on itself like makahiya leaves do, like a mouth. It drags me closer, jaws opening to reveal an eye surrounded by teeth.

Gusto mo siya? a voice whispers from within it.

While it's distracted, Chase snatches up the machete and finishes the job; with his swing the mouth cleaves in two, and the thing staggers back. Chase attacks again, depriving it of its head.

The rest of the tree retreats, melting into the walls and floors, until only the viscous puddle remains. The head withers to ashes. We're alone.

SIXTEEN

THE KNOCK

"Am I a bad person?" Chase asks, several minutes later. We both haven't moved from the couch; still sitting side by side, still watching the dried black liquid on the floor's rug like we're expecting it to coalesce into some fresh new horror. Askal is burrowed on Chase's other side, head on the boy's lap while his paws cling to the teddy bear.

"Why would you say that?"

"You said that the Diwata was only curious about me. But now—it doesn't feel like that. It feels like it's trying to frighten me. Was it—does it think I committed a—?"

"No," I say firmly. "He won't do anything to you."

"But how do you know for sure?"

"If He had marked you as a sinner, you would be seeing visions like the others."

Chase winces. "I mean, trees that try to tear out my throat seems like wanting me dead, right?"

"That's not what it said."

"Then what did it say?"

"Huwag mo siyang saktan. Don't hurt them."

He pauses. "Hurt…you? It thinks that I want to hurt you? I wouldn't! I like you!"

His confession echoes through my ears. After a moment, he looks down, embarrassed. "I liked you the instant I set foot on this island. But I was worried about approaching you because I didn't know if this was gonna be just some rebound. Rory and Jordan have been yelling at me to say something, and I *wanted* to, but every time I tried, I couldn't. Plus, I figured you weren't interested in me, anyway. But then Rory started convincing me otherwise, and then…" He raised his arms, sheepish. "Was that why? Because the god knows I feel something for you?"

I sigh. "No. It knows that I like you back."

Chase gapes at me for so long that I think the creature actually hurt him. "No, you don't," he says reasonably. "You pushed me away. Not that you shouldn't have. I moved too fast, and I didn't think to ask you first. I'm sorry."

"I can't."

"Can't what?"

"Have a connection with anyone else."

"But…why? Is it because of this island? Kisapmata won't let you start a relationship?" His voice rises, disbelieving. "So it *is* jealous?"

I have to smile. "It's complicated. If I left, He would have no ties

180

to the people here. As odd as it sounds, He's lonely too, and I am a good companion for Him. He's used to reading my thoughts, easy for Him to reach out and find others. The illusions that some of the crew see are proof of that. He's interested in you because He's protective of me, and He doesn't completely understand our relationship. So the easiest way to know what your intentions are, is to…"

"Terrify me?" A slow smile steals across his face. Askal watches us both, tongue out and looking oddly smug. "So, *our relationship*? You do like me?"

I swallow. "I—"

He raises his hands. "We don't have to do anything. I respect your space, and I respect the island…this god's, whatever's, space. But once we get out of here…do you think…? I mean, it's gonna suck since I'll be in LA, but if I could call you—"

"It's not about the distance. It's—" I look out the window. "I have other responsibilities here that I can't ignore."

I wait for him to protest, to insist we'll make things work between us. "Is it because of your father?" he finally asks. "You can't leave because of him, too?"

"It's different here. We don't just—I can't leave him because he's old. I wish I—sometimes I *do* resent that."

"I understand," Chase says. "Sometimes I get frustrated with Dad too, you know? It's like his job is the only meaning he has left in his life. He's never gotten over Mom dying. What about me? When did I stop mattering to him? But he's the only dad I've got. I know he's doing his best, despite everything. I'm sure that your dad's the same."

My gaze drifts back to the stain on the floor. "I guess."

Chase's phone lights up, buzzing. Surprised, we look at it for a moment before we realize the implications. Then Chase's hopeful look abruptly turns into a scowl when he sees who's calling.

"Riley? What the hell do you want? Look, you are the last person I want to—"

Riley interrupts him. She's not on video call, and her voice sounds terrified. "I said I'm sorry, Chase! Please believe me! I swear I won't bother you ever again. Just please, make her stop! Tell her to stop doing this to me!"

"What?" Chase is dumbfounded. "Riley, what are you talking ab—"

"It's not funny anymore, okay? I don't know who you paid to dress up like some deranged tree monster, but this isn't funny! Tell her to go away! I can't—oh my god. It's at the window. It's at the—"

The call ends.

Chase gazes open-mouthed at the phone. "Is the Diwata haunting Riley? Can it do that? Is it because—was it because I—?"

Chase yelled his frustrations into the cave. I'm stunned. The Diwata is protective of me. Was He trying to placate me by trying to solve Chase's problems with his ex? "I—I don't know. Maybe He was trying to help?"

"This is what he considers *help*?"

"He doesn't know enough about human relationships. And as you already know, He prefers a direct approach when it comes to confrontations."

Chase gulps. "He's not really gonna harm her, is he?"

"He won't."

The knock on the door is loud. "Chase? Are you okay?"

"The door's open, Dad." And then Chase pauses, dumbstruck. "Why is he knocking? It isn't even locked."

The door rattles again. "Chase? What's going on?"

Askal begins growling quietly. My gaze flicks toward the ceiling.

The beams are covered with makahiya, writhing quietly on the metal ledges.

Chase stands. "Dad, are your hands full or—"

He moves toward the door but stops when I grab his arm. "Wait," I whisper, a familiar dread creeping up on me.

"What? If that tree creature's still around and Riley is being bullied, we need to warn him—"

Quietly I point to the window before us.

Through the half-open blinds, we see Gries still some ways off, looking despondent and dirt stained, walking toward us from the direction of the cave; the rest of the search team is with him.

Chase is frozen, now with fear. "If he's over there, then who is at the—"

The doorknob rattles again. "Chase!"

The voice raises to a pitch that I've never heard Gries use before—a high whine, like an insect buzz.

"Get the fuck away from us!" Chase shouts. "Whoever you are, leave us alone!"

Nothing responds at first. And then—

"Chase." It's a different voice this time, feminine and light and sweet. "Chase, sweetheart. Please let me in."

Chase shakes so hard he would have fallen to the floor if I hadn't grabbed him. "No," he says, a near sob. "N-no. That's impossible. She can't. It couldn't have—"

"Chase," the voice croons, and I make the belated connection. "I've missed you. Come and kiss me. I'll tuck you in, and we'll read *Velveteen Rabbit* together like we—"

"No!" This time I'm the one shouting. "No! You're not going to make a mockery of his mother! Kung may gusto kang sabihin sa akin—sabihin mo na!"

The voice that sounds like Chase's mother breaks off unexpectedly. And then, horrifyingly enough, it is Chase's voice that begins to scream back at us.

"*Fuck you, Riley!*" It sounds so near, like the voice is in the room with us. "*I hope you get an STD, you cheating ho! Fuck you, Riley! I hope you get an STD, you cheating ho! Fuck you, Riley! I hope you get a—*"

"Wait!" Chase cries out, but I am already racing toward the door, steeling myself to face whatever I might find outside. Askal is at my side, hackles raised, prepared to do the same. I grab the doorknob, take a deep breath, and twist.

The door swings open.

There is nothing waiting for me there.

Breathing hard, I stare at the empty space. I turn back toward Chase, who watches me with fright. There is nothing amiss in the room. The makahiya on the windowsill are gone.

"Why did it do that?" Chase whispers.

I drop my head into my hands. "Because He wants to scare you away from me," I say quietly. "Because as soon as the sacrifices are done, He's going to open up a way to get out of this island, and He doesn't want you staying for me. And He's right. You're not going to want to be here when the ritual's complete."

Gries steps through the doorway, exhausted. "Hey," he says and then pauses, seeing the expression on our faces. "What's wrong with you two?"

***

The rescue team has yet to find Karl. We relay everything that's happened while Gries was gone, and he's horrified for Chase's sake.

"Why's it doing this to him?" he asks me accusingly. "You said this god spares the innocent. Chase is the last person it should be haunting!"

"He doesn't understand boundaries the way humans do," I say slowly.

"And it's haunting him because it's—curious about him? Wants to get him away from the island to protect him?" Gries lets out an incredulous-sounding laugh. "So this god thinks it's some sort of surrogate parent of yours?"

"The Diwata is protective of me, but He doesn't process emotions like a human. He heard Chase shouting about his ex. He might have thought that scaring her would stop her from harassing him further. He wants Chase away from Kisapmata. I know it sounds bad, but that's how He—"

"Chase, I forbid you to see Alon for the rest of the time that we're here on this island."

"Absolutely not!" Chase jumps to his feet.

I don't argue.

"Alon understands why I'm doing this."

"Do you really think that's going to make any difference? Do you really think that the island is going to ignore me, just like that? You didn't see it. It's powerful and scary as hell, but it listens to Alon. And now that I understand what it's trying to do, I'm probably safer with Alon than alone. Well, as long as it stops trying to help me. I'm not leaving without Alon."

Gries glares at Chase, then at me. "So you're going to ignore me and stick by him anyway, right?"

"I'm not the one in danger. You are!"

"Chase—"

"You're still obsessed with Mom's death! That's why you've been seeing her everywhere! The Godseye sacrifices people who can't let go of the past, the ones who've been violent toward the people they're supposed to care for!"

Gries rears back, looking stricken. "Chase, I would never do anything to harm you."

"Did you ever hit Mom?"

Gries doesn't respond immediately, though the guilt on his face is clear. "I never hurt her physically."

"What were you and Mom arguing about the week she died? At the time, you kept insisting that it was nothing. But now—now I don't think so. You act guilty, like you murdered her every time her names comes up in conversation."

"That's enough, Chase!" Gries roars. He shakes, rage and grief mixing on his face. He deflates before he even starts though, as if overcome by exhaustion.

"I just want to know how the plane wreckage wound up underground," he says. "Alon…"

"I don't know anything about that, sir. I'm sorry."

He sighs. "I'm not going to forbid you from seeing Chase. After Riley, you're definitely an improvement. But don't you think it would be better to avoid him until we get off this island? To keep him safe?"

I'm fully aware that Chase's eyes are pleading with me as I say, "I can't guarantee Chase's safety. But like he said, the Diwata listens to me. I can intercede on his behalf better if he's with me."

"I don't necessarily trust you, Alon. I don't think I could trust anyone who shares a connection with an entity capable of wiping out everyone on this island on a whim, however innocently you came into that relationship. Chase—we can talk later—"

"Leo? Are you in there?" Straw Hat's worried voice sounds outside the door, and I tense, noticing Chase do the same.

"Yeah, I'm here."

"We're going to need your help. There's been an emergency."

"An emergency? What's happened?"

"It's Steve Galant. He's gone bonkers. I don't know how it happened, but he worked himself free of his restraints. He's missing. Cameras show he's gone inside the cave."

SEVENTEEN

THE FACE

I INSIST ON ACCOMPANYING THE RESCUE TEAM INSIDE the cave. It is nightfall, and the idea of heading into the Godseye with only flashlights to guide us is unsettling to the others.

Oddly enough Hemslock, who advocated that I join the earlier cave expedition, is now against it. "I've been in the caves several times now and shit happens only when you're with us. You seem to attract these paranormal activities wherever you go. Who's to say that you won't make things worse for Galant if you're with us?"

"We may not know the mind of the god who dwells here, but Alon is good at calming it down," Gries points out, taking a completely opposite stance from before. "And I thought you would jump at the chance to record more ghostly activity."

Hemslock glowers at me but stays silent.

"I want everyone at the mess hall," Gries instructs the rest of the crew. "Stay together; if you need to use the bathroom or get something, go in pairs."

"We promise, sir," Straw Hat says nervously.

The new team consists of me, Hemslock, Gries, and the rest of Hemslock's bodyguards. The armed men calmly outfit themselves with thick vests and check their guns, as if traveling into caves to shoot at ghosts is a daily occurrence in their line of work.

"You two be careful," Chase whispers worriedly to his father and me.

As it turns out, we didn't need to travel very far into the cave to find Armani.

I almost do not recognize him. The executive producer has divested himself of his clothes. Naked, he lies atop the stone altar, gazing up into the hole in the ceiling as if in a trance. He does not stir as we approach. His physique has noticeably declined since he fell into the pit. Once a broad-shouldered man with a bit of a gut, he's grown emaciated. There are craggy lines on his face like he's aged thirty years within two days. He looks as desiccated as the balete around us.

"Reuben," he rasps as we approach, never turning his face away from the moon above. "That you?"

"You're gonna be alright, Steve," Reuben says reassuringly. "We're going to get you home. I'm sure that stone's comfy, but I think a nice soft bed would be more to your liking."

"I can't hear," the man whispers, oblivious to his friend's words. "I can't hear anymore. I can't see. And yet I *can* hear. I *can* see. Visions that I don't like, words that I don't want to hear. Can you see them, Reuben? The damned? The island has seen it all. More than we thought, more than we could ever dream."

He laughs suddenly. His cackle echoes through the cavern. "Am I dreaming? Are we all just dreaming? That's what it's telling me. That's what it's whispering in my ear. We're all dreaming, and we will all cease to exist when the god awakes.

"The fifth to serve. The sixth to lure. I understand now. They will root into our bodies and sprout like newborns. We are nothing but a mote in his eye, Reuben. We are nothing but dust underneath his feet. He will drink from us and then, if we are worthy, he will dream us into the next world.

"I am not worthy. I am not worthy. I am—" He begins to laugh harder, hysterical giggles he seems incapable of holding back.

"I am not worthy," he gasps out. "And Reuben, you—you are not worthy either—"

Hemslock springs. He grabs Armani's wrists, pins them against the altar's surface. His men jump into action, grabbing at the poor man's limbs to keep him still. Even then Armani thrashes about, nearly dislodging himself from the soldier's grip despite his weakened condition. At one point, he sits up and nearly makes a break toward the deeper recesses of the cave, only to be hauled back much more forcefully by the bodyguards.

"Bind him tight," Hemslock instructs them. "I don't want him breaking free."

"Shit," Gries says. He stares deeper into the cave, at something that the rest of us don't see. "I—I see her."

"Keep a hold of yourself, Gries," Hemslock says roughly.

"We've already got one mad person to deal with. Don't add to the score."

I see her as well. She doesn't come closer, content to hide in the shadows. But Gries shines his flashlight her way. Caught in its glow, her features are easier to make out. A pretty woman with long black hair and dark eyes looks back at us. She resembles Chase so closely that I know who it is.

"Why are you doing this?" Gries asks, the pain in his voice clear. "She never did anything to you!"

"Leo," the woman speaks in the softest voice. "Where is Chase? Did you remember to help him with his school project? I helped with the outline, but it's due tomorrow and I need to leave for the airport."

"No," I say, when Leo takes two steps toward her. "Don't."

But he is no longer listening, caught in the trap that always wraps around the island's guilty. "Elena, I'm sorry. I—"

"I don't want your apologies, Leo," the woman says sharply, turning from him. "You've made your decision. My lawyer will be sending the documents over in a few days, like you want. And I will be asking for full custody."

Leo's pace quickens. Before I can stop him, he grabs at her shoulder. "Elena, no. I shouldn't have shouted at you that morning. I shouldn't have threatened to—"

Chase's mother turns back to him, and she is no longer Elena. A flytrap of a mouth emerges from what used to be her face, something like a tongue curling around his wrist.

Gries screams. My machete slashes between them, severing the hideous, lolling protrusion that clings to him.

At the same time, Hemslock raises his gun, pointing it straight at the figure that wears Chase's mother's shape.

The woman's face explodes.

There is no blood. Instead, the same sap-like liquid that had covered the floor of the Grieses cabin bursts out of her, spraying the nearby walls. The creature drops to the ground, a chaos of writhing vines and roots.

But Hemslock doesn't stop. He walks over to the remains, firing angrily into the carcass of branches until it stills. He pauses and stares off into the depths of the tunnel, as if trying to see within the gloom. And then he laughs—a high-pitched sound similar to Galant's in its madness.

"I knew it," he says. "I fucking knew it!"

He begins to fire again—at whatever it is he sees in the dark. He continues to unload into the shadows until the click of his gun tells us that he is out of bullets.

"I knew it," he repeats. "You bitch. You really think you're fooling me?"

"Sir," one of the bodyguards speaks up. The soldiers look nervous, as the man paying their wages exhibits the same insanity that Armani has manifested. "Sir. There's nothing there."

Hemslock stares hard at the dark of the cave. "Not anymore," he says, reloading his gun but—to my relief—moving back toward the entrance, stepping over the tree creature's remains.

Its roots quiver—and then latch around his ankle.

Hemslock goes down with a yell. Six of his solders rush for him, drawing out heavy army knives. Expertly, they slice at the roots ensnaring their employer, who's frantically trying to kick free. One of the bodyguards turns his own gun to where the base of still-moving roots lay at their thickest. Several more blasts and the heap shudders to a standstill.

Two of the soldiers haul Hemslock forward, out of the cave. Two more carry Armani, and the rest form the rear, on the alert for any more threats as we run back toward the beach.

The film crew waits outside the cave, surprise on their faces. "That was fast," Straw Hat says in a bid to be jovial, but his features grow stricken when he sees Armani.

The medics rush forward. This time, Armani doesn't put up a fight as he is once more restrained. He only blinks and stares. "We are not worthy," is all he says, over and over again. "We are not worthy. Forgive me. I am sorry. Forgive me."

"He's as good as gone," Hawaiian Shirt says.

Hemslock has shaken off his bodyguards and stands upright on his own. "Get the case," he snaps, and two of his men leave.

"What the hell is the matter with you?" Gries asks him angrily.

"I saved your life," the actor says tersely. Whatever he saw within the confines of the cave still haunts Hemslock. I can see the strain in his eyes despite his effort to sound calm. "You would have been dead, or worse off than Steve."

"What the hell were you shooting at?" one of his soldiers asks him.

For a moment, a look of indescribable rage crosses Hemslock's face, and it is frightening to see. But it passes quickly, and he resumes his arrogant air. "That's not of any importance to you.

193

What's important is that we got Steve back without losing anyone else. Melissa, are we able to reach anyone on the mainland?"

"Communication's still down, sir. Internet isn't working."

"How are we going to know when the storm is over?" Gries explodes. "All I see is calm, serene sky with no rain in sight."

"We still have some business to take care of here," Hemslock insists. "You saw it, right? Guns work on these bastards."

The two soldiers return, carrying a wide, heavy briefcase between them. Hemslock gestures for them to set it on the ground. A deft flick of the straps opens it, allowing us a glimpse of what's inside.

"How did you even get these?" Gries chokes out.

"I know people who know some people. Look at these beauties." Proudly, like a doting father, Hemslock surveys the explosives within. "MI6s, AK-47s—nothing too fancy. Surprising how easy they were to bring in. They'll take out anything in a heartbeat, even a god. And then we've got our secret weapon."

"Hemslock, what the hell are you planning to—"

"What does it look like? Are you a fool not to figure it out by now, Gries? This island intends to kill all of us. These clear skies— they're just an illusion." Hemslock is busy, taking out more guns and tossing them to the other soldiers. "It's not going to let us go until at least three of us bite the dust. So I'm thinking we need to turn the tables, see what we have to bargain. Settlement ain't gonna be cheap."

Hemslock lifts a large flamethrower, grinning nastily. "This one is my favorite," he says. "What's the little god gonna do when I burn everything it sends after us?"

"You didn't bring these guns on a whim," Leo says. "You didn't hire a score of bodyguards because it's a part of your contract. You came here intending to destroy this island. You knew guns could hurt it."

"*Destroy* is such a misleading term. I'd like to offer Him an alliance, is all. If this god gave his power to these natives, then he can give it to us. Cortes said that the god prized strength most of all." He turns back to the caves. "So that's what I'm going to prove to him."

"Reuben—"

"I'm going hunting with my boys. This camera's still operational." Hemslock taps the helmet he's wearing. "Feel free to watch, but none of you are going to stop me. Let's roll, men."

"Are we really going to let him do this?" Chase mutters, watching Hemslock and his soldiers disappear into the mouth of the cave. I can hear Hawaiian Shirt and Straw Hat scrambling behind us, hurriedly setting up the laptop that connects to the camera Hemslock is wearing. Even when there is danger, some instinct motivates them to continue recording, watching, analyzing for a show that's endangering their lives. "Dad?"

"I don't think there's anything that would stop him."

With nothing better to do, we all crowd around Straw Hat's workstation. The dark cave comes once more into focus, Hemslock leading the way.

"We're heading back to the cavern with the writings," we hear him say. "There's something in the smaller tunnel beyond that it doesn't want us to see, so that's where we're going. Stay alert."

They pass the carved figure of the Godseye without incident. The ancient script underneath it seems to glow with its own unearthly light.

"Tight squeeze, careful," one of the soldiers murmurs as he slides through the narrow opening of the tunnel where we first encountered the creature. The heavy-duty flashlights attached to their guns are stronger than the ones we carried, and they illuminate the passageway, showing no new signs of supernatural activity.

Hemslock points his gun toward the ground, at roughly the spot where his bodyguards had gunned down the monster. Nothing of it remains—not even a root. "It's baiting us," he says.

They walk farther into the tunnel and reach the end without incident. "Holy shit," I hear another of the men say, and the camera spins abruptly.

On the beach, the crew gasps in unison at the feed.

It is the largest balete tree that I have ever seen, horrific in its majesty. It grows upside down from the ceiling and stands nearly a hundred feet high, its roots twined thickly together to form a massive tree trunk. The ground around the men is elevated and broken in many places—the branches strong enough to have fractured the island's bedrock, digging deep. The branches are full of living, breathing makahiya, unfurling and shutting at will. The finger-like tips of the balete's branches graze the ceiling, spiderwebs of brown ivy growing sideways despite the limits imposed on its height, gathering at the darker corners of the cave and expanding across the walls. They rustle, swaying in some unknown breeze that seems impossible so deep within the cave.

And at the center of the tree—

At the center of the tree is something that passes for a face, braided into reality by the thick quilt work of bark. Its eyes are closed. Its mouth is relaxed. More roots snake around it and pulse, breathing like a heartbeat.

"Almost like it's asleep," a soldier mutters.

This is not the only horror here. Scattered around the great balete lie human shapes, sculptures of smaller roots crisscrossed and braided to mimic two arms, a torso, a head. There are no faces on these grotesque creations, but their forms are frozen in mid-air, caught twisting in agony, trapped in some ongoing punishment that only they and the god within know.

"This is sick," one of the people in the cave grunts. "You telling me these used to be people? The ones it killed?"

"Spread out, but stay within sight," Hemslock instructs. They comply, each soldier picking an adjacent spot to the others as they continue their cursory investigation.

"Look at this." The camera shifts again. A soldier gingerly toes the base of one of the people-shaped briars. There is a crunching, brittle sound, and part of it falls away, crumbling at his feet.

"You gotta see this, sir." More scraping sounds as the man sweeps up some bits with his foot.

A few other soldiers edge closer for a look. "My god," one of them breathes. "That ain't dirt. That's bone."

"Bone?" Hawaiian Shirt asks frantically. "What does that mean?"

"Shut up," Leo Gries hisses at him.

One of the men in the cave takes out his hunting knife, testing the edges of the briar. "These ain't trees, Boss," he says amazed. "Kyle's right. There *are* bodies inside them. Just like that damn corpse tree outside."

"The victims who didn't make the cut," Hemslock says. "The ones that don't conform to the prophecy but died anyway because the god deemed them unworthy."

"Oh shit!" another soldier says and jumps back as the bone hedge in front of him begins to move. There are sounds of guns cocking as the men aim their weapons at the shaking patch.

"Wait," Hemslock says suddenly.

He smashes the butt of his gun against the bramble, sending up more fragments into the air. Like the balete, the strange formations are hollow. And within—

A hand, surprisingly human, flesh instead of bark, pushes its way out of the hole that Hemslock created. It grabs at his hand.

"He's alive!" Hemslock shouts. "Get him out!"

It's Goatee. He is naked and shivering and as pale as the smooth limestone around them, but he's alive and blubbering. They all get to work, frantically trying to break through the brambles to free Goatee, but with little effect.

"No," Goatee rattles. "No!"

"Save your breath," one of the bodyguards tells him. "We'll get you out of here."

"Shit," Straw Hat says.

"There!" one of the soldiers shouts. "Above us!"

We see it. We see a creature manifesting on the ceiling, branches and roots twisting and molding themselves into a grotesque human shape. Limbs emerge from that abstract of dead forestry, followed by a blank face, a mess of twig-hair and makahiya, its twisted mouth lined with thorn-teeth.

"It's on top of you, you assholes!" Straw Hat yells into the radio, though it seems no one can hear him. "Look up! Look up!"

Hemslock himself has already frozen, but his attention is not on the danger above them. The camera slides away from Goatee toward another figure that stares back from the darkness.

The face, or at least what face we can see of it in the dark, looks familiar. It's a woman with long yellow hair, carefully combed and parted down in the middle, though it hides much of her face. She's wearing a white cocktail dress. What we can see of her eyes is on Hemslock. What we see of her mouth is cruel.

"What's Hemslock doing?" Leo Gries asks frantically. He doesn't seem to see her. Neither do the others. But I do.

"You fucking bitch," we hear Hemslock snarl. "I knew it."

"I didn't want to," the strange girl says in a calm, clear voice. None of the other soldiers seem to see her either, even as she walks toward Hemslock. "You know I didn't want to."

"Shut up," Hemslock says. "You could have had everything with me. All you needed to do was shut the fuck up."

"Sir?" One of the soldiers asks.

Hemslock doesn't bother with a reply. He trains the gun on the woman, the tactical light mounted on the weapon briefly highlighting her pretty features, and pulls the trigger.

The shot is loud, echoing in the cavern. A red stain spreads across the woman's chest. She collapses.

"Sir!" An arm appears on the camera, grabbing Hemslock's wrist while another bodyguard attempts to calm him. "Sir, what are you doing—"

Those are the last words we hear. Suddenly, the man's head lurches forward, slamming into the camera lens. We have only a glimpse of his startled face, his bulging eyes, before he is viciously yanked back.

Tendrils close around his neck.

And then behind him, the creature's maw grins.

Both the soldier and Hemslock are thrown to the ground from the force. With a roar, Hemslock shoves hard at the man on top of him, and the creature obliges by dragging the bodyguard back. More tentacle-like roots spring from its face and wrap around the unfortunate man.

The soldiers whirl on the creature and then hesitate. Their bullets will hit their comrade. Their brief pause is all the thing needs to escape through another tunnel hidden to the left of the tree.

There is a horrifying thunk, the jarring sound of bone scraping through rock, as it drags the soldier into the hole with it.

Hemslock rushes to the opening, curses. "We can't fit inside this. Too small. Anyone see another way in?"

There is a furtive silence as the remaining four men search with Hemslock. Two keep their hold on Goatee. The others train their guns and lights upward, scanning the ceiling for signs of another attack.

"Nothing," Hemslock says in disgust. "Goddamn it. Goddamn it!"

He strides to where the woman in the cocktail dress fell, but she is no longer there. Hemslock stares at the spot for several seconds, and then kicks hard at the ground, sending up whiffs of dirt.

"Good riddance, you lying bitch," he says, and spits.

"What are we going to do about Carthorn, sir?" one of the soldiers asks.

"Forget him," Hemslock says. "We're heading back. Leave Karl here, too."

"But sir—"

"Do we look like we have a choice, Gunther? Have you seen the size of the hole that tree bitch pulled Carthorn through?" He points. "His bones are as good as crushed. If the unnatural angle he went in was an indication, he's dead. Be glad that he didn't suffer like Galant. We're heading back. They attacked us because we tried to break Karl free. But I know what we need do now."

"But sir—"

"You knew the risks of working with me. Said you wanted to hunt—and not just for sport, didn't you?" The camera shifts as Hemslock looks back up at the foreboding tree before spinning back to Goatee, still unconscious inside his thorn prison. "We're coming back," he says, and I can hear the smile in his voice. "With an offering."

EIGHTEEN

TOO SMALL

COMMUNICATION OUTSIDE OF THE ISLAND STILL DOESN'T work. The helicopter has yet to arrive. Hemslock has the crew continuously checking the connections, searching for equipment damage.

The storm should have passed by now. I sit and stare blankly at the sky. I can feel the heat of the sun shining down on me. I can feel the cool breeze brought in by the waters. Everything feels solid, real. It is easy to discard Hemslock's claims that this is all an illusion.

Several feet away, a new fight was threatening to break out between Gries and Hemslock once it became clear that the latter's attempts had done little to get us out of our predicament. Gries is still of the belief that rescue is coming. "You tried to kill it," he snaps at the actor. "It didn't work. Let's not push it. You already lost one man down there."

Hemslock shakes his head. He is preternaturally calm. "She was right," he muses. "It was just the sacrifice she got wrong. Once we go back—"

"Are you out of your mind?" Gries shouts. "Go back?"

"Yes," Hemslock says, eyes gleaming. "I know how to take its power for our own. And I *guarantee* it'll leave us alone once I'm done."

It is unnerving to see more of the crew side with Hemslock than with Gries.

"You know you're wrong," Hemslock points out. He's still wearing his guns, his bulletproof vest—he hasn't let go of any of his firearms since they emerged from the cave. "You know the Diwata's not going let us leave until it gets its pound of flesh."

"You're going to kill a lot of people by angering it."

"It's already angry. It'll kill us anyway. That's why we're going to need him." Hemslock points at me. "No offense, kid," he says. "But we're going to use you as bait."

"What?" Chase cries.

I jump to my feet but stop in my tracks when Hemslock points a gun directly at my head. I look around at the rest of the crew for support, but their guilty faces look everywhere but at me. Only Melissa makes eye contact with me. She's paralyzed with terror, terrified for my sake but unable to help.

"We've already discussed it," Hemslock says calmly. "You're our ticket to getting out of here alive. Seems like the god is sweet on you, so I'd wager the Diwata would be a lot friendlier if it knew you'd die if any of us did, right? Nothing personal. Shut your mouth and do as you're told, and we'll all make it out of here."

"Hey man," Hawaiian Shirt says nervously. "We didn't discuss anything. You said that the kid's going to be important, but none of us signed on for you to—"

"You're an ass, Gerry. You saw what they did to Karl. You wanna wind up in one of those little tombs, too? You wanna play nice and let it stick you in a balete tree, too? Turn you into a corpse like the first one we found? We're trapped here. We're all targets. As long as it knows the kid is safe—"

"Not all of you are targets," I interrupt.

"What the fuck did you say?"

"Not all of you are targets. But *you* are."

Hemslock sets the barrel of the gun against my forehead, and the click of the safety catch being released is loud in my ears. "You're really trying my patience."

"Shit, man," Straw Hat says, appalled. "You can't do this—"

"Shut up!" Hemslock shouts. "I'll do whatever the hell I want. I'm saving your sorry asses!"

"You are a target," I say again, quietly. The cold metal of the gun makes me sweat, but I do not move, do not let him know I am as scared as the rest of his team. "And if you kill me, the situation will get worse. The guilty see their significant others, families, lost loves—the ones they've hurt the most. You see yours, too."

"And what if I do?" Hemslock spits out. He looks down at me, gun still against my head. Then he begins to laugh, the loud boisterous laughter of someone with too much confidence in himself, the faint hysteria I can hear in his voice at odds with his bluster. "You really think I'm delusional, dreaming up images of that bitch who ruined my life wherever I go? Or are you in on the joke with the rest of the cast, too?"

Hawaiian Shirt says, "Reuben, what the hell are you talking about?"

"Don't tell me you don't know, Gerry. This is exactly something you'd cook up for the ratings." Hemslock trains the gun on him this time. "Where have you been hiding her?"

"Her?"

"Gail. Is she in one of the cabins? Or did you convince her to stay in the cave so you wouldn't have to sneak her in when I wasn't looking? Gotta hand it to you, Gerry. When she was with me, she would have turned her nose up at anything that wasn't five star. Hope you didn't break the bank paying her for your stunt."

"Reuben, again—what the shit are you talking about?"

"Do you think I'm a fucking moron? Did you really think I wouldn't know that this was all a setup?" Hemslock gestures wildly with his weapon before redirecting at Hawaiian Shirt. "You know how long I've been pushing you and Steve for the chance to do a documentary here? And how long Steve has been putting me off, telling me that a haunted island is so passé, it's not going to work with viewers? Then he calls me up out of the blue, telling me I've got the green light for a special? *After* my name had already been dragged through the mud? I read the gossip rags before I landed in this hellhole. The rumors from the tabloids that Gail had been spotted here. Coincidence? I think not. How much did you pay her to create this sham of a production? To make me believe that I'm seeing some ghost of her? Whose twisted entrapment scheme is this to get me to confess?"

"Reuben," Gries says, pale. "You're certifiably insane if you think that's what's happening."

"Everyone else's been seeing ghosts on this island," Straw Hat adds. "What makes you think seeing Gail here wasn't a figment of your imagination, too?"

"Because I haven't done anything wrong!" Hemslock shouts. "Karl ran over some girl! Leo caused someone to shoot himself! And let's not even start with all the things Steve's done! I'm a fucking saint compared to the rest of you, my name ruined by some bitches who only want money! The god of this island has no problems with me. Not when He knows I can make Him a star! When I can make Him feared and renowned the world over! The only thing that makes sense at this point is if you'd been conspiring with Gail to make me look worse!"

Mad, I thought, staring at Hemslock's eyes. He's gone mad, and he's the one with all the guns.

"Tell me: why the sudden interest in getting me a documentary so soon after Gail destroyed my reputation? You were so fucking critical when she first spoke out, Leo."

"My decision to be here has nothing to do with you."

"Ah, yes. Your beloved wife. You may not like me all that much, Gries, but unlike these other shitheads, I know you're not the type to stoop so low as to participate. Which must mean you were kept in the dark. Can't say much for Steve, Heussman, and the others. Hell I bet even Karl knows." He grins. "Backfired on you though, didn't it? You all came here thinking to put one over me. Well, I put ten shots into Gail in that tunnel. I'll tell the courts it was in reasonable fear of my own life. She'll never be telling lies again. None of you thought that the ghosts here were real, did you? And now you're struggling to make sense of what's a hallucination and what isn't. Now what are you going to do about it? Arrest me?"

"Gail was never here! The god's haunting you like everyone else!"

Hemslock shoots without warning. The bullet misses Gries, burying itself into the wall of one of the cabins. The sound makes everyone jump, makes some cry out.

"I'm your only ticket out of here," Hemslock says calmly. "I know how to appease the god and get us out of this mess. It isn't a coincidence that it's been sprouting balete trees all over the place. You all saw that abomination underground. There's gonna be two more sacrifices. And we're gonna appease the god by making both happen."

"You're going to make things worse," I say quietly.

Hemslock grins at me. "Kid," he says. "You ain't seen how much worse I can be."

"Mr. Gries!"

One of the medics staggers toward us. His whole shirt is wet from blood. Hemslock shifts targets, the gun now trained on the newcomer.

"What happened?" Leo gasps.

"It's not mine," the man wheezes, as other crew members help him sit. "Not most of it. It's Steve Galant. He chewed his way out of the restraints and attacked us. Amy and I were guarding his tent— he knocked her out and took a chomp out of me before running off."

"That shithead is going to ruin everything," Hemslock says tersely. "Where'd he go?"

"The mess hall, I think."

Hemslock gestures at his men, and they head for the cabin.

"Is he just going to leave us?" Hawaiian Shirt asks nervously.

"What are we going to do?" Gries says angrily. "I don't think we can stop him. We just stay out of his way. Until the helicopter comes."

"But what if no one comes to rescue us?" Chase asks. "Then what?"

"We'll find a way. We'll use Alon's boat and make for the mainland if we have to." Leo turns to me. "What does he mean by a peace offering?"

"He's going to finish out the prophecy," I say grimly. "He's going to recreate the ritual."

"I had no idea Hemslock was an unhinged loon," Hawaiian Shirt says shakily. "What the hell was he going on about? What entrapment scheme with Gail?"

"He's on a psychotic break." Gries glances back at the mess hall. "He's so convinced he's done nothing wrong, nothing to anger the god that accusing us of a hoax is the only way he can explain his ex's presence on the island."

"What do we do, sir?" Straw Hat asks worriedly.

A shot rings across the clearing.

"Shit," Leo says, already running. Chase and I sprint to keep pace beside him. The others do not follow.

We reach the mess hall at the same time. Inside, Hemslock and his bodyguards are cornering Armani in the kitchen.

None of them see us, and instinct tells me not to announce our entrance. I conceal myself behind the door, tugging Chase to my side. Gries quietly follows my lead.

Armani looks possessed—naked again, and even more emaciated, though scarcely a few hours has passed. He's holding a knife that is covered in as much blood as the rest of him.

One of his eyelids hangs strangely.

Armani does not act like he's in pain. In fact, he's smiling from ear to ear.

The soldiers surrounding Armani look disgusted. Their firearms are trained on him, though there is already a bullet hole in the wall behind the man.

"Steve," Hemslock says. "What the fuck?"

"I can hear you, Reuben," Armani says in a calm voice that is stark contrast to his appearance. "I can finally hear you. I can still hear them. They live inside me now. They are one with me, and I am one with them. Soon, you all will be one with them, too."

"I'm almost tempted to shoot you here and now," Hemslock snaps. "I'm choosing not to in honor of our old partnership. Come quietly with us. You'll get the treatment you need."

"I'm already cured," comes the chilling whisper. "We are alike, Reuben, you and I—always thinking we know better than everyone else. We are all asleep. We are all dreaming. But He will wake. There is no meaning in this life but Him. There is no meaning until He has awoken. Then we will be saved. See. Look." He lifts his fist, and slowly opens his hand for us to see what lies in his palm.

With horror, I see a bloody eyeball. His bloody eyeball. He's removed it from his own head.

"I no longer require my eyes to see," he whispers. "We will need nothing else. You are close, Reuben. Already I can see the signs around you. You will understand soon: His love for you. His love for all of us. I do not need eyes to see. You do not need eyes to see. Let me show you. Let me show—"

He steps toward Hemslock, his knife raised.

Hemslock puts at least five bullets into his former friend. I lose count with the hail of bullets that follow from the other soldiers.

Armani jerks and the knife drops from his hand. He's dead before his body hits the ground. Hemslock keeps his gun trained on the fallen man, inching closer.

"Fuck," he says without any emotion.

Askal growls quietly. I place a hand on his head to stop him from making more noise.

"What do we do now, sir?" one of the men asks.

"One of you go to Galant's cabin and grab the biggest blankets you can find. We're bringing him to the cave."

"What? Why—"

"I don't pay you to ask questions, Dalton. Get to it."

When he returns, at Hemslock's instructions, the men bundle up the body and head out.

"Return to the others," I tell Chase and Gries.

"Alon," Chase begins.

"Trust me."

After a moment's hesitation, he nods reluctantly.

I follow the soldiers. Askal tags behind me.

They bring the body to the cave. I discreetly follow them inside and crouch behind a rock. I watch as they unwrap Armani and hoist him onto the altar, splaying his arms and legs over the small holes carved into the stone.

Hemslock bends over the corpse. He takes out his knife.

"What are you doing?" one of the soldiers asks. "What..."

He falls silent, seemingly stunned, as Hemslock begins his bloody work. The rest of his men fall back, several looking sickened, as Hemslock cuts into the corpse's chest.

Finally Hemslock lifts his hands, holding a bloody heart.

"*He who offers the sacrifice,*" Hemslock quotes, "*controls the Godseye.*"

Askal bares his teeth but makes no sound. I brace myself.

Armani's body jerks without warning, his back arching. Some of the men swear; all train their guns back on the altar.

Armani's mouth falls open, jaw loose. His fingers curl, stiffen.

And then his body is sucked *into* the stone, through the opening at the center of the altar. With horrible, cracking noises of bones breaking, flesh is forced through the too-small crevice, the corpse's back and waist bending unnaturally to fit. The guards fall back, watching in horror as the body slowly disappears. Armani's head is the last to be yanked through, grinding loudly against the rock as it grates into the tight space.

For an instant, I could have sworn that Armani's remaining eye opened one final time to stare at Hemslock. Something reaches up from inside the hole and wraps around his head. I remember the strange plants we've encountered, the ones whose flesh peels back and writhes like makahiya, with an eye at their centers.

And then Armani is gone, leaving only bloodstains in his wake.

Hemslock drops the heart down into the hole after Armani. It disappears into the nothingness.

"I told you this shit is real," he says. A wide smile stretches across his face. "Do you believe me now?"

He raises his arm, folding his fingers onto his palm. As if in answer, the makahiya growing quietly along the sides of the altar mimic his movements, closing and opening.

"The god has accepted my offering," Hemslock says. "Two more sacrifices to go."

NINETEEN

CONTROL

CHASE AND GRIES ARE HORRIFIED WHEN I TELL THEM what happened inside the cave. "Do you mean that the god gave Hemslock some of its powers?" the older man asks, ashen. "Why?"

"Only the sacrifice matters," I say heavily.

"So he's going to gain superpowers?" Chase demands. "We can't let him shoot anyone else! How do we stop him? What do we tell the others?"

"I'm not sure the others are going to believe us if we tell them. If this is the Diwata's will, then it is what it is."

"Are you even listening to yourself? Why would the Diwata give Hemslock anything? He only completed one sacrifice—we have to stop him before he can do the rest!"

"Do you trust me?"

Chase pauses, looking back at me. "Yes," he says, albeit uncertainly. "I do."

"Then we have to let this play out." I look up at the sky. "It's too late for anything else now."

Straw Hat has been looking through every instance of footage that they have collected for the show, trying to find any clue to get them off the island faster. There is little else to do. Hemslock has imposed heavier restrictions on the rest of the crew, forbidding anyone from leaving the camp. He insists that we take our meals together, and always sends one of his soldiers to accompany anyone needing to use the bathroom. The crew is as much Hemslock's prisoners as they are the island's.

I know that the crew still see the apparitions. Occasionally I hear their startled gasps, catch them fixated on something in the distance, turning pale.

Occasionally I see an apparition, too. An old woman with decaying teeth, her bright eyes peering out from behind one of the tents. A man with a disfigured face, blood dripping down his jaws. A bullet-ridden boy, staring aimlessly.

"It's angry," Melissa whispers. "It's trying to see which of us it can pick off first."

Many in the group don't see these ghosts. Or if they do, none of them say anything.

"I've logged at least five hours sifting through videos," Straw Hat says, gesturing at the clock on the bottom right of his laptop. "It's almost 6 p.m. The sun should have set by now."

"You're kidding me," Gries says. "Are you telling me that it can manipulate time, too?"

"Didn't the old woman say that?" Melissa asks. "I've been

reviewing notes from that interview. She said time has no meaning on the island. Maybe the Diwata can trap us in a pocket dimension or something. Maybe the world is moving on beyond this island, but we're stuck in this particular moment."

"How did you figure that out?"

"I watch a lot of horror movies."

"You're not helping, Melissa."

"Well, that's another reason—besides the storm—help won't be arriving," Straw Hat casts a nervous glance back at the cave. Hemslock and his soldiers have disappeared back inside for Goatee. They went without cameras. "He really thinks Karl's still alive in there?"

"I don't know what he thinks anymore," Gries says darkly.

I drift away from the rest of the group to idle by the beach with Askal, watching the waves lap up to shore. I wonder if it is proof that time still moves forward. But even as I wait and watch, the tide never comes in. The waves ebb and flow, but the water doesn't rise or fall.

Askal whines. I scratch his head absently.

Anong ginagawa mo? I ask the waters silently but receive no answer.

"Room for one more?" Chase asks from behind me.

I make space, and he sits beside me. "What if we're stuck here forever?" he asks. "What if this our version of purgatory?"

"You're not going to be stuck here. We're going to find a way out." But as I say the words, I know they sound hollow. Despite my knowledge of the island, I don't know what comes next. This has never happened before. "I'm sorry."

"What's there to be sorry about? It's not your fault. You're not the reason we're here." He leans closer. "I know Dad still sees Mom. I see the way he stares. I know he doesn't say anything because he doesn't want to worry me. But I can tell."

He looks down. "They argued a lot the week she died. I didn't know about what. When I heard Mom's voice back at the cabin— was that really her?"

"Everything on this island is an illusion," I say. "It's the people who decide what is real or not."

"You know more about this than you first said, don't you? Like with the cultists. You say you don't know what happened to them, but I think you do. You just don't want Hemslock to know."

"What makes you say that?"

"Just a hunch. You didn't seem surprised by all the information they discovered about the cult."

I stare out at the sea. "I was told that the cult had brought a woman to sacrifice to the Diwata the same way Hemslock did. Watson cut out her heart on the stone altar."

His hand on mine feels warm and comforting. "But the Diwata didn't like the sacrifice she'd made. So it forced her to return the body of the woman she'd killed back to her family, and then took her instead."

"Just like the old lady said. But how do you know she's telling the truth?"

"'Tay told me."

"He was the island's caretaker when it happened, right? And that's what you meant when you said you couldn't leave. You're worried that without your presence the island might just—take whoever it wanted? The god needs worshippers to complete the sacrifice, but He could kill anyone He deemed sinners. You thought that staying here with Him would mean fewer casualties."

"I'm sorry I didn't tell you sooner."

"I understand. We are the interlopers. You are trying to keep us from getting killed. What do you think's going to happen now? What do you think we ought to do?"

"I would have advised following your father's suggestion and waiting until help arrives—but Hemslock's taken that option out of our hands."

I look down. I'd subconsciously drawn a symbol in the sand. The eye figure from the cave. "The only way out is to give the Diwata what He wants."

"Dad still sees Mom. Are you saying he's a potential sacrifice?"

"Unfortunately."

Chase considers that carefully. Then he smiles—a determined, grim look. "How do we help Him choose Hemslock, then?"

His fingers feel nice. Gentle. "I don't know if we have any say in that anymore."

I don't realize that I've fallen asleep, only that I am dreaming.

I dream of the cave. I dream of Hemslock and his men pushing their way back toward the tree with the curiously carved face. I want to scream at them to stop, but nothing comes out of my throat. I am forced to watch, helpless, as they draw closer.

"Keep your eyes peeled for more of these beasts," I hear Hemslock instruct. He turns toward one of the twisted roots, the one that holds Goatee.

It takes some time, but the men manage to dig out Goatee a second time. Nothing else attacks them.

Once freed, Goatee kneels on the ground, looking around him with an odd detachment, like he hasn't spent the last few days trapped here. His voice sounds muted, like he's speaking from somewhere farther away. "You should have left me to dream."

"My quota for unhinged madmen has been reached for the day, Karl. Don't tell me you're gonna start babbling nonsense like Steve did."

"I dreamt inside the tree," Goatee says. "It changed me. It was wrong of us to come to the Godseye, Reuben. It was wrong of us to desecrate the island. But my mind is clearer now. I was full of anger when I came here, just like you. Angry at my ex-wife. Angry about the divorce, about her taking custody of my kids. I sinned. I killed a young thing who wouldn't let me go, the girl I cheated with. I was never arrested for her murder. But that doesn't matter now. Cleanse yourself of your anger, Reuben. It's the only way to live."

Hemslock aims his gun at Goatee. "Are you even Karl? Or did some fucking pod person replace you inside that goddamn tree?"

"You always think the world is out to get you, Reuben, and sometimes there is a reason for it. I was *glad* that I'd gotten away with killing her. You're the same way. You never think about how you hate. You always looked at Gail as being beneath you. And all the other women who accused you of harassment—Hannah,

Josie, Brenda. You hurt them, and then you blame them instead of yourself."

The gun in Hemslock's hands trembles, just slightly. "How the fuck did you know Josie? Or Brenda?"

"The god knows everything. It sees into your soul, manifests your fears and dreams into life. It has looked into your heart, Reuben, and it only sees hatred. Anger about the things you yourself had caused." Goatee bows his head.

"And that is why He will take you, too," he says. "Your sacrifice of Steve Galant is in vain. Even he repented in the end. He embraced Him wholeheartedly. It will not be the same for you. Like Cortes. Like Alex Key. He knows what you did to Josie. He knows that they are not the only ones. Leave your anger, Reuben. You will suffer through the—"

Nobody expects the gunshot. Goatee slams against the wall, blood running down his face from the bullet-sized hole at the center of his forehead.

And yet—and yet—for a few moments Goatee remains upright. The shot should have killed him immediately, but it does not. Instead, his eyes meet the other man's.

"You should have let me sleep, Reuben," he says.

And then he falls.

"Christ, Hemslock," one of the soldiers says. "You should have—he wasn't acting hostile—"

"He's been compromised," Hemslock says brutally. "You saw the state Galant was in when he died. Stay on guard."

"Sir—"

"If you think that's bad, Kyle, look away like a coward because you're not going to like what I'm about to do next."

He takes out his knife and turns to Goatee's body.

This time Hemslock is more certain of himself. He butchers with less hesitation. The others turn away, nauseated, until he is done with his grisly task.

Hemslock stands, Goatee's heart in his hands. He turns toward the gigantic tree, presses the heart against the bark—and the heart sinks through like it was intangible.

Something crackles from inside. The roots unravel and open, revealing a hollow.

Hemslock gestures at one of the men, who shines his flashlight into its base.

Something lies within. It is a blackened husk, a mummified corpse. The roots of the tree tangle around it, like they have been binding it in place.

I see its face. Unlike the corpse tree in the sinkhole outside, this figure still has eyes, and they are wide open, staring. It is the only recognizable feature in that sunken, withered form.

Its chest has been torn open. Inside, a heart beats steadily against its ribs. I can see it through the translucent skin.

"Shit," a soldier says.

Hemslock raises his hand, closes it into a fist. "Move," he commands.

The corpse jerks up, and the others rear back. Hemslock moves his hand slowly back and forth.

The dead body copies his movements.

"Damnit, Hemslock," one of soldiers says. "What are you—"

"It's accepted two of my offerings," Hemslock says. "Now we need one more to waken this Dreamer."

The corpse blinks.

With a shrill scream, it lunges forward, toward Hemslock. A blast from one of the soldier's guns flings it back inside the tree, and the other join in, firing haphazardly into the balete.

The corpse jerks, then staggers toward the opening once more.

Roots wrap around it unexpectedly, bind it against the ground. With a hiss, it struggles. Hemslock's laugh is long and loud. "You don't like me, little godling," he says. "But that doesn't matter now, does it?"

I wake up to a loud explosion. I don't remember falling, only that there is sand between my teeth and Chase is at my side, turning me over. "Are you okay?" He asks frantically. Askal nuzzles the side of my face, barking when he realizes I'm awake.

There is a throbbing in my head—like my skull is about to split open. Like something that isn't me is inside of me, screaming all the hurt into my bones to rid itself of that pain.

"Give me a second," I gasp. As intense and as sudden as it was, I can already feel my dream starting to recede. I stagger to my feet, aided by Chase. "We need to go back to camp," I manage to say, and to his credit he asks no further questions.

The group emerges from the cave just as we reach it, and they're breathing hard like they've been running. The explosion must have caused them to flee. Hemslock sees me and smiles cruelly. "Thought your pet god would kill us?"

"He didn't stop you because you're a psychopath who would have shot any of us if we had tried to," Gries says sharply.

"I'm the psychopath who *saved* you," Hemslock snarls. "Your guide has been so thoroughly brainwashed by the fucking demons in this place that he was about to serve you all on a platter to appease this holy fucking cannibal."

"What the hell, Reuben," from Hawaiian Shirt.

"He's been lying to us all this time. Before we lost all communication with the mainland, I'd been sending letters, asking the team to verify everything they can about ol' Alon here."

"And then I thought, what if we checked our tour guide's background, to see how this kid knows so much about the island and its curse when so many other local residents didn't. No one seems to even know where the family lives, or why they've got free rein over the island. Wanna know what I found?"

Nobody speaks. Chase quietly reaches out to clasp my hand.

"This father who's been sick for the longest time? The reason the kid even took this job with us, to help pay off the bills for his treatment?" Hemslock leans forward, his gaze never leaving mine. "No one knows who he is."

The crew moves uneasily, glance at each other, and then at me, as if hoping I would proclaim my innocence. I don't.

"The locals know who you are, kid, but nobody knows where you're from. Certainly not from any of their villages. The fishermen you befriended admitted to seeing you often, but word is they fear you as much as they fear the curse. But I'm willing to bet that they know, and that they're protecting you. They stood by and let Lindsay Watson and her followers get killed because they didn't want some foreigner gaining the god's favor. You didn't like that I performed the rituals before you could. You wanted to sabotage us right from the start. That's why you kept lying, saying you didn't know shit about anything."

The gun is back, once more aimed at my face.

"No!" Chase exclaims, pushing me so that he is between me and Hemslock.

"Chase!" Gries cries out, rushing toward us.

"You really willing to die for this liar?" Hemslock says with a laugh. "After gaslighting you into believing this little shit was on your side? When all this time our own guide was planning to betray us to this demon god? All the other villagers we talked to, from the mayor to that damn grandmother—they knew. She said they all worshiped the Dreamer, didn't they? Pretending to warn us off the island, but was actually fattening us up for it. Just like your hero, Lapulapu, with Cortes.

"Your father sacrificed Alex Key. That's why the creatures in this island leave you alone. I'm willing to bet your father also served up Lindsay Watson, and then the rest of her cultist friends for dessert. And now that he's too old to continue, you've taken his place. You let that corpse tree claim Steve under the pretense of saving him. You sat back and let Karl's ghosts drive him crazy.

"And *you* knew, Leo. You were there when I got the report, when you learned that we couldn't find any trace of his father, or of his family. You knew he was lying to us!"

223

"Yes," Gries says. "I knew. And to be honest I was worried that Alon was getting too close to Chase." He turns to the others. "But if Alon's intention was to see us dead like Hemslock claims, then we'd be dead. Alon did everything they could to protect us. Only the ones who didn't listen—Galant, Karl—they suffered."

"Yes," Melissa says softly. "I trust Alon, too."

No one else seems ready to speak, at first. But then Hawaiian Shirt nods.

"Alon is all right," he agrees. "I still don't know what the hell's going on, but I don't believe the kid's out to get us."

Slowly the others nod.

"Are you all fucking fools?" Hemslock shouts.

Hawaiian Shirt shook his head. "Kid, explain yourself so we're all square, right?"

I lick my lips. "I'm not lying. My father's been sick for a while, but most of the villagers wouldn't know where we live."

"Well, there you go, Hemslock," Hawaiian Shirt says. "It's a reasonable explanation. There're far too many islands around here for everyone to know everyone else. Just extend your search and I'm sure you'll find all the pertinent information you need."

"You're a goddamn simpleton if you actually believe that," Hemslock spits out. "Didn't you see anything strange about the kid while we were inside the Godseye?"

"We didn't notice," Gries says. "We were all busy thinking you were out of your mind. Fuck, Hemslock. What if the god isn't getting weaker? What if you only made it angrier?"

Hemslock's eyes flick toward Chase's. The latter meets his gaze head-on, undeterred. "I was with Alon the whole time, and nothing happened," he lies.

The actor smiles coldly. "So that's how it's going to be, is it?"

He gestures at a nearby balete, cutting it—and a branch abruptly breaks off. The rest of the tree takes on a sicklier appearance, as if growing more brittle and withered.

And then, with a moan, it moves.

"Come," Hemslock commands, and it obeys, shuffling to his side as the others watch, terrified. The man laughs. "It works. It really fucking works. That's how Lapulapu did it. He sacrificed two enemy chieftains and Cortes, and in return the god gave him power. He gave the man fear and control of these fucking creatures to do his bidding. No wonder he nearly wiped out the Spaniards."

"What did you do, Reuben?" Gries asks with alarm.

"What the rest of you were too chickenshit to dream of. What Lindsay Watson couldn't."

"What the hell?" Hawaiian Shirt demands. "You said you killed Steve Galant in self-defense. You said you couldn't find Karl. And now you can control these fucking trees?"

"Just because you sacrificed them," I say, "doesn't mean you've succeeded. The creature inside the cave resisted your control. It tried to attack you."

"How did you—?" Hemslock recovers swiftly. "So you know about that. Did the god tattle? Cry about getting his ass kicked?"

"The missing pages in Cortes's journal describe the ritual. How to control the Diwata. Lindsay Watson tried to do the same thing, and now you're following in your aunt's footsteps," I say.

Dead silence. The crew turns disbelievingly toward Hemslock, who refuses to give ground.

"Yeah," he says. "Lindsay Watson was my aunt. You were snooping, weren't you? Always wondered if you were the one who'd mucked up my cabin. How did you know?"

"You referenced an 'eternity within a dream' four months ago in one of your emails. That was only mentioned in Cortes's journal, and *that* was found within the last two months. Page thirty-seven of the journal—one of the missing pages—was in your room. And I assumed you had the rest. The handwriting on the margins looked the same as in the photos of Watson's notes."

"He said he had an Aunt Elle," Gries says, eyes widening. "It was Aunt L, short for Lindsay. That mugshot of her, I knew her expression looked so familiar—"

"My mistake," Hemslock says, still smiling. "I should have known not to be careless. You pieced together the story pretty well, kid. Aunt Elle sent me a care package after her death. She'd been smart enough to keep Cortes's journal pages in a bank vault for me to inherit. I've been chasing after her ever since. Where did you think I got my obsession for ghosts? Her theory, like Cortes's, had always been that Lapulapu sacrificed to the Godseye and gained the power to repel the Spaniards from his island. But she miscalculated. The victim had to be someone worthy of punishment, not simply one to fit the riddle. Ironically, killing the woman made *her* worthy in the eyes of the god. I've since learned from her mistakes. I gave it Steve, I gave it Karl, and soon I'll give it you, Leo."

Gries freezes.

"My dad doesn't deserve punishment!" Chase shouts.

"Did you tell him about the dozens of people you let go because you didn't like how they looked, or because you were in a bad mood and wanted to take it out on someone else? Did you tell him about that man who begged you for a second chance? You had him thrown out of your office like he was yesterday's garbage. Then he went home and shot himself."

Chase's mouth falls open.

"You turned your nose up at Karl, but you've hired attorneys and paid bail for stars who've done more than a hit and run. You're a hypocrite for calling me out, Leo. You had a reputation with women yourself. I've seen you at some of those events. You pretend to be the angel, but I *know*. And when your wife about had it, you threatened to take full custody of your son and exhaust all her finances at court."

Chase stares at his father, incredulous. The look on Gries's face is enough to know that Hemslock is telling the truth.

"But that's no longer the point. This god of yours is not going to let us go until we complete the sacrifice. So I'm going to do something drastic."

And then, without warning, he fires at me.

TWENTY

ULTIMATUM

I STAGGER BACKWARD. ASKAL IS FRANTIC, TORN BETWEEN keeping close to me and snarling at Hemslock. The man points the gun at him. "Shut him up, or I'll shoot him, too."

Someone grabs at my injured arm. It's Gries.

"Stop this, Reuben!" He's scared. They all are. Even Hemslock's bodyguards are taken aback, though none of them break ranks.

Chase is taking most of my weight, all but carrying me. He shakes with anger at how close I'd come to being killed.

One of the medics approaches us, ties a strip of gauze firmly around the lower, fleshier part of my arm to serve as a tourniquet. "It looks a mess," he whispers, "but it's not as bad as it looks. The bullet only grazed you." Askal whines, turning away from Hemslock and putting a paw on my leg.

"Are you listening to me, you immortal piece of shit?" Hemslock screams at the sky. "I can finish the ritual. I can give you what you want. Let me fucking *help* you."

"Hemslock, this has gone far enough," Leo says. "You're going to kill us all if—"

"And what if I am?" Hemslock says. "You were happy to kill my career for ratings. You thought making me confess on camera was going to be the gotcha of the year. By this island's own rules, you're all guilty of punishment. Maybe if I lob enough bodies at its door, the Diwata'll allow my men and me to get away. Galant's sixth to lure. Karl's seventh to consume. Who'll be the last to wake?"

He trains the gun on me again. Chase steps in front of me again. Askal follows suit, teeth bared and growling low at the actor.

"Chase," Leo chokes.

"I always knew you had a soft spot for our guide," Hemslock says.

"Gail Merkan said no," I say quietly. "They all did."

Hemslock eyes me again. The sneer has leached out of his face, leaving something far less human in its wake. "That ain't my problem anymore," he says, raises his gun at me, heedless that Chase's standing between us, and fires again.

Something unspools itself from the ground and rises up. It's a fast-growing balete tree with the same thickly intertwined roots, forming a shield between Chase, Askal, and me, as well as the bullet, which hits the center of the newly spawned clump of branches. It engulfs the ammunition until it becomes lost within the dense roots.

"What the f—" Hemslock begins.

More trees sprout up around us, leafless branches and dead twigs, furious and angry against the wind. Spindles lash out, the closest one striking Hemslock across the cheek, drawing blood. With loud curses, he turns on the offending branch, firing at where it's thickest, puncturing it until its weight can no longer hold. With a loud crack, it topples to the ground.

Askal is howling. The rest of Hemslock's men waste their bullets on the other moving trees, gunning them down before they can reshape themselves into the frightening creatures with the snapping mouths. Leo Gries throws his arms around both me and Chase, pushing us out of the line of fire and back toward the mess hall, with Askal close behind. I see the rest of the crew follow.

It feels like hours, though it only takes minutes. The gunshots finally stop.

Straw Hat is the first to look out through the window, nervously. "They killed those monsters," he whispers. "Nothing is moving. There's only branches and bark on the ground."

I shift to look myself, ignoring Chase's warning grip on my hand.

Hemslock is laughing. The sprawl of wreckage on the ground from this vantage point looks almost human, though black bile seeps out into the ground instead of red blood. His men are sifting through the tree corpses, keeping their guns ready should anything else move.

"Now that's how you do it," Hemslock chortles. "Hey, kid! Your supernatural friend's not as strong as it likes to have us believe, eh? What a waste of power, keeping to this fucking island when you could conquer the world. Who knows? Maybe I'll take its place.

Imagine what I could do. What I could take. The cultists got it wrong, letting all this get away because they let the curse fuck with their heads. I—"

He stops, staring. "Sam, what the hell's up with you?"

One of the soldiers has doubled over, coughing. "Got something in my lungs," he wheezes. "Went down the wrong way. I can't—I—"

He stiffens without warning, staring at something over Hemslock's shoulder. The actor spins around, but there's no one there.

Sam opens his mouth again—and a black sap-like liquid pours out. He gags and stumbles back, clutching at his throat, as the veins in his arms and face begin to protrude, his eyes bulge in fright.

And then, with a terrible, flesh-ripping sound, a thick root as long as an anaconda and half as thick, emerges from his back.

Hemslock shows him no mercy and he picks up his flame-thrower. The blast knocks Sam's body backward. A ball of fire surrounds the soldier, and he disappears within the red heat.

The body drops to the ground, still burning, still twitching, but appearing more tree than human.

"Shit," one of the soldiers growls. "Mask up. They can get into you."

Hemslock stands over the remains of a fallen tree. "Rise," he says.

The branches by his feet stir.

"Rise," Hemslock says again, and he almost has it. The roots shudder. The branches rise, reassembling before him. They're similar in shape to the woman-like tree creatures that have attacked us, but also completely different. Their forms are much more slender—thin broomstick-like shapes—and unnaturally tall, like they've been stretched beyond proportion. Wordlessly, they take their place beside Hemslock.

"How the fuck are you doing this, Hemslock?" Hawaiian Shirt gasps, stepping out of the mess hall.

"I'm doing exactly what Key says it would do—and we called him a fool for it. It's been right in front of us this whole time. You thought he was a madman, but I knew better." Hemslock is sweating. Whatever strength he used to summon these monsters is taking its toll on him.

"You're not going to control the Diwata," I say, following Hawaiian Shirt. "You're going to destroy this island and everyone else on it. The Diwata won't let you leave."

Hemslock lowers the flamethrower to his side and takes out his gun again. I stand my ground.

He pulls the trigger. There is a faint click.

"You're lucky I'm out." He nods at one of the men. Before Gries can move, he's sucker punched. He slumps, then is hauled up onto one soldier's shoulder.

"What are you doing?" Chase shouts, but this time it is I who hold him back.

"We're going to do a little experiment," Hemslock says. "We both know that Leo is a prime candidate for one of the sacrifices, Alon, and your god thinks the same thing. We're heading back into the caves and getting what I'm owed, and this time, ol' Leo here is gonna be our surety. Surety that you'll be on your best behavior while we're inside, because we'll shoot him if you attempt anything.

I'd be more inclined to take you too, but I suspect your god's going to attack us if it thinks I'm going to kill you. I'll mend fences with your Diwata by presenting it with the final sacrifice we need. So you all be good and quiet, and stay here."

"You're seriously going to sacrifice him?" Melissa cries out.

Hemslock smiles. "I'd sacrifice the world if it would get me exactly what I want."

We can only watch as they drag Leo into the cave, the tree creatures Hemslock controls barricading the entrance with thick roots to keep us from rescuing him.

"What are we going to do?" Chase asks, frantic, once they disappear from view. "We can't let him kill Dad!"

Straw Hat and Hawaiian Shirt look at each other helplessly. "Hemslock and Gries worked together for years," Hawaiian Shirt says, in a bid to be comforting. "I'm sure Hemslock's bluffing."

He doesn't succeed.

"He killed Steve Galant," Chase says. "He killed Karl Rosmussen."

Hawaiian Shirt flounders. "Er. It's—"

"I don't know what we can do, Chase," Melissa says. "They've got all the guns. Maybe they'll have it out with the god and wind up killing each other. And—and it kinda sounds like Mr. Gries was even worse than Mr. Hemslock in a lot of ways, you know? I don't know if the god's gonna let him go."

Chase looks down, unable to contest that.

Melissa turns to me. "Would the god protect Mr. Gries? He regrets what he's done, right?"

My throat is tight when I respond, "That might not be enough."

"Seems to me there's a lot of shit going on here that you knew about but didn't share," Hawaiian Shirt says angrily. "What the hell is Hemslock going on about? How did he control those *things*? And he's related to fucking Lindsay Watson?"

"He's just as unhinged as his cultist aunt," Straw Hat says. "I ain't getting paid enough for this shit."

"I bet he has all of Lindsay Watson's research and that's what makes him so sure he can..." Melissa mutters. "If he can sacrifice all three—then he could potentially—"

She stops abruptly because we all hear it: familiar roaring sounds from above, growing louder with each passing moment.

"Holy shit!" Hawaiian Shirt is off toward the beach, waving his hands above his head, yelling frantically at the helicopter that has appeared from behind the clouds. It's heading directly toward us. In a flash, Straw Hat, Melissa, and Chase are by his side, whooping and yelling. The others run to join our efforts.

We draw back as the helicopter finds solid ground, the rotors slowing to a stop.

"The Hollywood crew on the mainland sent for us," says the pilot. There are only two people inside—him and a medic in uniform. "There was a bad storm, and we couldn't fly out earlier."

"You have no idea how glad we are to see you," Straw Hat says fervently.

"It'll take two or three trips to get everyone out of here safely. Is this all of you?"

The others exchange glances, as if not sure how much to tell him. Hawaiian Shirt is the highest ranked of the crew, and he takes charge. "We'll tell you everything you want to know after we're all back in Leyte," he says brusquely. "And man, do we have a story for you. Come on, y'all. Get on board. Injured first."

He extends his hand to me, but I shake my head. "I can't leave. Not yet."

"You out of your mind, kid? Hemslock's lost. He's only going to shoot you again—"

The medic is already out of the helicopter and assessing my wounds. "You'll need to have this treated," she says, "and I doubt the facilities here are enough. What happened here?"

I ignore the question. "I'm not going to leave this island until Mr. Gries does."

Melissa looks worried. "Are you saying—do you mean—?"

I lower my voice. "I don't know what's going to happen to them if the Diwata senses me leaving."

Chase swallows hard. "I'm not leaving until we rescue my father."

"What's this?" the medic asks again, accompanied by the pilot's irritated, "Didn't you guys say you wanted to *leave* this place?"

"Believe me, we very much do," Hawaiian Shirt says quickly. "Two or three trips, you said? Get anyone else who's been injured out first, and maybe you should send a boat for supplies while you're at it."

"You don't have to do this," I say quietly to Chase, as the argument begins over who gets to board that first flight. "I swear to you that I'm going to find your father and make sure he's here for the next trip. You should get out while you can."

"You're the one with the injuries," he shoots back. "I'm not going to leave you here, and you know it."

235

I wait until the medic is done, until she leaves to check on the others. "I don't want you going inside the cave with me. There's no telling what might happen."

"Like I told you before, you're going to have a hard time shaking me off. Your god can try to scare me off as many times as he'd like, but he doesn't know how stubborn I am. You're stuck with me, Alon, whether you like it or not. And besides—this is my father." He takes my hand. "Would *you* abandon *your* father?"

I look at him. My fingers tighten around his. "No," I say. "I suppose not."

TWENTY-ONE

SCRAPING

No one tries to stop us. I think the other adults have given up on changing our minds. Now that help has been assured, they're more concerned with leaving the island before anything else happens.

Only Melissa remains trusting and optimistic, though worried. "I told them I'll take a later trip out," she tells us. "They should be back with more helicopters and boats now that they know what's been happening here. But I cannot in good conscience leave you two without at least some adult supervision, even if that adult has to be me. I don't think anyone else will. They all want off the island at this point."

"I don't want you involving yourself in this," Chase says fervently to her. "This is personal, between Alon and me, and Hemslock." Askal barks. "Askal, too."

"They still have guns," Melissa points out. "Maybe you should wait to pursue them until the next helicopter comes? I'm sure there'll be authorities swarming in once they learn what he's done. Let them take on the danger."

"Guns aren't going to help where we're going. But thank you."

Hawaiian Shirt, whom I had not liked at the first meeting, is surprisingly adamant as well. "You can get on the helicopter right now, you know," he offers me. "You're hurt. And now that the word's out, they should have the authorities swarming the island soon, and I don't know what that's going to do to your, uh, god—"

"That's not going to be a problem." I look at some of the equipment still on the island, at the crew hurriedly trying to carry as much of it to the beach as they can, *still* seemingly thinking about the possible repercussions for their jobs. "I'm sorry you weren't able to get the film footage you wanted."

Hawaiian Shirt grins weakly. "We'll see what we can splice together. And even if we can't—we're alive. That's something, right? No documentary is worth dying for."

Chase and I wait until the first of the crew begin boarding the helicopter and then leave, Hawaiian Shirt and Melissa following. We head toward the kitchen, the only place that might have supplies to defend ourselves with. "We should have pepper spray at the bungalow," Chase says as we steal inside. "Should we go and get some there, too? I know Dad has a couple for emergencies—"

His voice trembles over the last sentence.

"You should get on the flight while there's still time," I say again gently.

Chase glares at me. "Like hell no. You don't get to change my mind because I got a little—nervous. Let's do this."

In the short time we've been away from the mess hall, everything has changed.

Vines and roots cover the room when we step in. The brisk-moving foliage is slowly but surely covering the walls in their entirety as we watch. Chase gasps. Hawaiian Shirt cuts off a shriek, clamping a hand over his mouth to muffle the noise.

The thick roots around us writhe and throb as if with a life of their own. There are some similarities to the giant balete tree growing in the cave; the roots are connected, braiding into a large tangle of branches that drop from the ceiling, makahiya scattered across its numerous branches. At certain angles, the tangles resemble arms and legs. At certain angles, faces seem to look back at us. They have no mouths or noses but stare at us with blank gazes.

"What is this?" Melissa chokes out.

"The Diwata's power is growing," I say quietly. "He knows that rescue has come and that more people will know about the island and its supposed curse. If it goes on like this, then the island may no longer be accessible."

"What do you mean?"

"If Hemslock succeeds, then the god will no longer have any use for an island."

An odd keening noise interrupts us. Something in the center of the balete's base begins to open, the bark peeling back like petals.

A large eye blinks back at us from within.

239

Melissa gasps and Chase nervously raises his fists. But I step forward, carefully picking my way through the roots.

"Anong gagawin mo?" I ask it quietly when I am near enough.

The eye stares back at me. Something else moves within the wood.

A face forms among the brambles, a familiar one. A woman with long black hair and sad eyes appears. Her head twists slowly as she stares at us.

"Holy shit." Hawaiian Shirt is hyperventilating. "Holy shit. Holy fucking shit."

"No," I say. "He's gone. You can't use her anymore."

The face twists. The lips stretch wide and the eyes bulge out. Liquid dribbles out of the wood like white paint being washed away. The rest of the woman melts as well, something similar to the corpse on the balete tree taking its place.

"You're Lindsay Watson," I say. "Or what's left of her."

The corpse stirs, moans. The desiccated jaw stretches. *Forgive me*, it whispers.

"Is this Hemslock's doing?" Melissa asks.

I answer. "No. The sacrifices directly fuel the Diwata's power. This is His doing."

"I don't trust Hemslock," Hawaiian Shirt says guardedly. "But it looks like he was right about you withholding information."

"Is that what you're most concerned with right now?" Chase asks heatedly. "Alon has been protecting us."

"There's another fucking *corpse tree*, and I was already about to lose it with the one we already discovered."

"What do we do?" Chase asks from behind me. "Do we kill it?"

We should. Death would be kinder than the miserable existence this creature leads.

"No," I say. "This is out of our hands now."

"Hemslock controlled some of those creatures," Melissa points out shakily. "Is the god granting him those powers?"

"Not for long."

"How sure are you of that?"

"I know I haven't given you a lot of details about the island. But on this one, I want you to trust me. He won't have those powers for long."

The face metamorphoses back into the large eye, which swivels toward Chase, who freezes.

"Yes," I tell it.

"What is it asking?" Chase asks nervously.

"If I really do like you."

Chase moves past me, crouches before the creature. "I swear I won't do anything to hurt Alon," he tells it. "I mean—I've never had to ask permission from an, uh, eye before, but—"

The tree creature shakes, branches rattling. And then the eye closes and disappears, bark closing back on itself.

"Did I offend it?" The boy asks worriedly.

"No." I crouch down beside him, smiling. "It's letting us be."

Chase's hand closes over mine. "You don't have to do this," he says. "I—I can understand why the Diwata wants to punish my dad. Why he would be a sacrifice. But this isn't your responsibility. I should—he's my—"

"No," I say. "I'm more involved in this than you know. I want to bring your father back."

"Even if you're going against what the Diwata wants?"

"Even so." I squeeze his hand. "We're in this together."

<hr/>

We take all the useful equipment we find in the cabins and the mess hall—flashlights, several coils of rope, an extra mace from Melissa. I have my machete, and we locate more hunting knives from the soldiers' stash.

Hemslock barricaded the cave after he and his men entered with Gries. Beyond the stone altar, vines have slithered across the passageway, blocking our way. I swing at them with my machete, only to uncover a thicker swathe of roots beneath.

"Looks like Hemslock's not going to let us have access to the treasures Cortes stole," Hawaiian Shirt says. Unexpectedly, he begins to laugh. "Treasures. Jesus. We came here to look for the gold Cortes stole, but I almost forgot about that. The sanest thing to do would be to get out of here. Get back to the helicopter, let the authorities handle this."

But Chase and I already know where we have to go.

<hr/>

"You kids positive you know what you're doing?" Hawaiian Shirt asks nervously, peering over the edge of the pit, eyeing the corpse tree worriedly.

The balete does not move, content to simply be.

"Poor ugly bastard," Hawaiian Shirt says.

"Are you deliberately trying to antagonize it?" Melissa hisses.

242

Chase and I are tying ropes around our waists, and she's helping us, making sure the harnesses we're making are strong enough not to slip free. "You are two of the bravest people I've ever had the pleasure of knowing," she says. "Although I don't know if it's courage, or if you're just out of your minds. But I have to come with you. I'm not going home and telling people that I let two kids into a haunted hole while I sat back and watched."

"No," I say quietly, giving my rope a good tug. "The fewer people involved at this point, the better."

"That's not on you to decide," Melissa says. She glares at Hawaiian Shirt. "Back me up here."

Hawaiian Shirt looks like he wants to argue with her but doesn't know how to without looking bad. "Was Hemslock right?" he asks instead. "Do you really have some kind of weird mind meld with this god?"

"I trust Alon," Melissa says firmly. "Save the questions till we're all out."

"Alright," Hawaiian Shirt agrees, summoning his courage. "You've been telling us to stay away from this island since day one, and it's our fault for not listening. We're coming with you. This doesn't sit right with me."

"You said you knew nothing about caves," I say.

"Well, we can't leave you here, either. Did Hemslock and his men leave any guns and bullets we can grab?"

"There aren't any," Chase says. "And we'd likely shoot and hit something we shouldn't."

Hawaiian Shirt sighs heavily. "Let's get this over with." He looks down at Askal. "And you want him along? Won't this put him in danger?"

"Trust me," I say again, and he sighs.

Chase and I lower ourselves into the sinkhole first, the adults waiting to pull us back up at the first sign of danger. I hold on tightly to Askal with one arm. He endures the descent patiently.

"You've done this with your dog before, haven't you?" Hawaiian Shirt asks warily but refrains from further comment. Askal simply wags his tail and yips importantly.

The descent is quick enough. We cling to the sides, taking care to stay as far away from the balete as we can, and shimmy down into the darkness. Melissa found us the flashlight helmets Hemslock, and his men used, and we flick them on once we reach the bottom, about a hundred feet down.

Chase stares up at the corpse tree and shudders. "We need to find Dad fast. Unless Hemslock's already killed him. Like that might be for the be—"

He catches himself, biting his lip. "Hemslock's a fucking liar, but he was right about what my dad did, wasn't he?"

"You guys okay down there?" I hear Melissa call out.

"We're good." I shine a light down the tunnel, the one the robot tank had explored. Nothing stirs, though I know that doesn't mean safety.

"I still think this is a bad idea," I hear Hawaiian Shirt say loudly.

We don't hear Melissa's response because a sudden earthquake nearly knocks me off my feet. Chase stumbles and collides into me, and I hear the exclamations above us as they, too, struggle for balance. Askal begins to bark frantically.

244

I look back, and my heart freezes in my throat. The balete is turning; the corpse and its perpetually screaming mouth is slowly tilting to look at us.

It begins to heave itself off the ground.

It is the first time any of us have seen the balete in its entirety. Its roots detach from the soil one by one, curling back into themselves as the tree rises higher, the corpse jerking forward in detached, rapid movements. There are no feet—the corpse has been fused with the hollow of the tree for so long that I do not doubt its lower body assimilated long ago. But that does nothing to stop its quickness. Its gnarled branches lower, the thin branches flattening and gripping the ground like centipede feet—and the tree begins to crawl toward us.

"Chase! Alon!" Melissa screams, horrified by the sight. "Get out of there!"

But it stands between us and our way out of the sinkhole. There is no way we can reach the ropes for Hawaiian Shirt and Melissa to pull us up without getting caught in the tree's roots, which are already multiplying at an alarming rate.

I grab Chase's hand and pull him deeper into the cave as the roots begin to fill the entrance of the tunnel—yelling at Melissa to leave, to get help. Askal guards our rear, howling at the tangled roots.

Our flashlights helmets illuminate what they can of the passage before us, and we run. Askal catches up to us quickly enough, slowing down so as not to leave us behind. We can hear the corpse and its balete slipping in briskly after us, the rasping of its bark as it scrapes against the walls a terrifying sound, like the sharpening of knives.

We don't know how far we go or how long. We don't stop until we are gasping for air. And we slow only after there is no echo of its pursuit, until we are alone with the silence of our enemy.

"We're screwed," Chase gulps. "We are, aren't we?"

"No," I say. "If it hadn't wanted us to go into the cave, the balete would have stopped us. It didn't want *the others* inside."

"Great." He lets out a sound that is halfway between a laugh and a sob. "Why? Why does it want only us? I mean—I understand why it wants you here, but why me?"

Askal inspects us both carefully with his nose and lets out a satisfied bark of approval when he finds no injuries or bruises.

"Because Hemslock has your father," I reply. "And while it might not seem that way, the Diwata is on our side."

I'm not the most confident in my reassurance, but Chase nods, straightens his back. He takes my hand and squeezes it. "Once we get Dad out," he says, "you'll leave the island with us? And I can call you and stuff?"

I smile at him and squeeze back. "If we can get through this, yes."

He nods. "Let's get his over with, then. Wouldn't be polite to turn down the Diwata's offer of hospitality, huh?"

TWENTY-TWO

THE PLANE

WE STAY ON GUARD, LISTENING FOR ANY TELLTALE SIGNS that the corpse tree is behind us. I don't know if separating us from the others was its only intention, but we force ourselves to walk faster, just in case it's following.

We see little else along the way, at first. The passageway is not one created by nature; it looks to have been dug out, though I am not sure if the work was done by human hands. There is very little debris as we walk, the ground swept clear. I am more than aware of the roots that climb across the ceiling. They appear just as we'd seen in the videos the production crew's robot had provided before it had been destroyed. It's dark enough here, but makahiya continue to bloom, multiplying the deeper we go.

"They're connected to the balete outside, aren't they?" Chase asks. "They must be."

"I think all the balete on this island come from one main

source." My attention focuses on something glinting on the ground. At first glance it looks like a shiny pebble, but a closer inspection reveals that it's a piece of glass, its sheen not yet obscured by dust.

In the darkness beyond lies the little robot tank that Hemslock sent into the sinkhole. It's on its side, broken and shattered. A generous heaping of its electronics has been ripped out of its body, then scattered across the ground.

Chase crouches down to look at the robot's remains more closely. His hands find something else.

He stares—and begins to tremble.

It's a small diamond earring.

"Mom's," he chokes. "I've seen her wearing this. But why—how—"

As he holds it, the earring decays before our eyes, turning into a small, gnarled root. Chase drops it.

"I don't—what—"

"An illusion," I remind him quietly. I touch his shoulder, and he leans into me.

"Okay," he says, calmer. "Do people who die here leave bits of themselves behind on the island independent of the Diwata?"

"I think they do."

He nods, and I can see that this helps him. "Let's keep going."

It's a long walk. Our phones have stopped working, and we don't know if it's been thirty minutes or two hours since we started. Have Melissa or Hawaiian Shirt alerted the others to our disappearance or kept quiet?

We push on doggedly and finally step into another cavern larger than the one we left. And it's familiar.

It's the cavern where Hemslock and his men sacrificed Goatee.

But something has changed. The misshapen human forms made of roots have been reduced to burnt ashes and smoke, the tang of it fills my nostrils.

The massive tree still takes up the center of the cavern. But broken roots hang overhead, and crushed ones lay underfoot. Twigs and branches are piled high where the corpse used to be, a gaping hole in its chest. The heart that the actor fed the altar is now several feet away, no longer beating.

Chase sucks in a breath. "Oh, God. Why did they burn it?"

"Because they wanted to diminish the Diwata's power." I stand before the body, gazing down at what remains of it—its shriveled form, its eyes that have not closed, even in death. I had not known this man—if he was one of the earlier sacrificial victims, or if it was ever even human—just as I still don't know the identity of the corpse in the balete tree outside. "It rejected Hemslock's offering," I say. It was why the Diwata attacked Hemslock instead of obeying his commands, though I doubt the man was even aware of it.

"You mean it rejected Karl Rosmussen's heart? Karl isn't one of the sacrifices?"

"It appears so." And I point.

Goatee's body is sprawled on the small stone altar. His eyes are open, though there is nothing left for him to see. There is a bloody hole in his chest, where Hemslock had carved out his heart.

"Should we...do something?" Chase asks nervously.

"The Diwata rejected the sacrifice," I say. "That's why He didn't take the body away like He did the producer's."

"But why wouldn't He accept?"

"Because there are others on the island that would make better offerings."

As if on cue, roots slither out from underneath the stone altar. They wrap around Goatee's body, spinning it into a thick cocoon of twisted branches. Speechless, we watch the roots shift from the altar, fixing the undead seedling on a spot several meters away and flowering almost immediately from the top down. Soon the plants have taken over the corpse, forever trapping Goatee's body within the banyan, swiftly covered by the ever-moving, restless makahiya. It looks no different than the other balete outside.

"Those plane crash investigators were digging all over the island, looking for bodies," Chase says. "But they never thought to check *inside* the trees. Oh, God…"

I look at the slowly forming tree that had once been Goatee, knowing that I should feel pity, although I do not. "Yes," I say quietly. "Oh, God."

Askal begins to growl, his haunches now raised. I look to see what he's angry about, and freeze. "Don't move, Chase," I say harshly. "Don't step on them."

"Don't step on what?" Then Chase yelps, once he sees what I mean.

Hemslock and his men have set up explosives among the branches.

"He's going to blow up the island if it won't give him what he wants?" Chase asks shakily. "What'll happen to the god if he does that?"

"I don't know, and I don't want to find out."

"I don't see any other passageways beyond the one we just used. Did we miss something?"

I look past the dead body, into the darkness of the hollow. "No we didn't." I take out my machete and cut away the remains of the tree to widen the hole around it. Askal stays close to me, staring into the hole as if expecting something to attack us.

I see disturbed soil there, and something behind the corpse that is darker than the rest of the cave wall.

"What are you doing?" Chase asks worriedly when I step into the hollow, but I already see what I've been looking for.

"There's another passage." It's wide enough, tall enough for a grown man to pass, and I have no doubt that this is where Hemslock and his men forced Leo Gries.

Chase pales a little, but squares his shoulders, resolute. "Okay. If that's where we gotta go, that's where we gotta go. Let's find Dad and get out of here."

The passageway is damp and smells faintly of mold, as if fresh air was a luxury it couldn't afford. I forge ahead with Chase keeping close behind me, my steps sure despite the slippery stones. The tunnel is much more humid here, and it clings to our clothes.

I spot glows in a soft, subdued greenish light ahead, similar to the splay of lanterns the crew hung to illuminate the path between the cabins. But as we approach, I see that they are made of something else entirely.

The nebulous lights come from the hundreds of balete trees that surround us when we step into the new cavern. From the ends of their wizened branches hang strange cocoons wrapped in thick roots and held together by black sap, the resulting shape only barely human. The dim brightness is concentrated somewhere within those mummy-like forms; whatever they were pulses with quiet energy. Occasionally they rustle, as if there is something alive within.

We are careful to pick our way through the heavy roots, some of which are so massive they've broken through the cave rock. And we stare.

Before us lies the wreckage of an airplane, mangled and partly blackened by fire. Trails of smoke are still evident, rising from its remains.

Chase sinks to the ground, in disbelief. "No. How could the whole plane be—?"

There is no sign of Hemslock or his bodyguards, but Leo Gries is there. He digs frantically through the wreckage, heaving broken pieces of metal out of his way. "Elena!" He calls, grief-stricken, too caught up in his nightmare to hear us shouting for him.

Chase runs to his father. A thick trunk bursts up through the ground in front of him, blocking the path.

Leo.

A woman steps out from the shattered airplane cabin, through a gaping hole where the doors should have been. She is a small, brown-haired woman with a bright smile and dark eyes. *Leo,* she says again.

"Mom?" Chase whispers.

"Elena!" Gries cries out. He begins to shove shattered steel out of his way in his quest toward her. "Elena, I'm so sorry..."

"Are you, Leo?" the woman asks sharply. "Are you truly sorry for everything you've done? Were you sorry when that poor man killed himself? Did you feel guilty when you fired people just because you could?"

She wavers, disappearing—and then steps out of the shadows from behind Gries. "Are you sorry for all the drinking? All the cheating? The nerve of you to claim that Chase wasn't your child? That young actress you threatened? Your other ultimatums to take full custody of our son and leave me with nothing?"

"Yes." Leo Gries is openly weeping. "Yes. I'm sorry. I didn't want you to leave me. I should have never used Chase against you. Forgive me. I'm sorry. Forgive me."

You must pay, Elena Gries says. Her features warp; the black of her eyes protrude, and her mouth purses, twists, and then opens far too widely. Something long slithers out past her charred, bark-like lips. She opens her arms.

Leo Gries, oblivious, stumbles into them.

"No!" Chase shouts.

The creature that calls itself Elena Gries straightens, and she is human again, smiling, pleased. *Chase*, she says. *I miss you, Chase. I'm sorry I couldn't be with you. Come and hug me, love. We can be together.*

She drifts closer to Chase. From underneath her dress more roots slither out.

Let me be your true parent, she says. *Care for you the way I care for my Alon.*

"No!" I plant myself between them. Not one to be outdone, Askal leaps in front of me, barking.

The mother hovers. *He misses his mother*, she coos. *Let me be that for him the way I have been for you. I gave you my blessing. I know he will be happy here. With us. You want that as well.*

"You frightened him. This isn't how you should be treating people you say you care for."

I deeply regret it. I was curious why you were interested in him. But his father is guilty. He deserves a better family. We could be a better family for him.

"Please," Chase chokes out. "Please let Dad go. I know he screwed up, and I know he hurt so many people, including my mom...but please. If you say you care for me, please let him go. He's all I have left."

Then stay with me. Stay with me and Alon. The woman's voice changes. It's more than Elena's now—there is an undercurrent to it, darker and harsher, as if something else is using her mouth to speak. *I will be a better parent. We can be family. We are family.*

"No!" I step forward and seize the woman's wrist. Underneath her flesh-like exterior, it feels like I'm holding a tangle of worms that shift and move in my grip. Elena Gries smiles past me, at Chase. *We can be family.*

"'Wag!" I shout again. "'Wag mo syang pakialaman!"

The woman reels back. *Prinoprotektahan kita.*

"And I want to protect you, too." I say the words in English, for Chase's benefit. "You looked out for me. You want to be just. But this isn't justice. And you can't make that decision for him."

"I just want to go home," Chase whispers. "With Dad. Please."

The man is worthless. Elena Gries twists against me. *The boy is too young to know justice.*

I tighten my grip. "That's a part of being human," I shout back at it. "You can't force people, even if you're looking out for them! You have to let them make their own decisions. You can't have them do whatever you want just because you want it! I've always obeyed, but that doesn't mean others should if you're in the wrong!"

The woman smiles, her face crinkling when she does—only to fold in ways that a human cannot. Her skin begins to slide off, her smile and her eyes and the rest of her features slipping off with it.

I keep my hold on the woman's wrist, even as the now-familiar tree creature inclines its faceless mouth to look at me. It ululates slowly, the teeth within that carnivorous flower-like mouth shifting and grating.

You have never gone against me before, she whispers. *These humans are bad for you. I will take his father, and he will dream with us. It is for his own good.*

"If you do that," I respond angrily, "then I *will* leave with Chase."

There is a snap. Elena Gries's limb comes off. It takes a step backward, but already the roots are reforming and reshaping, the torn arm slowly being reabsorbed back into the creature.

The world will hurt you, the creature whispers. Now it is revealing its true nature; the woman's face loses its animation as her body grows more wooden, becoming like the balete with the crudely defined faces on its bark. *I protected you your whole life. 'Wag mo akong iwan.*

I lean closer, unafraid. The Diwata watches me through the woman's alien gaze. "I won't leave you," I say softly, "but I can't obey you this time."

A large baton strikes the tree creature squarely in the center of its head. I step back in surprise as it staggers, but Chase does not let up, swinging his weapon at it again and again.

"I'm not afraid!" he shouts. "I miss her but I'm not afraid of you. And I won't let you use her against me!"

His last upswing shatters the tree creature. It crumples to the ground, and something at its core unfurls. The form dissipates, sprawls out into roots that run tangled across the ground, joining the others that lie twisted and decaying in this cave, and remains still.

Breathing hard, Chase stares at what's left of it, as if expecting a new form to reconstitute and rise up again. But the broken roots continue to decay, splintering slowly on their own. "I didn't kill it, did I?"

"No. But I think the Diwata got the message."

"I guess." Chase looks down at Askal. "You're always up everyone's ass, but you didn't even bark at the tree this time, boy." He lets out a shaky laugh. "Were you as scared as I was?"

Askal lets out a little snort, clearly taking offense, but allows Chase to pet him. The boy looks around and sucks in an abrupt breath. I follow his gaze.

The airplane is disappearing. Or rather, it is transmuting from broken steel and metal to bark and wood. The wreckage untwists itself, crumpling until it becomes a large mass of writhing roots and branches. And soon even they surrender and ungroup, sliding away into the hidden corners and small dark holes they had come from, leaving the clearing to us.

256

"No," Leo Gries says hoarsely. He rushes to where the plane once stood and falls to his knees. "I'll take whatever punishment she gives me!" he shouts, weeping openly now. "I deserve it. I deserve everything. If only I was better for her—better for you. Chase, I'm so sorry."

Chase rushes over and yanks his father into an embrace. Hoping to give them what little privacy I can, I turn away, and make the mistake of looking up at the cavern.

"Alon?" Chase asks when I don't say anything for a while. I respond by pointing upward. His gaze follows my finger—and he gasps.

There are easily thirty or so of the tree creatures gathered at the ceiling, hanging upside down, watching us with their lack of eyes, their Venus flytrap mouths that slowly open and close, sampling the air with their sharp root-tongues.

"Are they gonna come after us?" Chase asks slowly.

"No," I say. "They won't."

"But why would they look at us like that if not to—"

"They've always been here. But they're not for us. They know that they can't get to you. They're—waiting."

"For more people like me," Leo Gries says, sounding exhausted. "I'm going to be one of the sacrifices. If that will let you and Chase leave—"

"I'm not going to let them get you, Dad," Chase interrupts fiercely. "And I know Alon feels the same. So they're not gonna attack us?"

"No," I say carefully. "And since they're letting us pass without comment, let's not antagonize them."

"Chase," Leo Gries says again.

"You're not allowed to say anything else until we leave this cave, Dad," Chase says firmly. "I don't know what Alon said to it, but if the Diwata's letting us go, let's take advantage of that."

"It might," another voice says, "but we won't."

Hemslock is back, surrounded by his men. Their guns are pointed right at us. "The god might be soft about letting you go, Gries," the actor says, "but I'll be damned if you're going to fuck this up for me again."

TWENTY-THREE
BALETE

They usher us into another tunnel, Hemslock boasting all the while. "Seems like we've finally gotten in the god's good graces," he says, grinning. "Practically no attacks on us all the way here. It hit Leo hard, though—really pulled out all the illusions for him from the way he was carrying on about his wife. Figured we'd leave him and let the god handle him how it saw fit, then collect his corpse once it was all over. But then you kids had to come along and ruin the good thing we had going."

He shows us a breathtaking sight: a balete tree at the center of the next cavern we enter, even more immense than the one they burnt. There is no face carved into its center this time, but the massiveness of the tree dwarfs everyone within its vicinity. The ceiling it dangles from is hundreds of feet higher than the others, and a constellation of branches dips down toward us, as thick as a hedge maze.

And seeds. This is the only balete on the island that has foliage on it; I can see the thick green above us, large and wide like banana leaves. Dense nestles of rope-like plants cling to the ceiling and wrap themselves around the healthier-looking branches like strange ivy, proof something is capable of flowering and thriving in this place.

Two of Hemslock's men are setting up explosives around this giant balete.

"Pretty, right?" Hemslock gestures at the massive tree. "We're going to need a hell of a lot of flamethrowers to take this down. As it is, knives and bullets bounce off it like they're nothing, but I've still got a lot of dynamite on hand."

"You need to leave immediately," I say. "If you value your life, you will abandon this attempt to kill the Diwata and go. A helicopter has arrived, and they're taking crew members off the island. By the time you return, there'll be more rescue teams waiting."

Hemslock looks unconvinced. His bodyguards glance at each other, more nervous than before.

"Kid has a point," one of them says. "Would be easier if we could call for backup, return to the island when we've got more support. We're struggling, what with Kyle and Bren gone and—"

Hemslock rounds on the man, furious. "That ain't an option."

"But—"

"I said that ain't a fucking option! As soon as word gets out about this place, every asshole is going to come to take whatever treasures they can find, and then we're fucked. Don't you get it?"

Hemslock points at Leo. "He's what it wants. Galant was the sixth to lure. Rosmussen is the seventh to consume. He'll be the eighth to wake. Grief made a shell of you, Gries. You ain't been a father to your son, and you've been shit at work. Thought this show was your chance to pull yourself together, help you find closure with your dead wife. But that's not working, is it? At this point, it's an act of kindness to put you out of your misery so you can be with her." Hemslock's eyes gleam in the darkness. "You still don't get it, Gries. About Cortes."

"Cortes?" Leo asks hoarsely.

"He was set up. Aunt Elle sent me copies of the last few pages of Cortes's journal. I can recite his last entry word for word: *I have learned all from Lapulapu's men, enticed some with strings of bead and the salvation of the one true God, instead of this demon lurking within the cave. The god of the Godseye is pledged to honor any who sacrifices to him. That was how Cilapulapu gained his powers. No longer. Tomorrow I strike, offer him up as a sacrificial lamb myself. I will take his heart and plunge it into one of the trees that grow upside down within the Godseye, and then I will claim this land for my own, triumph with what has long been denied to me by Magellan. And then* everyone *shall bow to* me. *I will be a god.*"

He pauses for effect, smiles. "Cortes knew about the ritual. My aunt did. And now I do. And once I sacrifice Gries, the world's my oyster."

"*Take their hearts and sacrifice them to the Tree,*" I quote softly, "*and you will find eternity within the dream.*"

"My aunt died trying to discover the god's secret. No doubt those grotesque balete had been warped in her image. So you see, kid, like you, I am very much invested in helping your god achieve his dreams—quite literally. I came to the Godseye to help him.

The fuck do I need another documentary when I can gain so much more?"

"Someone pushed Galant into the sinkhole," Gries said. "He said so before he lost consciousness."

"Don't tell me you're sorry for him. Steve was a rich ass who had too much of Daddy's money to play with, and if anyone deserved death it was him. Who did you think leaked that shit about him in the first place?" Hemslock's grin is vicious. "No one's going to cry over an old rich pedosadist who's had an accident in some far-off island whose name no one can spell. But his death will ensure that everyone knows about this show. About me. You're going to get a huge bump in visitors, kid. *The sixth to lure.* I was rather pleased with myself when I figured that out. Your god's all for the ratings."

"And then Karl," Gries says with growing understanding, and horror. "He was your friend."

"Karl was a blessing in disguise. If the god was willing to grab him, then that's one less problem off my plate. You saw him staggering around, drunk as hell. He's a lost cause. He ran over some chick he'd been sleeping with when she wouldn't let him go. Don't know how he was still able to function. His own demons have been eating at him for so long. Get it? *Seventh to consume?*" Hemslock chortles, but of the group only he finds this funny. "I couldn't exactly leave him to his fate when the cameras were trained on us, so I made my contribution more compelling—by killing him first chance I got. A shame, though. First time I'd ever seen him that sober, even if he was spouting all that preachy nonsense."

"And you mean to make Dad the last sacrifice," Chase says angrily.

"*Eight to wake.* Kind of a poetic justice. Your dad's been asleep ever since your mom died. He lost all his edge. The last few shows have been utter flops. No one thinks he's got the touch anymore. He used to be so—unapologetic. Vicious."

"You mean he shirked people out of money for profit," Chase says flatly. "He cost people jobs while giving himself and others like him bonuses for laying them off. He ruined his marriage out of selfishness."

"I didn't see you complaining when you were enjoying his wealth, boy."

"He changed after Mom died."

"And look where that's gotten him. Poor ratings and bad decisions. You're his son. Of course you'd defend him. But no one likes weakness in Hollywood. No one will miss your father."

"I've done things I'm not proud of," Gries says quietly, "and things that I regret. If the god of this island wants to punish me for that, then I'll gladly pay. But don't take this out on them, Hemslock. They have nothing to do with this. My son has nothing to do with this."

"But not Alon? So you believe me when I say he's got deeper ties to the Godseye than he lets on?"

Gries looks at me, then glances away.

"He was rejected," I say.

"Still defending Leo because you have a thing for his son?"

Chase quietly simmers, but I ignore the insult. "No. I meant your other friend. The Diwata rejected him as an offering."

"And how the fuck would you know that?"

"Because when you sacrificed him, it attacked you instead. The roots didn't drag his body underground like Steve Galant."

Hemslock's smile wavers. "You're wrong. I know more about the legends, about what the riddle requires, more than you ever could."

"Yes," Chase says, vibrating with extreme sarcasm despite everything. "You know so much better than a boy who's been living here all his life, the only one the island had ever welcomed."

I am no longer watching Hemslock and Gries. I am watching the ceiling above us, where the roots and tiny hair-like twigs have slowly begun reforming into a wide eye staring down at us.

Hemslock sees the movement, his eyes flicking upward. "You accepted my offering!" he shouts. "You took Galant *and* Rosmussen! You rewarded some fucking brown monkey when he killed Cortes for your sake! I brought the last of the three sacrifices you need! You were ready enough to take them until they intervened! I gave you what you demanded—now pay me what you fucking owe!"

The soldiers have spread apart, their guns trained upward at the writhing mass of branches.

Hemslock's gun is pointed right at me.

"If your little pet guide makes any move to harm us," he says, "I'm going to kill you."

"It's not going to matter that you offered the Diwata those sacrifices," I say quietly. I take a deliberate step toward him. "It doesn't matter because you're part of what it wants. It knows the demons that plagued Karl are nothing compared to the demons that haunt you."

A muscle ticks in the actor's jaw. "You're pushing it, kid."

I risk another step. "The cultists were punished not because they were mistaken. They were punished because the god saw that Lindsay Watson was the better choice for sacrifice than the woman they were offering."

Hemslock doesn't move.

"The Diwata knows what you did to Carol, and Lee."

His face hardens.

"There were more of them than the news reported. That's why you were so paranoid. You think that the people in your studio knew about the others, and that they're all against you. That this is a setup to earn more profit from your confession than a ghost investigation documentary. That's the only reason you can come up with, after you started seeing her everywhere."

"I see her everywhere because she's in this goddamn cave!" he roars. "I shot her!"

"No, you didn't. This isn't a setup. You're blaming other people for your own guilty conscience. You must leave. All of you. There's still time to save yourselves. He won't give you what you want. But he won't take your lives."

Hemslock smiles, and this time I am close enough to see how unhinged he is. The reality waiting for him outside these caves is worse than anything he can imagine happening within them.

"Kid," he says, "if he won't give me what I ask for, then I'm going to make it impossible for the Diwata to say no."

And then everything else ceases to matter because he shoots me.

TWENTY-FOUR

BREACH

THERE'S PAIN.

All I know is the hard rock underneath me, where I am now flat on my back, struggling to breathe. There is a peculiar wetness on my chest that I dimly recognize is blood. It is spreading far too quickly for me to slow or stop.

I can hear Chase shouting, frantic. I feel pressure pushing down on me, and know he is trying to staunch the flow, though I don't know if he'll be successful.

My vision is growing dim. The pain is unbearable.

And yet, at the same time, I can see everything. I see, from some heady distance, a bird's eye view of my own body, of the soldiers who had not moved when I had fallen, of Leo Gries looking horrified, and Hemslock not at all.

With a loud, angry snarl, Askal leaps for Hemslock, and manages to take a huge chunk off his leg. With a shout, the man tries to kick him free, but Askal clings stubbornly. Hemslock turns the gun on him.

There is another shot.

"The fuck are you doing, Hemslock," Gries whispers, face white.

"Don't be such a pussy, man," Hemslock says, calming, shoving the now-unmoving Askal to one side with his boot, then speaking directly to me. "I aimed it pretty carefully. It's going to hurt like a bitch, but unlike your little mutt, you'll live. Or you might not, with my next shot."

"What the hell are you doing?" Gries chokes. "You really think you're going to get what you want by shooting a teenager and a dog?"

"Don't you get it yet, you fool? Lapulapu uses Spaniards like Cortes to feed his god, and in exchange he gets to be the most powerful brown bastard in this region. Who's to say that this little shit hasn't been doing the same thing? That everyone in this fucking country isn't in on it and mad that I keep making the necessary sacrifices first? Why do you think this so-called tour guide has been willing to help us when everyone else had been warning us away? I bet you all this talk about a sick father was simply a sob story to gain our trust."

"Alon's literally bleeding out, you psychopath!" Chase shrieks at him, still pressing down hard on me. "And you killed Askal!"

"Unfortunate collateral damage," Hemslock says coldly. His eyes flick somewhere behind Gries.

"How the fuck did you—" he snarls, then doesn't bother to finish. He moves his rifle, the light attached to it catching on a tree creature standing by the passage to the other cave. A woman's face lies juxtaposed over its inhuman features.

267

Some of the soldiers keep their guns pointed at the ceiling, at the swirling mass still multiplying above; two join Hemslock, firing at the balete monster who is adroit enough at avoiding their hail of bullets—scampering into the shadows, flickering in and out of their line of fire.

None of them seem to see the cave wall behind them beginning to pulse like a heartbeat as thick roots gather and intertwine to form another massive, hollow tree. None of them notice the roots on the ground splaying out from the construct, spinning and twisting toward them, until it is too late.

There is a cry. One of the thick roots has latched onto one of the men's boots, and suddenly he is on the ground, struggling frantically as the tangles drag him toward the opposite end of the cave, where another knot of squirming tree-tentacles lies in wait. The others turn and begin firing at where the knot lies thickest, some aiming for the roots that are pulling their comrade away. Their shots tear off bark, but don't deter the balete.

The man is yanked into the hollow, still screaming, still shooting blindly, to no avail. The hole closes behind him, and the man, the tree, is quiet, as if he never existed. The branches endure a few more seconds of gunfire from the rest of the mercenaries before they untangle abruptly on their own, scattering away like rats, revealing a solid cave wall with no sign of the soldier.

There are soft moans. More tree creatures form from the center of the twisting eye above them—the same hair-like tendrils and slim, razor-sharp branches for hands and gaping maws for faces.

They are quicker than before, deadlier now that their sanctuary has been breached. They avoid the hail of bullets, scampering upside down as they skirt along the sides of the cave, some posing as a distraction while others leap at the soldiers from behind. Another man goes down, and then another, screaming as the knife-like fingers tear into them, ripping through their vests to get at the tender flesh beneath. Their screams are abruptly cut off when those large, teeth-filled mouths snap down onto their heads.

Gries grabs at my shirt, helps Chase drag me behind a large boulder to shield us.

"Stay together!" Hemslock screams at his men.

"Is Alon alright?" Gries whispers.

"I don't know," Chase says frantically.

Gries shrugs off his jacket, pushes it under my head. He pushes his hands down hard against the wound on my chest. "We need to get you to a medic as soon as possible," he says raggedly.

That's unlikely, given the gunfire around us and the journey back out. I try to speak, but no words come out.

"Don't talk," Chase whispers. "Save your strength. We're going to get you out of here."

Another high-pitched scream is cut off by a horrific grinding sound. One of the tree creatures has found another victim. Blood is pooling around the lifeless soldier; his eyes staring at nothing while the monster begins to feast.

There is a whooshing sound, and the thing catches fire before it can gnaw its victim any more.

Hemslock has the flamethrower in his hands. Crazed, he swings it haphazardly.

"Stop it, man!" one of the remaining soldiers shouts in fear. "The explosives! We'll all die!"

Hemslock isn't listening. When the other man tries to deter him, the actor spins and shoves the weapon right into the man's face. He launches again.

With a scream, the soldier catches fire, twisting and turning frantically before dropping to the ground and rolling, trying to put out the flames covering him.

"You're not going to get me," Hemslock shouts. "I'm going to fucking torch this whole island unless I get what I'm due, you fucking prick!"

He strides toward us. Chase clings to me, refusing to let go, even as the flames draw closer.

"I'm going to burn them to death if that's what it takes," he snarls.

Gries leaps at him from behind without warning, his weight catching the bigger man off-guard. Both hit the ground.

Gries tries his best, but Hemslock is heavier, stronger. The actor punches the other man's face, grunts when his opponent manages to get in a knee, but he's on an adrenaline high. He continues pummeling Gries once he gets the upper hand, the latter sagging under the force of his blows.

Chase props me against a large boulder then grabs his baton and runs at Hemslock, slamming the weapon against his back. "Leave him alone!"

It barely even fazes him. With a snarl, he punches Chase, sending him stumbling back. Then Hemslock slams the younger boy to the ground, his hands around his throat.

270

"I'm doing you a favor," he snarls, fingers tightening. "Since you're going to be a fucking orphan soon—"

He stops. His hold slackens. Blood drips from his mouth. He staggers back.

I stand behind him. In my hand is a heavy branch, its sharp end plunged through Hemslock's stomach, in almost the same place he shot me.

Askal stands beside me, bearing no wounds. His jowls are pulled back, his teeth fierce, and he is growling.

Hemslock swings at me, his fist missing when I duck. Askal takes that opportunity to latch onto his arm, teeth digging in deep. With a scream, he spins, trying to shake him off.

Leo Gries has regained his footing, the flamethrower secure in his grip. My eyes flick toward Chase, but he is already sitting up, his hands pressed against his throat and his eyes glaring murder.

"I knew it," Hemslock says, breathing hard. "I knew you were in on it."

Both Gries and Chase look at me, take in the thick root that is now wrapped around my waist, staunching my injuries. They watch as the remaining tree creatures gather behind Askal and me, silently awaiting orders.

"You lied, didn't you?" Hemslock wheezes. "You're just like these monsters. You're some tree freak evolved to look human."

"I *am* human," I say. "I have a sick father. I stayed on this island to try and prevent all this from happening."

"And that's why these fucking monsters are at your beck and call, right? Were you controlling them all this time? Did you cause the sinkhole and the corpse tree? Take out our comms, mess with our equipment, try to kill us that first time in the cave?"

"That was never me. I told the Diwata not to. I wanted him to leave you alone, to find some other way."

"Him?" Even heavily injured, Hemslock cannot stop taunting. "Your little demon god?"

A harsh grinding sound echoes above us, like something massive is moving. Drawing closer.

Askal's face abruptly splits open, but this time it is of his own doing. A mass of frothing tendrils springs from his head. His paws shift and, in the blink of an eye, become writhing, thick roots. My pet dog slowly comes apart, revealing what he really is for the first time. His tail wags, pleased by their reactions, before it drops off, branch-like protrusions forming in its place.

"No," I say quietly. "Not my demon god. My father."

TWENTY-FIVE

RITUAL

A VOID THAT CONTAINS BOTH NOTHING AND EVERYTHING AT once; that was how Alex Key had described the Diwata. *A demon that wears nothing but an eye,* is how Cortes had written of him in his journal, the journal that the hero Lapulapu had claimed and passed down generations until it was hidden away for everyone's good.

But he had always been Tatay to me.

And now they see Him in all His glory. The branches from the growing trees above us fuse and connect, binding together to form something that boasts no human shape. The foliage around it thickens until oval-shaped leaves look down upon us like a canopy— still forming the shape of an eye, but an eye that is now flowering, growing evergreens. It shifts and twists and *breathes* like a living thing.

A huge portion of the tree—half the height of the cavern— detaches itself from the cave wall. But when it lays a hand on my head, it is gentle. As always. 'Tay's hand feels leathery, but cool to the touch.

With an angry roar, Hemslock snatches the flamethrower from Gries, but it is not powerful enough to blast the ceiling, and Father remains unscathed.

Cheated of his target, Hemslock spins back to us, the flames aimed our way.

"I'll burn everything down," he threatens. "I'll destroy the whole island, turn it into a barren wasteland."

I don't move. I don't need to.

The attacks come. Massive roots rise in the air like anacondas, tails ending in sharp stakes. Hemslock burns the first dozen, but he is too slow against more. They tear into him, and he drops his weapon, the flames sputtering out. I can see him struggling, trying to summon the power to force the creatures to carry out his will. None of them listen.

I say nothing; I concentrate.

The roots wrap around him more securely, his arms bound tightly against his body until all you can see of him is his stark, enraged face staring back at us. I gesture with my hand and more thick vines encircle his legs.

A growl echoes from deep within the ruins of Askal's face. A thick root sprouts up from its center, something sharp like teeth at its end, drawing closer to Hemslock's face.

"It was you," Chase whispers. "When I was attacked in the cabin—the vines beat them away. That was you."

"I don't understand," Gries rasps. "You can control them?"

"No." It takes immense effort to focus, to make sure that my hold over them doesn't slip. It's fortunate that the rest of the soldiers are no longer fighting, their bullets gone. They stand petrified with terror. "Only when he lets me."

"Your father is the Diwata." It hurts to hear Chase speak like this—like I've betrayed him, though that's exactly what I've done. "When you told me that he was weak—that he'd been sick for a very long time—this was what you..."

I don't look at him, not wanting to see his face now that he knows how I'd misled him. I look up at the moving, twisting darkness above me. "Does it have to be this way?" I ask Him. "We have a sacrifice already. Enough to sustain you for a long time. Surely that's enough?"

The cave walls shift, a ripple going through them like they were made of water. With it comes a heavy, rustling sound, like that of a thousand makahiya opening and closing, leaves scraping against each other.

"Pagod na ako, 'Tay. Sobra na ang kamatayan dito."

More rumblings, murmurs from around us.

"What did you say?" Chase asks. "What is he saying?"

"I told him that I'm tired of all this death. He says that it is not on me to plead for who dies and who does not when they are all guilty. That I am here because I am His child and His conscience, but it is He who punishes."

I turn back to the cave. "I am your conscience," I affirm in English this time, again for Gries's and Chase's benefit. "You said you feared that your long absence had turned you cruel, that you would no longer listen. The cruelty is what they will remember of you. Gods forgive because they see humans for what they are: foolish. Please forgive them."

A rattling sound from above us.

"Yes, 'Tay. This is what it means to be family. To listen to those who care for you. I've never asked you for anything before. Please."

The roots overhead writhe quietly, the balete's movements slowing as Father mulls my words. And then another rumbling, almost a purr, resounds throughout the cavern.

The cocoon dissipates, and Hemslock sprawls on the ground.

The teeth retreat back into Askal. The mass of roots disappears, and flesh shifts back into Askal's dog form. He barks smugly.

"You're too kind," Chase says. "If I were a god, I would have murdered him without guilt." Another rumble sounds, and he looks alarmed. "Not that I'm disagreeing with your decision!"

"Yes," I say, smiling now. "He knows."

A choked laugh from Hemslock interrupts us. "The deaths of the cultists had always been a mystery...but it *was* you. The years line up. I should have realized it sooner."

"What does he mean?" Gries asks.

"Your precious little guide. The baby that was thought to have been sacrificed nearly two decades ago along with his mother." Hemslock staggers to his feet, still weak. One of his soldiers approaches him, but he waves him off. "Always wondered what happened to you. Wondered why my aunt was brought to that old woman when the god could have killed her on the island. There had to be a reason, and now I know. Your god sent Lindsey Watson back because she had to send *you* back—not a dead baby, but one alive and well."

"Alon?" Chase asks, stunned.

"That's why you have free reign of the island. Why the villagers speak little of you and where you came from. They're all in on it. Just like how they shut up about Alex Key. This god is *fond* of you. He feels responsible for you, doesn't he? Like a parent, since your mother died for his sake. The Diwata is using you to reestablish a connection with humans." Hemslock no longer looks homicidal, brows furrowed as if he is newly contemplating all that happened. "And you think sparing me was gonna be your act of kindness? I would have killed you. Should have. Wouldn't have thought twice afterward."

"I know what it's like to be surrounded by death." I look around, at the tree creatures who are still silent, still paying reverence to Father. "All this isn't worth it. My father didn't need sacrifices because I was here with him. But he won't spare you a second time. Leave while you still can."

"Hey." Chase's hand splays across my sides. The vines have dropped away from me, revealing my now-uninjured stomach. "How...?"

"Balete and their healing properties, or so the legends say," Leo Gries says, understanding. "Are you immortal?"

"I don't know. I'm aging, but I don't know what that means in the long run or if that will stop one day. Father doesn't always explain. He wants me to learn on my own."

"It's true, then. The cult believed that they could gain something

277

from the ritual. But the powers they thought they would receive were transferred to you instead."

Chase's voice trembles. "But your grandmother—you knew who she was when you saw the video. Does she know about—"

"Yes. She wouldn't have said anything. She raised me for the first half of my life. She knows." I look to Chase and take his hand. "I'm sorry. I knew you would never have trusted me, but I didn't know how to explain without giving away my secret."

"I'm already over it." His hands slide up to my face, cradling my cheeks gently. "And I understand why you had to do what you did. You—you stayed with him because you wanted to teach *him* compassion. I mean—who the hell does that?"

"I only helped Him relearn it."

"And—Askal?"

"They used to bury pets on the island after they die. Askal and I grew attached to each other." My dog beams.

"Still too humble for your own good," Chase says, smiling. "I've never actually kissed a demigod before, you know. Rory and Jordan are constantly telling me to try something different, and this sounds about as different as it gets."

My smile fades. "Chase—I can't—"

Hemslock leaps for us without warning. He's out of bullets and his flamethrower has been taken away, but he pulls a hunting knife from his boot. With a growl, he lunges his blade at me—

—and something rips open within him in response. He freezes, mouth dropping open. Copious amounts of blood fall from his lips, splashing onto the floor.

A large root has extended from Askal, his puppy facade disappearing briefly to reveal his true nature once more. He impales the man cleanly through the chest, the sharp tip sticking out from his back. Hemslock dangles in the air, his feet kicking uselessly as he gurgles.

As is his nature, the Diwata chooses violence.

I don't feel anger, only sadness that it had to come to this, that the man had not learned from his reprieve. Hemslock glares at us with hate-filled eyes, still struggling to form words for one last rage-filled tirade about what he did or didn't deserve. We never get to hear it. The light slowly fades from his eyes, his body sags, and his head lowers as the last breath leaves him.

I look at the other soldiers, on the off chance that they are tempted to follow their leader. But they seem to understand that the fight is over; the last four survivors slowly lower their weapons to the floor and raise their hands.

"We're done," one of them says. "We want out of here just as much as you do."

With a sickening sound, Askal drops Hemslock's body onto the ground.

"Did you do that?" Chase asks softly, though something in his voice tells me that the question is strictly rhetorical.

"No," I say quietly. "Askal has always done what he wanted to do."

Askal whines happily, settling back into his dog shape.

"Chase, Alon." Gries gestures urgently at the cave. "We have to go."

Chase steps toward his father.

I don't. "No."

Chase turns, surprised. "What do you mean? They should have another helicopter here by now. Maybe even boats. We gotta let them know we're okay and that Hemslock is—"

I am already shaking my head. "No. I can't go with you."

Chase stares at me. "You can't," he says, voice hitching. "Why would you stay here after everything?"

"Because he's my father. I can't leave." I lift my hand. Roots from the ground crawl up my leg, curl themselves against my palm. "You know what's going to happen. The island will draw attention now. Whatever the show would have done, this will be bigger. They'll want to know who I am. I'm not blind to see how the media will take this. One of Hollywood's celebrities died on this island. They'll bring more people here. There'll be more deaths. I need to stay and protect him."

"You can't protect the Diwata on your own!"

"Yes, I can. By barricading this island. By making it impassable so it will be difficult for others to attempt. By using whatever means I have to make sure there will be fewer deaths if they risk it anyway."

"I don't understand," Leo Gries says. "Your father *wants* there to be more deaths. Didn't you say that those eight sacrifices will fully awaken him? Why would you want to delay that?"

"I know it's inevitable. There will always be people like Hemslock, who are greedy and power hungry and will never listen. But I can prevent the deaths of those who don't have to die. 'Tay's been sleeping for a very long time. He can sleep a little longer."

Gries nods slowly. "You could have finished the ritual by letting it kill me. Instead you saved my life. Seventh *to consume*. Hemslock let his rage consume him, but I let my grief over Elena consume me too—it's the same thing, isn't it? It could have been either of us. It could still be both of us."

I don't say a word as he stands there, processing. "I think your wife will agree with me," I finally say, gently, "that your son needs you now more than ever."

"No," Chase shoots back. "We can't leave you here! Even if you're right about people coming to find the treasure or the god for themselves, you'll still be in danger. I can't—I don't want to leave you!"

I lean toward Chase and kiss him. He clings to me greedily for a minute, as if he never wants to let me go.

Another unexpected earthquake sends both father and son stumbling. I remain upright and grab Chase before he can fall.

Some of the trees still burn, though most were on their way to being extinguished. One has toppled over without warning and triggered the explosives—likely set as a failsafe on Hemslock's part.

I look back at the large eye above us, the writhing branches. And I know: 'Tay will never let me leave. Will never let me spend the rest of my life outside of Kisapmata, with Chase.

But I also know what I have to do.

"Please," Chase begs. "Please, come with us."

"Thank you," I tell him, smiling. "I was alone for the longest time. I thought I didn't mind. But you are the first outside of my family to care for me. You made me understand that I can be much more than I was. And I will always be grateful to you for it. Now go."

I push him back to his father, just as another tremor rocks the cave.

The ground between us splits, and another sinkhole appears, rapidly widening. Gries yanks Chase out of harm's way, the growing distance between us ensuring that my decision is final.

"Thank you," Gries calls out to me. "Thank you so much. We won't—we'll try—"

"I'll find you again," Chase shouts back at me as his father pulls him into the tunnels, the soldiers quick on their heels. "I don't care how long it takes! If you intend to park your hot, immortal ass inside this cave and wait for your dad to wake up, then I'll come back and drag you and your dog out myself!"

They disappear into the passageway as the walls continue to tremble. The trees watch them leave, content to sway in an unseen wind, waiting for everything and nothing at all. With Askal alert and expectant at my side, I turn back to Hemslock's body, the machete in my hands.

I see them. I see rescuers guiding them toward a waiting helicopter. I see both Melissa and Hawaiian Shirt still waiting for Chase and his father, holding true to their promise not to leave the island without them.

I see Melissa talking to Chase. I see Chase, heartbroken, shaking his head. I watch Melissa's face fall.

Before long they are all on the helicopter as it readies for its final journey away from the island. I see Chase turn his head to look back one last time.

He sees the roots growing over the entrance of the cave, wound so thickly and tightly that no gaps show through, preventing anyone else from entering.

He sees the sinkhole and the corpse tree entombed within, slowly gathering in sand and soil, until the sand lies smooth and even, like no hole had ever existed.

And then he sees me standing on top of the cave, on the one lone mountain on the island rising hundreds of feet above the trees. I watch him fly away from me as the helicopter rises higher, until the clouds obscure his view of Kisapmata, until there is nothing but an eye of an island staring up into the sky from waters of unwavering blue.

TWENTY-SIX
TO WAKE

Deep inside the caves, 'Tay and I sleep.

The world spins outside, and I drift through memories that lie scattered within Kisapmata. I see brief glimpses of what unfolds outside our little home, of what the future might bring.

Kisapmata is gone. There is no visible sign of the island anywhere on the map now. Scientists believe that an underwater volcano erupted, destroying Kisapmata in its aftermath. More months of testing will prove that to be false, but it is enough to fill the news for days.

There is no recovered footage of the tree creatures or of Tatay, but I know videos of the corpse tree will be all that is needed to draw fascination. So would recordings of Steve Galant—raving and blind, screaming for mercy in his final days. Unable to see or hear; unable to do anything *but* see and hear.

I wander through these half-forgotten thoughts, into the dreams of those who have never left the island. Airplane wreckage and boardrooms. Lights and cameras. Anger and speculation. Glints of gold coins. Cultists still nestled inside hollow trees, serving as sources of nourishment for 'Tay's other children, who are undiscovered by even the most recent expedition.

I do not see Chase anywhere amid all this chaos, and that comforts me.

I hope he does not return.

But I know others will come. Humans are foolish. I said as much to 'Tay. Their goals will be no different the next time. Hunger and greed. Occasionally compassion. Kindness. But I know that is not always enough.

Chase's stuffed bear is cradled loosely against the crook of my shoulder. Askal is curled at my feet.

They will try again, and 'Tay will wake one last time. And the world will change, perhaps for the better. Perhaps not.

Until then, we dream.

ACKNOWLEDGMENTS

ALL MY GRATITUDE AND SUPPORT AS ALWAYS TO MY agent, Rebecca Podos, without whom I would have never gotten this far. Thank you for always being an amazing person to work with, and just being an amazing person in every metric.

My thanks and appreciation to my editor, Annette Pollert-Morgan, for her invaluable and lovely insights and work, as this book would be all the lesser without her guidance. Also my grateful acknowledgment to the rest of the Sourcebooks team, without whom this book would not have been possible—Beth Oleniczak, Madison Nankervis, Chelsey Moler Ford, Neha Patel, Liz Dresner, Kelly Lawler, Leonardo Santamaria, Laura Boren, and Danielle McNaughton.

My love for all things horror started when I was six years old, when I picked up a book with a cat on the cover and thought it was going to be a marvelous story about pets—and it turned out to be *Pet Sematary* by Stephen King, so I suppose that technically I was right. But unlike most other parents who would take the book away and look for something a little more age-appropriate, mine continued to encourage me to read all the kinds of books I wanted no matter the genre. And now here we are!

For my partner, Les, who hates scary books but would watch all the horror films I wanted with me regardless. I know you're not going to read this one, either, but I love you all the same. And also for my eldest, Ezio, and my youngest, Altair, the latter of whom has already shown a similar love for all things horror even at three years old.

As a rather eager ghost hunter but foolish young adult in my early twenties, I once stayed overnight at an underground cemetery for a travel gig and was soon romped into ghost hunting with a few other like-minded friends once they learned. While I am suspicious by nature and have never believed in ghosts myself, much less seen any (though not for lack of trying), I have always loved the idea of creepy places and staying in haunted mansions that no sane person would willingly go to. Many things in this book were inspired by the old cave and island haunts I used to explore then, which is why this is also a shoutout to my old ghost squad and our weird fascination for the unseen, the unholy, and the things that go bump in the night— Liv, Annabelle, Mark, Nestor, and Alph!

ABOUT THE AUTHOR

RIN CHUPECO IS A Chinese-Filipino writer born and raised in the Philippines. They are the author of many young adult novels, including The Bone Witch trilogy, *The Girl from the Well*, *The Suffering*, The Never-Tilting World duology, and The Hundred Names for Magic trilogy, along with an upcoming adult gothic vampire series, Silver Under Nightfall. They write full-time and live with their partner and two children in Manila. Find them at http://www.rinchupeco.com.